D0975638

"I want to caution whoever reads this diary to remember that our earthly treasures are fleeting, but our heavenly treasure exists where moth and rust do not destroy. As I draw closer and closer to my eternal home, knowing all that is in store for me there, I have no doubt that the real treasure is yet to be found."

—Anna Coles, January 31, 1788

The Hidden Gate
A Fallen Petal
Double Trouble

Savannah Secrets

Double Trouble

Gabrielle Meyer

Guideposts
Danbury, Connecticut

Savannah Secrets is a trademark of Guideposts.

Published by Guideposts Books & Inspirational Media
100 Reserve Road, Suite E200
Danbury, CT 06810
Guideposts.org

Cover and interior design by Müllerhaus
Cover illustration by Pierre Droal, represented by Deborah Wolfe, LTD.
Typeset by Aptara, Inc.

Printed and bound in the United States of America

10 9 8 7 6 5 4 3 2

Chapter One

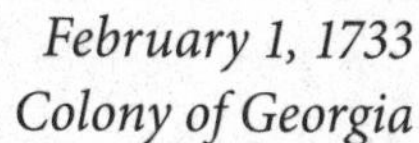

February 1, 1733
Colony of Georgia

Tonight, I write by the light of a single candle as my husband, Joseph, and my thirteen-year-old daughter, young Anna, sleep restlessly beside me. There is but little room in this cold tent we share with five other families. I sit on the hard earth, my traveling desk on my lap, with this small, leather-bound diary before me. What will unfold in this book? What story will it tell for future generations?

Both the desk and the diary were a gift from my father upon my marriage, and he encouraged me to write, though life has given me little to write about—until now. This afternoon, after sixty-one days at sea and another month of preparation in the Colony of South Carolina, we have finally arrived at the place we shall call Savannah. The day has been long and grueling, yet sleep does not visit me. My mind and heart are too anxious with questions my husband has refused to answer. I do not know why we have come, nor what Joseph hopes to accomplish in this wild place. What I do know is that the hostile Spaniards to our south and wary Indians to our west do not want us here.

I do not want us here.

We have neither the skill nor the experience to be among these colonists, and it makes me wonder why General James Oglethorpe allowed us to come. Did Joseph lie about our qualifications? The colony is intended to help the worthy poor who are suffering unjust treatment in England's debtors' prisons, and to act as a buffer between the Spanish in Florida and the English colonies to our north. My husband and I are neither debtors nor soldiers. General Oglethorpe made a call for laborers and tradesmen to establish the colony, yet my husband is neither of those things either. He has never worked with the soil nor built a structure in all his born days. He is a wordsmith, a gatherer of information, a writer, and a learned man. He is not a farmer or builder. His hands are stained with ink and not calluses. How will we survive this place I have heard so little about? Disease, hunger, and enemies at every turn threaten our precious lives. What could we possibly add to this colony but more mouths to feed?

The wind blows around our musty canvas, and the snores of two dozen worthier colonists mingle in a strange symphony. There are a hundred and fourteen women, children, and men, plus General Oglethorpe, a doctor, and a minister sleeping in six tents this evening. We are high on a bluff over the Savannah River. Today, we climbed a set of wooden steps built by the Tythings, a group of guards led by General Oglethorpe who came ahead of us to clear the land.

When we reached the top of the bluff, we had a breathtaking view of the surrounding area, including the village of the Yamacraw Creek Indians. The only thing I know about the Yamacraw is that Governor Johnson, whom we met in South Carolina, is afraid of them. They attacked Charles Town some fifteen years ago, and since then, he has wanted a colony between the Indians and himself. What does that portend for us tired and hungry colonists? How could we prevent an attack now? Our only hope is to build a fortification on the bluff overlooking the river, which we shall commence to build on the morrow.

General Oglethorpe has told us that we shall all live in communal harmony, each man working for the good of the others. He believes he has identified the four reasons there is trouble and unrest in England and has made it clear he will not tolerate them in his new colony. There shall be no alcohol, since he believes alcohol leads to laziness. There shall be no slavery, because he believes slavery is unjust. There shall be no lawyers, because he believes lawyers are dishonest and breed hatred and discord. And there shall be no Catholicism because of the trouble it has brought to England these many years. He also says no one shall own their own land or work for their own interest. Everyone must put forth the same effort—yet, I have already witnessed a vast difference in the work ethic of those in our group. My husband, I am afraid, is the laziest of the lot, and I find myself working twice as hard to make up for his lack. He would much prefer a book in his hand, not a hammer or a hoe.

He turns in his sleep beside me, and I wonder what dreams—nay, nightmares—plague his mind here in this uncivilized place. What does he plan to do, so far from home? Surely, he has no wish to colonize Georgia or defend the English colonies from the Indians or Spaniards, nor does he hope to farm. Joseph is a man driven with a desire I cannot explain and a focus I dare not question—though it has nothing to do with taming this new colony.

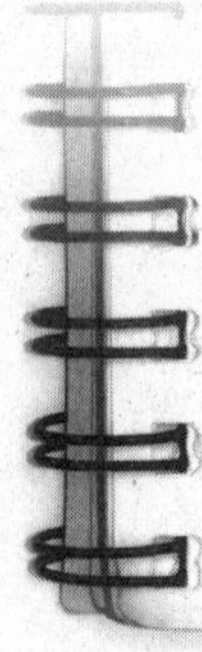

I have my suspicions about why we have come, but I cannot voice them here, in a diary that might fall into the wrong hands. For now, I will keep my thoughts to myself and pray to God I am wrong. Because if we have come for the reasons I so dreadfully fear, we will have more than Spaniards, disease, and hunger to contend with.

Sunshine glimmered through the leaves of the live oaks and magnolia trees as Meredith Bellefontaine sat beside her son Chase, who drove her SUV through the historic streets of Savannah. Since losing her husband, Ron, almost two years ago, she had come to cherish these rare moments with her grown son even more and tried not to take them for granted.

Outside, the July sun baked the brick sidewalks of East Charlton Street, where Meredith had lived since she had inherited the three-story row house from her great-granddaddy. Inside the vehicle, the air-conditioning felt pleasant, but more importantly, the cool climate would help protect the integrity of the priceless heirlooms riding in the back seat and on her lap.

"Careful," she said to Chase for the fifth time since leaving the Savannah National Bank. "Maybe we should have buckled the writing desk in before we left."

Chase only smiled at Meredith's fretting and carefully turned right onto Habersham Street. Her house sat on the corner of East Charlton and Habersham, and boasted access to Troup Square, one of the smaller and lesser known of the twenty-four squares laid out by the founders of Savannah. An afternoon bridal shower was in full swing, if Meredith guessed correctly. A whole host of women wearing large hats were seated in white chairs at white tables replete with beautiful floral arrangements. They eagerly watched a young lady open a pile of gifts. Behind the bride-to-be was the Victorian armillary mounted on six bronze turtles. The large structure looked like several circles intertwining in a globe, representing the celestial relationships.

In one corner of the square, opposite Meredith's stucco Italianate home, was the quaint brown Unitarian Universalist Church, which was rumored to be the location where organist James Piermont wrote the beloved Christmas song "Jingle Bells." And in the center was the popular cast-iron pet water fountain. Troup Square wasn't the grandest or the most beautiful of the squares, but it was Meredith's favorite, and its gravel paths, lush green grass, and cozy benches always made her smile.

"The writing desk will be fine," Chase reassured her as he took one more right turn onto Macon Street and parked the car in Meredith's spot directly behind her house. His voice grew deep in mock seriousness. "As long as I can get it into the house without dropping it."

"Don't tease." Meredith put her hand on his arm, her pulse picking up speed even though she knew he was joking. "Two hundred and eighty-six years of family history are represented in that desk."

"Not to mention centuries of mystery that will finally be revealed." As a history professor at Emory University in Atlanta, Chase was just as excited to examine the family heirloom as Meredith. It had been in the bank safe since the late 1950s when Ron's aunt, Temperance Bellefontaine, had inherited it and then hidden it away again. She had refused to take it out, no matter how many times Meredith and Chase had asked. Now, after her death, she had left it to Meredith in her will. Even though Meredith was only a Bellefontaine by marriage, Aunt Temperance had wanted it to go to her because Meredith had been the president of the Savannah Historical Society and would eventually pass it on to one of her sons, keeping it in the Bellefontaine family.

"I wish I could stay for the weekend to look over the desk and the diary," Chase said as he put the car in PARK. "But hopefully I can get back here in the next few weeks." He had made the three-and-a-half-hour trip from his home in Atlanta to accompany her to the bank but had to leave within the hour to return for an important meeting.

The diary he spoke of lay in Meredith's lap. With white cotton gloves, she had removed it from the writing desk at the bank and slipped it into an acid-free envelope. "I've been longing to get my hands on this diary for years," she said. "Maybe now we can have it properly preserved."

"And finally learn about Anna Coles and her connection to the pirate Blackbeard." Chase wiggled his eyebrows in anticipation. He loved history, but he also loved historical lore, especially pirate legends. "I heard the buzz about the diary all the way in Atlanta. A lot of people will be excited to find out what the diary has to tell us."

"I'm not as concerned about the pirate connection, since I doubt there is any," Meredith said. "I'm more excited to learn about the early days of Savannah." She opened her door and gingerly held the diary as she stepped out of the vehicle. "So little is known about the original colonists, it's a shame Aunt Temperance kept the diary hidden in a safe these past sixty years."

"And her mother before her." Chase also exited the car and opened the back door. Meredith came around the vehicle to watch as he gently removed the small writing desk from the back seat. Closed, it looked like a simple rectangular box made of walnut. Brass handles on either end, as well as a brass lock in the center, were the only adornments. Over the years, it had been scratched and dented, but it was in surprisingly good shape. It opened in two halves at the hinges and presented a sloped, hard surface to write on. Under the writing surface was a compartment for paper and books. The other side had wooden squares meant to hold ink bottles and pens. "I wonder why each generation of Bellefontaines chose to keep it hidden."

Meredith shrugged and cringed when the desk bumped into the side of the car as Chase pulled it out. "Maybe they just didn't care."

"That can't be true."

"Then why didn't Aunt Temperance talk about the diary or let us read it?" The older woman had refused to discuss the diary—and almost appeared scared of it. Meredith had never understood her reticence.

When the desk was clear of the vehicle, Meredith closed the door and walked ahead of Chase to the brown wooden gate at the back of the row house. She slipped the key into the lock and pushed the gate open into a small courtyard with a wall fountain. The delicate sound of trickling water and birds tweeting in a nearby magnolia greeted them.

"Maybe we'll finally find out why they kept it hidden." Chase waited for Meredith to go ahead of him and open the back door into the house.

"I've already been contacted by five different newspapers in Georgia, Florida, and South Carolina." Meredith unlocked her house door and opened it for Chase to walk into the back hall. "There's so much speculation about the diary and its contents. When news leaked that Aunt Temperance had died and I was the heir to the diary, I spent hours staving off curious people."

"What have you said?" Chase asked.

"I've declined to answer until I know more about the diary." The back entry wasn't very large, with its tile floor and ornate hooks on the wall. Four steps led down to the raised basement and seven steps led up to the main floor of the house. "But it hasn't stopped them from reporting on the little that is known about the diary. Most of it is hearsay and rumors."

"Some of my colleagues have read the articles online. Everyone thinks we'll finally find Blackbeard's long-lost treasure. It's believed to be the largest pirate treasure still hidden today." Chase's blue eyes, so like his father's, twinkled with the prospect.

"Don't tell me you're getting gold fever." Meredith tried hard not to chastise her adult sons, but sometimes the mother in her couldn't be controlled.

"Wouldn't it be fun to find it, if for no other reason than the historical value?"

"This diary and writing desk are the only treasures I need." Meredith closed the back door and indicated the steps leading to the lower level. "I want to keep the desk in the study."

Chase maneuvered toward the stairs, and Meredith found herself holding her breath again. "Be careful."

Thankfully, Chase was patient with her apprehension and took his time going down the stairs.

The house had been updated just before Ron passed away. Meredith had kept the character and integrity of the 1870s home intact but had updated the colors and the flow of the layout. At the bottom of the steps, they entered a large family room with a low, beamed ceiling, dark wood floors, and comfortable furniture. A redbrick fireplace, white built-in cabinets, and plush rugs gave the room a homey feel. At the far end, facing East Charlton Street and the front of the house, a bright study beckoned. Large windows let in the south-facing sunshine.

"Are you sure you want this in the study?" Chase asked as he entered the cozy room.

"I think it's best." Meredith moved some papers on her desk aside and made a spot for the writing desk. "The safe is in here."

Behind the gold-gilded picture frame of *Washington Crossing the Delaware*, a hidden safe was tucked into the wall. It wasn't large, but it held Meredith's most important documents and would be the perfect place to store the diary.

A shadow passed just outside the bay window facing East Charlton Street. It wasn't uncommon for pedestrians to walk in front of Meredith's home, especially so close to Troup Square—but this person caught Meredith's eye. Something about the way he walked and carried himself brought a twinge of grief to her heart and forced her to look closer. The man was tall, his shoulders broad and solid. Everything about him, from his salt-and-pepper hair to his strong jawline, looked strikingly similar to Ron.

With a racing heart and sweating palms, Meredith moved closer to the window.

The man had stopped at the base of the curved stairway that led from the street to the front door. From where she stood, she could only see the side of his face as he looked up at the house.

"Mom?" Chase sounded concerned. "What's wrong?"

Meredith couldn't find her voice. It stuck in her throat like a lump, choking her and cutting off her air.

The man turned and met Meredith's startled gaze. His eyes, the exact shade of Ron's and Chase's, grew wide.

Without stopping to explain, Meredith rushed out of the study, up the stairs, and into the main floor entry.

"Mom?" Chase was close behind her. "Where are you going?"

Meredith fumbled with the locks on the front door and finally yanked it open. She stumbled onto the stoop, but the man was no longer there. She looked toward Troup Square, and then down East Charlton Street, but he wasn't there either.

"You're scaring me," Chase said when he stepped onto the stoop and put his hand on Meredith's shoulder. "What's going on?"

Meredith started to move down the steps, but Chase held her back, forcing her to turn and face him.

"What is it, Mom?"

Swallowing around the lump, Meredith took a deep breath. "Your father."

"What?" Chase shook his head, a frown marring his handsome face.

"I—I just saw him, at the foot of the steps." She pointed at the spot where the man had been standing. "But he left."

"You saw Dad?" Concern filled Chase's eyes. "Mom, you're not making any sense."

"It looked just like him." She continued to scan the street, desperate to see the man again.

"Mom." Chase repositioned himself to stand between her and the street so she was forced to look at him. "You know it wasn't Dad. He's gone."

"I know he's gone, Chase." Her heart was still pounding hard, but the initial shock began to wear off. "I'm not given to flights of fancy—but I'm not blind either. The man looked exactly like your father."

"There are probably a lot of men who look like Dad."

"This man could have been his twin."

"Maybe Dad had a twin he never told you about." Chase's soft voice teased and it was likely meant to make her smile, but she couldn't bring herself to oblige him. He was her peacemaker, always trying to ease a tense moment with his sense of humor. He turned her toward the house and gently nudged her back inside. "Don't let it bother you, Mom."

How could it not bother her? She'd just seen a man who looked exactly like her dead husband standing outside her house.

It was the most bothersome thing she'd ever encountered.

Chapter Two

"Have a seat," Chase said to Meredith as he escorted her through the entry and into the living room. "Do you want something to drink? Some cold water?"

Meredith took a seat in a wingback chair and put her hand to her forehead. A cold sweat chilled her skin. It wasn't like her to get so upset. She was a private investigator, after all, and had faced more harrowing circumstances before. "Water would be nice."

Chase squeezed her shoulder. "I'll be right back."

He left the long, narrow room and went into the kitchen at the back of the house.

Meredith usually found her home a comforting place, but right now, very little soothed her mind. The living room had high ceilings, ornate, painted woodwork, and two beautiful fireplaces against the wall. When Meredith had remodeled, she'd taken out the wall between the small living room and dining room and made it one room. Wainscoting, neutral gray-painted walls, and well-placed antiques were just some of the things she loved about the house.

But, at the moment, none of it mattered.

"Hello!" Julia Foley, Meredith's business partner, opened the front door and entered the house without knocking, knowing she'd be welcome. "I'm itching to see that diary, Mere."

"In here." Meredith's mama would be mortified if she saw her daughter now. A proper lady would rise to greet her guest, but Meredith's legs felt too weak to stand.

Julia blew into the room as she usually did, her straight, shoulder-length silver hair combed to perfection. She wore slimming gray pants and a matching suit coat with a light pink blouse underneath. Elegance followed Julia wherever she walked, and it was no different now. "Meredith." She paused at the edge of the rug, her smile turning to a frown. "You look like you've seen a ghost."

Taking a deep breath, Meredith met her friend's concerned gaze. "I thought I saw Ron. He was standing outside the house."

Julia didn't speak for a moment. Her eyes revealed that she calculated several different thoughts before she seemed to settle on the most logical. "You imagined it?"

"No." Meredith shook her head. "That's the problem. He was just as real as you and I."

"Ron?"

Meredith sighed. "It couldn't possibly be Ron. I haven't lost my senses. But the man looked just like him."

Julia continued into the room and took a seat on the chair across from Meredith. "Who do you think it was?"

"I don't know. But he seemed pretty intent as he looked at the house—like he was searching for something."

"Or someone." Julia crossed her legs at her knees and pursed her lips as she thought.

"Why did he run off when he noticed me looking at him?"

"He ran off?"

"When I went to look for him, he was gone."

"That's strange."

"All of it is strange."

"Don't let Mom worry you," Chase said as he returned with a glass of ice water and handed it to Meredith. "We've determined it's my dad's long-lost twin brother."

"We've done no such thing." Meredith took the water and shook her head, finally allowing herself a hint of a smile. "Could you imagine what your grandmother would think if she heard you say such a thing?"

"After hearing about your first two cases"—Chase crossed his arms and looked from Meredith to Julia, one eyebrow raised—"I'm almost expecting some sort of tantalizing family secret to be unearthed." He grinned, his lopsided smile as charming as the rest of his personality.

"What brings you to Savannah today?" Julia asked Chase, a knowing gleam in her eye. "Anything—or anyone—in particular?"

Meredith suspected her friend was teasing Chase about his recent encounter with Carmen, the feisty office assistant they'd hired for their investigation agency. A few weeks ago, Chase had come into Meredith's home, and Carmen thought he was an intruder. Carmen had just pulled a peach upside-down cake out of the oven, and she proved that a rolling pin was as effective for self-defense as it was for making piecrust. Ever since then, Julia had taken great pleasure in teasing Chase about the encounter.

"Chase offered to come to the bank with me today to retrieve the writing desk and diary," Meredith said, changing the course of the conversation before Julia could embarrass her son.

"How could I forget?" Julia stood, expectation in her face. "Where is it? What does it say? Does it actually talk about Blackbeard's treasure?"

"We haven't had a chance to look at it yet." Meredith took a sip of the cold water. It ran down her parched throat and melted away the lump that was still lingering.

"We would have looked at it, but we were sidetracked by Dad's doppelganger." Chase winked at Julia.

Meredith tried not to take his teasing as an insult to her intelligence. He was just trying to ease the situation.

"Can we look at the diary now?" Julia asked.

Meredith set the glass down on the coffee table and forced herself to stand. "We put the diary and the desk in my study."

The three left the living room, walked through the entry, and started down the front stairs leading to the basement but were stopped by the sound of the doorbell.

Meredith glanced up at Chase, her heart thrumming again. Had the look-alike returned?

"I'll see who it is," Chase said to his mom.

Julia and Meredith watched with curiosity as Chase opened the large front door. "May I help you?" he asked.

"Is this the home of Mrs. Meredith Bellefontaine?" An older gentleman stood on the stoop wearing a dark gray, three-piece suit. His white hair and matching white mustache were striking against the dark suit.

"It is."

"I'm Anthony Stone, Miss Temperance Bellefontaine's attorney." He handed a business card to Chase.

Meredith had not met the lawyer but knew who he was from several social functions she'd attended over the years. She had corresponded with him and his secretary through emails over the past few weeks regarding Aunt Temperance's will.

"This here is a friend of mine," Mr. Stone continued as a second man stepped up to the door and extended his hand to Chase. "Conner Pearlman is an antiquities appraiser who specializes in rare books and diaries."

"Come on in," Chase said.

Meredith and Julia moved forward, greeting the men and introducing themselves.

"What can I do for you?" Meredith asked.

Conner Pearlman was much younger than the lawyer. He wore a pair of khaki pants with a navy blue polo shirt that matched his eyes almost perfectly. The handsome man looked like he was better suited for a golf course than a library full of rare books. He carried a hard-sided briefcase and had a quick, charming smile.

"I'm here to ensure y'all have retrieved the writing desk and diary," Mr. Stone said with a genteel Southern drawl, appearing to be in no particular hurry. "And to complete the transition with an official appraisal for insurance purposes."

Insurance purposes? "Isn't that my responsibility?" Meredith asked.

"Perhaps." Mr. Stone smiled, and his white mustache lifted. "But I wanted to offer this service, in appreciation for the many years of friendship with Miss Bellefontaine."

Meredith glanced at her son to get his opinion, but he just shrugged.

"I'll give you my card." Mr. Pearlman set his briefcase down and pulled a wallet from his back pocket. After retrieving a white business card, he handed it to Meredith. "I work mostly with rare manuscripts, but I do appraise diaries as well."

His card gave an address in Atlanta.

"Chase also lives in Atlanta," Meredith mused.

The two men studied each other.

"I thought you looked familiar," Chase said. "Have you done any work for the Atlanta Historical Society? I serve on the board of directors and work at Emory University in the history department."

Mr. Pearlman nodded enthusiastically. "Yes, of course, that's where I've seen you before."

"We have several rare manuscripts in our collection at the university," Chase said to his mother and Julia.

"When would you like to look at the diary?" Meredith asked Mr. Pearlman.

"Is now a good time?"

"Conner is in town on another piece of business for me," Mr. Stone quickly explained. "And I suggested we stop by here on our way to another meeting. I do apologize if this is an inconvenient time."

"Not at all." Meredith smiled. "I was just about to show the diary to Julia."

"Wonderful." Mr. Stone waved his hand. "Please lead the way."

Chase closed the front door, and Meredith showed the group down the enclosed stairway. "We've—"

The doorbell rang once again.

"Now who could that be?" Chase asked, a little impatiently.

"You've suddenly become a very popular person," Julia teased Meredith. "I'll see who's at the door, and you can show the men the diary."

"Sounds good." Meredith continued down the stairs, through the family room, and into the study. She paused when the men entered, both of them narrowing their gaze on the writing desk. The diary was beside it, still in its acid-free envelope.

Mr. Pearlman's eyes shone, and he shook his head in amazement. "I'm not embarrassed to admit I'm a little more eager than I should be to see this diary. I did some research on it once Anthony asked for my assistance." He looked at Meredith. "Is it true that no one has seen it for sixty years?"

"That's true."

"And have you or your son read it?" he asked.

"We haven't had the chance yet."

"Yoo-hoo!" A high-pitched, overly enthusiastic voice wove its way through the rooms and into the study. "Meredith, darling, it's Beatrice."

Meredith closed her eyes briefly and forced herself to put on a smile. The new director of the Savannah Historical Society, and Meredith's so-called replacement, had a unique way of irritating her.

"I rushed over here the moment I heard you were in possession of the diary." Beatrice continued talking even before she entered the room. Her pixie-style haircut was meticulously groomed, and her bright yellow sundress almost hurt Meredith's eyes. "I have a proposition for you, dear—" She paused when she saw everyone standing in the study. "Oh my lands." Her Southern accent, which she had perfected since arriving in Savannah, deepened, and she fluttered her eyelashes. "I didn't realize you were entertaining gentleman callers."

"I'm fairly certain I mentioned that upstairs," Julia said dryly.

"Fiddledeedee." Beatrice giggled and shrugged. "And here I am, going on and on when there are introductions to be made."

Meredith quickly made the introductions as her study grew smaller and smaller with the addition of the bubbly newcomer.

"An antiquities appraiser!" Beatrice's eyes grew large as she sidled up to Mr. Pearlman. "I have a unique collection of rare diaries from important Southerners. I've been meaning to get them appraised."

Mr. Pearlman removed another card from his wallet and handed it to Beatrice—putting a little more space between them.

"Thank you kindly, sir."

Julia shook her head directly behind Beatrice. She was even less patient than Meredith with the fake Southern belle.

"Is there something I can do for you?" Meredith asked Beatrice.

Beatrice clapped her hands together, her eyes shining. "I've come to make you an offer you cannot refuse, Meredith, dear." She took her purse off her shoulder and reached in to remove her checkbook. "I'd love to add this diary to my growing collection and will spare no expense at acquiring it."

"The diary is for sale?" Mr. Pearlman and Mr. Stone asked in astonishment, at almost the same moment.

"Of course not." Meredith frowned. "The diary is a priceless family heirloom. I would never think to sell it." Suddenly leery of all the people gathered around the book in question, Meredith lifted the envelope off the desk and held it to her chest.

"I'm in a position to pay whatever you ask," Beatrice said with a syrupy-sweet tone. She glanced sideways at the men. "Nothing is too outrageous for me."

Julia bit her lip, and Meredith suspected that her friend had a quick retort.

"If the diary is for sale," Mr. Pearlman said eagerly, "I'd also like to make an offer."

Meredith shook her head, all eyes on her. Pain began to build in her temples, and she suddenly felt more tired than usual. The events of the day were starting to wear on her, and she was ready for the lawyer, appraiser, and Southern belle to leave. Her cardiologist had warned about excessive stress, and at the moment, it was all a little too much for her. "I'm sorry for the inconvenience, but perhaps we should schedule a different time for you to appraise the book, Mr. Pearlman. I'd like to look it over first."

"You really should have it insured as soon as possible," Mr. Stone advised, a bit breathlessly. "It isn't safe to have something so rare and valuable lying about uninsured."

"It won't be 'lying about,'" Meredith promised. "I plan to keep it in my fireproof safe until I've decided on a more permanent home." She pulled the painting of Washington away from the wall on its hinges to reveal the hidden safe behind.

"What sort of permanent home are you thinking?" Beatrice clutched her purse, her gaze shifting from the safe to the diary in Meredith's grasp. "Possibly the Savannah Historical Society?"

"Possibly."

A shadow fell over the room, and everyone looked toward the window.

Meredith's pulse picked up speed once again. The man from before appeared on the other side of the glass, this time in full view of everyone in the room. He stared at Meredith, his blue eyes focused solely on her.

Meredith trembled from head to toe but could not tear her gaze from his. "It's him!" she whispered desperately to Chase.

Without waiting for his mom to ask, Chase left the room in pursuit of the Ron look-alike.

The man turned on his heel and started down East Charlton Street, faster than Meredith expected a man of his age to move.

Julia put her arm around Meredith's shoulder. "It'll be okay, Meredith. Chase will catch up to him and find out who he is."

"It's uncanny, isn't it?" The pounding in Meredith's head increased with the beat of her heart. "It could have been Ron."

"I've never seen any two people who weren't related look more alike," Julia agreed. "Are you sure he's not a relative?"

"I'm sure. I've been a part of the Bellefontaine family for over forty years, and I've never seen this man before."

"Now, about the diary," Beatrice continued, hardly noticing the sudden tension tightening the room as she took a step toward Meredith.

"I think we're done for today." Julia placed her hand on Beatrice's arm and nudged her toward the door. "Meredith has had a big day, and she'd probably like some time to herself."

"Of course," Mr. Stone said. "Sorry for the intrusion, Mrs. Bellefontaine."

"Don't hesitate to call my office when you're ready for the appraisal," Mr. Pearlman added. "I'll be available whenever it's convenient for you."

"Thank you." Meredith's response was quiet and shaky. "But I don't believe I'll have it appraised until I've had a chance to read it myself."

"Don't wait," Mr. Stone advised. "You wouldn't want anything to happen to it before it's insured."

"I'll see everyone out, Meredith." Julia smiled at her friend, ignoring the others. "Call me later."

Meredith nodded, thankful for her calm, levelheaded business partner, wondering what would happen when Chase found the look-alike.

***

"Are you sure, Mom?" Chase stood in the back entry a couple of hours later, just after sunset. He had run after the look-alike, but the man had disappeared again. "I'd be happy to spend the night."

Meredith put her hand on his elbow and urged him out the back door. "You already missed your meeting on my account. I don't want you to miss the rest of your weekend plans."

"I can rearrange my sche—"

"When your father died, I made a promise to myself." Meredith smiled at her youngest when he turned in the courtyard and looked back at her. "I would be a confident, independent woman and I wouldn't demand my sons take over their father's role. I've been living here alone for almost two years. I don't need you to spend the night."

"It's really no problem. You've had quite a scare today, and until we know who that man is, I'd feel better if you weren't alone."

She looked over the courtyard wall to the dark shadows in Troup Square. The wind had picked up in the past hour, and it pushed and pulled the trees in a dizzying dance. Rain threatened, and if Chase didn't leave soon, he'd have to face the worst of it on I-16.

A gust of wind rattled the trash cans at the back of the row houses, sending a shiver up Meredith's spine. "We may never know who the man is." Meredith spoke with more confidence than she felt. "But I can't live my life in fear of anyone or anything—especially in my line of work."

Chase shook his head, love and admiration on his face. "If Carter was here, he'd probably get upset at you again for opening Magnolia Investigations and suggest you find a less threatening line of work."

Meredith's older son, Carter, had not been a fan of her chosen profession and had made his opinion known from the start.

Chase leaned forward and placed a kiss on Meredith's cheek. "But Carter's not here, and my personal opinion is that you should follow God's leading and do what makes you feel like you have the most purpose."

"Thank you, Chase."

"I'll be praying for you, just like I always do. Let me know if you see that man again, and don't hesitate to call the police if he keeps coming around."

"I will." She hugged him. "I love you. Thanks for all your help today."

"Love you too, Mom." Chase walked through the courtyard and opened the back gate. "Have fun looking through the diary. I wish I had more time to read it."

"Come back whenever you'd like. I'll have it for a long time."

He paused. "Don't forget to lock all the doors and windows before you go to sleep."

She smiled. When had the child become the parent?

"Good night." She waved to him and stepped back into the house.

Everything inside was still and quiet, while outside the wind continued to howl. Even though she spoke with confidence, she hated living alone, and missed Ron with every waking moment.

She locked the back door—double-checking to make sure it was secure—and then turned to go through the rest of her house.

GK Chesterson, the beautiful Russian Blue cat she had purchased from one of Chase's friends a few years ago, appeared at the head of the back-entry steps. He had made himself scarce most of the day, during all the activity, but now he meowed at Meredith, looking for some attention—and his supper, no doubt.

"What would I do without you?" Meredith scooped him into her arms and nuzzled her nose into his soft fur.

In response, he meowed again and began to purr.

Meredith ran her hand down GK's spine as she made her way to her kitchen at the back of the main level.

The kitchen was one of her favorite rooms of the house and the space where she had spent the most time and attention during the big remodel. When Ron was alive, and she was the president of the historical society, she had loved to entertain and throw parties. Now, it was just she and Carmen who used the massive kitchen. The biggest gatherings she had each year were hosting holidays with her sons and her grandchildren. Maybe one day she'd have another party—but the thought of hosting it alone didn't hold the same excitement as before.

She set GK on the floor, then flipped on the light switch and went to the cabinet where she kept his food. A movement near Troup Square caught her attention and made her pause. Her kitchen windows looked out on the back deck and beyond to Macon and Habersham streets. They gave her a stunning view of the square by day, but at night, it was a bit harder to see.

Lights from Habersham Street cast eerie shadows into the square, especially with the wind blowing the tree branches to and fro. A man stood just under one of the live oak trees, but it was hard to discern what he was doing. It wasn't uncommon for people to walk the square with their dogs in the evening. For the most part, the neighborhood was safe at any time of the day, though Meredith didn't like to be out alone after dark.

Forcing herself not to be afraid—and to assume the man was in the park with his dog—Meredith quickly fed GK and then made herself a cup of herbal tea with honey.

He was still standing under the tree when she finished, but there was little she could do to find out what kept him there. Instead, with her teacup in hand, she went through her entire house, from top to bottom, and checked every door and window to make sure they were locked.

When she went into the lowest level, she entered the study and turned on the light. After she closed the window shades for privacy, she opened the envelope and pulled out the old diary. She was still amazed that it was finally in her possession. What mysteries would it unravel? What questions might it answer? The possibilities were endless.

With her teacup beside her, the wind howling around the corner of the house, and the diary in her cotton-gloved hands, Meredith curled up in Ron's favorite reading chair and opened to the first page.

It was late, and she was exhausted from the day's activities, but her curiosity was insatiable. The writing was faded, and the lettering was slanted and a bit hard to understand at first. Anna Coles had written in small, precise penmanship, filling the page as full as possible. The paper had aged and yellowed, though it was remarkably well-preserved—which was probably a testament to the years in a dry safety deposit box, away from the elements.

After almost three hundred years, though, the book was fragile, and Meredith was thankful for her training with old manuscripts in college and at the historical society. She held it carefully and almost reverently as she began to read the first page out loud.

"'Tonight, I write by the light of a single candle as my husband, Joseph, and my daughter sleep restlessly beside me.'"

Excitement bubbled up in Meredith's chest, replacing the fear and anxiety that had resided there for most of the day.

She spent over an hour reading the early accounts of Anna Coles and her small family. Anna's husband was a writer, just like Anna's father. She feared he would not last long in the colony, since he had no real skills, but it was the unspoken fear that Anna harbored concerning his reason for coming to Georgia that intrigued Meredith the most. If he hadn't come to farm and colonize, why had he come? What would the pages of the diary reveal?

Another concern Anna shared in the early pages of the diary was about her thirteen-year-old daughter, also named Anna, though she referred to her as Ann. Young Ann was being pursued by a man who was almost twice her age. Meredith knew it wasn't uncommon for women to be married as teenagers in colonial times—and a man twice her age would only be twenty-six—but Anna Coles understood how tender and unprepared her daughter was for matrimony. Anna poured out her heart, including her fears and her hopes for their lives in Georgia, and was much more open and personal than Meredith had expected. It made for a remarkable account, though Anna wrote so many details, Meredith almost felt as if she were intruding on the woman's privacy.

When the clock in the family room struck ten, Meredith closed the diary and slipped it back into the acid-free envelope. She hadn't gotten far, taking her time to savor all the little details, not feeling the need to rush through reading it. There was no hurry. When she was ready, she would put it on permanent loan with the Savannah Historical Society and possibly help them create an exhibit.

With great care, Meredith opened the safe behind the Washington painting and gently placed the diary within. After closing the safe, she spun the knob and then put the painting back in place.

GK had found her and now followed her out of the study, through the family room, and back up the stairs. She smiled at the cat, but her mind was on old Savannah and the first group of colonists who had arrived from England.

What was Savannah like before time and technology had changed her for good? Meredith loved her hometown, loved its southern hospitality, historic downtown, and charming squares. She loved almost everything about it, but still wondered what it looked like, sounded like, and smelled like before it was overcrowded with people and buildings. Maybe, as she read Anna's diary, she might get a glimpse of that long-forgotten world.

After Meredith slipped into her pajamas and went through her nightly routine, she climbed into bed and snuggled under the covers. The rain began to pour outside, and the wind continued to rattle the windows. GK jumped onto the bed and kneaded the comforter with his front paws before settling into place near her feet.

All the lights were off, and the noise from the storm filled her house with all sorts of unfamiliar sounds. A shiver covered her body in gooseflesh, and she had to force herself not to let her mind wander.

Instead, she turned her thoughts to her prayers.

"Do not be anxious about anything." She whispered one of her favorite Bible verses from Philippians. "But in every situation, by prayer and petition, with thanksgiving, present your requests to God. And the peace of God, which transcends all understanding, will guard your hearts and your minds in Christ Jesus."

She was safe, her house was secure, and she had nothing to fear.

Chapter Three

May 20, 1733
Colony of Georgia

A little more than three months have come and gone in this foreign land, and I am even more certain we should not be here. Daily, we face hardships of every kind. Accidents, fatigue, hunger, abandonment, Spaniards, and ineptitude are our greatest enemies. Of late, a disease has ravaged our small colony, one unlike any we witnessed in England. Mrs. Musgrove, the Creek wife of trader John Musgrove, has come to Savannah to treat those who are ill. She calls it the Yellow Fever and says it will get worse as the summer continues. It has stolen the lives of eight people already, friends and neighbors we have grown to love and depend on in this uncivilized place, and made many others sick.

Even now, as I take a moment of precious daylight to capture my thoughts, I watch young Ann move about our small, one-room cottage. I constantly look for signs of the disease, fearing she will be next. I make myself sick with worry, and there is no one with whom I can share my concerns. No mother, sisters, or even a husband who seems to care. Instead,

I use this diary as a trusted friend. A safe place I can share my deepest fears.

The weather has turned hot, and I've been told it will get hotter. As I write this, General Oglethorpe meets with at least fifty Indians in the stockade built for our protection. This is their third day of meetings, and we hope a treaty will soon be signed. Tomochichi, a trusted leader of the Yamacraw Indians, has become a friend to General Oglethorpe, and we are hopeful that there will be nothing to fear from his people. It will be good to have allies in this strange place. A second group of colonists arrived recently, bringing with them much-needed supplies and more help, should we need it if the Spaniards decide to attack.

Daily, there are militia drills on the squares at the center of each ward. If we are attacked, we hope to be ready. Soon after we arrived, General Oglethorpe and Colonel Bull laid out the plans for Savannah, much like a military camp. We live around four communal squares named Johnson, Percival, St. James, and Decker. Each square is used for common purposes, and the lots to the east and west of each are intended for churches, schools, and businesses. To the north and south are the tithings, which are areas broken into forty residential lots. We were assigned a lot on Johnson Square and had to live in our tent until it was our turn to build a small home with the help of our neighbors. Everything we do, we do as a group effort, so we helped the others and then they helped us.

For the first month, Joseph did his share to help where he could, though he gave but little effort. He wielded a hammer, practiced military drills, and even helped to break up the soil where we planted our gardens. But as soon as our home was completed, he began to take trips outside the colony. The first few times, it was for a day or two, and then, as the months progressed, he began to leave for several days at a time. Even now, he is gone, though I do not know where, nor when he will return. He takes only his bag, his traveling desk, which is similar to mine, a musket, and a loaf of bread. When he leaves, I cannot help but worry if I will ever see him again. Should he go missing, how long should I wait to look for him? And where would I even begin? I ask him where he goes and what he does, but he refuses to answer me.

Several people have started to comment on his absences. General Oglethorpe has even come to speak to Joseph and advise him not to leave the colony on his own. But Joseph is a free man and he still leaves, though I have begged him to listen to the general. He tells me it is not my concern, but I disagree. He has brought young Ann and me to this place, without our consent, and now he leaves me for days on end to worry about how we will survive. If that is not my concern, then pray tell, what is?

When it is Joseph's turn to work in the fields, and he is away, it is I or Ann who must go. But it is not only Joseph who neglects his duties. Several others have shown themselves to be lazy and ill prepared for colonial life.

A bugle has just blown at the fort, and the men have been called to convene in Johnson Square. I pray a treaty has been

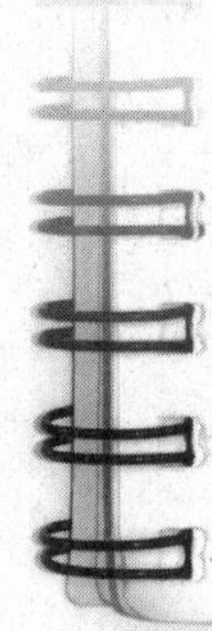

signed, but Joseph is not here to go and learn the details. I must wait until someone else tells me. No doubt John Gready, the farmer who has shown an interest in marrying my Ann, will come by to share the news. For now, I will tuck this diary into my writing desk and pray that God is watching over my little family here in this desolate place.

Sunlight peeked through the shade in Meredith's bedroom early the next morning as GK stood and arched his back, his front paws stretched out, his claws extending as he yawned. Meredith blinked several times to make her eyes focus and then glanced at the clock next to her bed. Almost seven.

Rolling onto her side, she reached out and petted GK for a moment and then pushed the covers to the side and sat up, her feet hanging over the edge of her bed. Ever since Ron had died, mornings were the hardest, especially mornings when she didn't have any particular place to go. Since they had wrapped up the investigation into Harlowe Green's long-lost brother, there had been very little to keep Meredith and Julia busy at the agency. Carmen had her hands full digitizing Ron's files and answering curious emails and phone calls, and there were the occasional questions from Arnold Mains, who was finishing the remodel on Ron's office, but that was the bulk of their work. Maybe she would text Julia to have breakfast with her at the Downhome Diner and catch up with Charlene, or stop in to see Maggie Lu for a bit.

GK rubbed up against Meredith's back and began to meow. He was a creature of habit, much like Meredith, and would expect his breakfast.

Meredith reached for her robe and slipped it over her satin pajamas, then she grabbed her cell phone, which she charged by her bed at night. She usually took it to the kitchen, where she read the *Savannah Morning News* and checked her Snapchat to see if Carter or the children had snapped her.

After putting the phone in her pocket, she walked toward the door, tying the robe belt tightly around her waist and yawning.

Memories from the night before returned to her, and unease crawled up the nape of her neck. Part of her hoped Ron's look-alike was far away today and she wouldn't have to see him again—but the other part didn't think she'd rest well until she knew who he was. Maybe she should call Ron's sister, Gwyn, and ask if there was a relative who looked exactly like Ron that Meredith might not know. It seemed unlikely, but it might answer a question.

With a newfound purpose for the day, and another mystery to uncover, Meredith walked down the stairs and into the foyer with GK close at her feet.

At the bottom of the stairs, she paused, surprised to feel a bit of humidity. The air-conditioning was on, which usually kept the moisture at bay. Even this early in the morning, especially in July, the air outside could be thick with humidity—but never inside, unless a door or window was open.

Meredith's chest began to rise and fall in short, shallow breaths. She was certain she had checked every single window and door in the house before she had gone to bed. From where she stood in the front entry, there was nothing out of place. The door was locked and secure, the windows were all closed, and every piece of furniture was exactly as she'd left it.

On shaking legs, she walked toward the back of the house and opened the door that led into the rear entry. The moment she did, she was met with more heat and humidity—and found the back door ajar and the lock broken.

Meredith stepped back and almost tripped over GK, her breath becoming choppy as her pulse accelerated. Someone had broken into her house—and that someone could still be inside with her.

She reached into the pocket of her robe and grabbed her cell phone. With shaking hands, she dialed 911.

"911, what's your emergency?" asked a woman on the other end.

"I'm Meredith Bellefontaine, and I live on East Charlton Street, near Troup Square. I believe someone broke into my house."

"Is there currently an intruder in your home, ma'am?"

"I'm not sure." Meredith's heart pounded so hard, she feared for her health. "I secured all the doors and windows last night, but I found my back door open and the lock broken just a moment ago."

"Ma'am, I'm going to ask you to step outside your front door and wait for the police officers to come and assist you." The dispatcher was calm and cool as she spoke to Meredith, almost nonemotional. "If there is an intruder in your home, do not approach the individual. Do not attempt to search your home, and do not hang up until the officers have arrived."

"All right." Meredith gave the dispatcher her address as she rushed to the front door and fumbled with the locks until she was able to get the door open. Stepping outside, she shivered, despite the heat.

"Meredith?" Harlowe Green stood on the sidewalk, out for a morning stroll, apparently. He frowned, his wrinkled face showing his surprise—probably at seeing her outside in her robe. She rarely stepped out of her house without being properly dressed. "Is everything all right?"

"Did you hear anything during the night?" the dispatcher asked on the phone. "Any unusual sounds? Any unusual activities outside your home?"

Meredith rubbed her left temple as she tried to think past the fear. She forced herself to nod and smile at her elderly neighbor, not wanting to alarm him, while trying to remember everything that had happened yesterday.

"I did see a man hanging around my house several times yesterday. He looked just like my dead husband."

There was a pause on the other end, and then the dispatcher asked, "You thought you saw your deceased husband, ma'am?"

"No, of course not." The last thing Meredith needed was the dispatcher to think she'd lost her mind. "Just someone who looked like him. My son even went after him the second time we saw him. And last night I saw someone lingering in the square outside, but it was too dark to see if it was him."

Harlowe continued to stand on the sidewalk with his walker, his brow furrowed as he listened to Meredith talk to the dispatcher.

"The police officers should be there within three minutes." The dispatcher continued speaking in her calm tone. "Are you in a safe place?"

Meredith glanced up and down her street. Several cars passed, and she saw a few pedestrians with their dogs on leashes. She couldn't help but search their faces for signs of Ron's look-alike.

Nothing.

She caught Harlowe's eye, again, and was thankful for his presence—even if he was twenty feet away and well beyond his one hundredth year. He would offer very little in the way of protection, but it was reassuring to have him there. "I'm safe," she said.

A few minutes later, a police car drove toward her on East Charlton Street. The officer pulled up to the curb in front of the house, dark sunglasses hiding his eyes. Next to him sat a female officer. She inspected the street with a cursory glance and then unlatched her seat belt.

"The police officers have arrived," Meredith assured the dispatcher. "Thank you for your help."

"If you need anything else, don't hesitate to call back."

Meredith pressed the red button and slipped her cell phone back into her robe pocket.

"Will you be all right, Meredith?" Harlowe asked.

"Yes, thank you." She waved at her concerned neighbor and then faced the police.

The officers were an interesting contrast. The driver was tall, with wide, muscular shoulders and dark hair. His partner was medium height with a thick blond braid and piercing blue eyes.

"Mrs. Bellefontaine?" the man asked. "I'm Officer Isaiah Clemmons, and this is Officer Hayley Ellis. We've been told you suspect an intruder broke into your home?"

"Yes. My back door is open, and the lock is broken."

"Have you noticed anything missing?"

"I didn't check."

Officer Clemmons took out a pad and pen and began to take notes. His eyes were still hidden behind his dark glasses.

"Can we take a look?" Officer Ellis asked.

"Of course." Meredith led them into her house, still shaking, but feeling more confident with them near.

They went to the back door and examined it. The lock had clearly been broken, and there were muddy shoe prints on the tile floor that she hadn't noticed before.

"It was raining last night," Meredith said. "The prints lead toward the lower level."

Officer Clemmons took off his sunglasses and bent to touch one of the prints. "It's dry. Whoever came into your home did it several hours ago."

They followed the prints down the steps, across her family room floor, and into the study.

Meredith inhaled a sharp breath when she saw the picture of George Washington pulled away from the wall, the safe door hanging open.

The officers followed her line of sight as Meredith stepped over to the safe.

"Anna's diary." She covered her mouth with her hand. The diary was gone—and, if she was correct, it was the only thing missing.

Nothing else looked disturbed, though she would need to look through all the papers just to make sure.

"Who is Anna?" Officer Clemmons asked as he jotted something on his pad of paper again.

Meredith quickly explained the diary and how it had come into her possession only yesterday.

"The pirate treasure diary?" Officer Ellis asked. "I read about it in the *Savannah Tribune* just this morning. You're the owner of the diary?"

"Pirate treasure?" Officer Clemmons shook his head. "I haven't heard about it."

"The diary is rumored to hold the key to Blackbeard's long-lost treasure." Officer Ellis's eyes glowed with interest as she looked at Meredith. "Did you read the diary?"

"Only the first part—but it didn't say anything about a pirate treasure."

Officer Ellis sighed. "Well, whoever took the diary knew exactly where it was stored." She looked inside the safe and then glanced around the room. "And from the looks of the safe, they knew exactly how to crack it." She looked back at Meredith. "Does anything else look suspicious?"

The writing desk still sat where Chase had put it yesterday. None of the books or furniture was disturbed. Other than the muddy prints, the room was pristine. "No."

"Do you have any idea who would have known where the diary was?" Officer Clemmons asked.

She thought back to yesterday. "There were only a few people. I hadn't even had the diary for twenty-four hours."

"Who are those people?" His pen was poised over the paper.

"My son Chase and my business partner, Julia, were here. There was also a lawyer, the one in charge of my aunt's estate, Anthony Stone. He brought an antiques appraiser from Atlanta with him, Conner Pearlman. The only other person was the president of the Savannah Historical Society, Beatrice Enterline." Officer Clemmons wrote down each name as she spoke. "But I can't imagine that any of them would have taken the diary."

"If they're the only people who knew where it was, then it's very likely one of them took it." Officer Ellis studied Meredith with a steady gaze. "Was there anyone else?"

Meredith shook her head and was about to say no when she recalled Ron's look-alike. "Yes," she said. "There was a man standing outside my house." She pointed to the window where she'd last seen him. "He looked just like my late husband, Ron. When we saw him the second time, my son went after him, but he disappeared." She also told them about the man standing in the park late last night, though she didn't know if it was the same man.

"We'll write up a full report, take pictures of the safe, the shoe prints, and the back door, and do more investigating around the house, in the square, and outside." Officer Clemmons wrote a few more notes in his book. "We'll also call all these people for questioning."

Meredith nodded. She knew Chase and Julia were innocent, and she suspected the other three who had been in her home were innocent too, but it wouldn't hurt to question them. If they could just find out who the look-alike was, then she was almost certain they'd find the diary. But what would Ron's look-alike want with the diary?

"If you don't mind," Meredith said to the officers, "I'm going to call my colleague, Julia Foley, and have her come over. She and I are private investigators with Magnolia Investigations, and I'd like her to be here."

The officers looked at one another. Officer Ellis raised her eyebrows and then shrugged.

"I've heard good things about your agency," Officer Clemmons said. "I don't see any reason why not."

While the officers wrote up their report, Meredith called Julia and quickly filled her in on what had happened.

"I'll be right there," Julia said immediately. "Give me fifteen minutes."

Meredith ended the call and took a deep breath. She didn't know what upset her more—that Anna Coles's priceless diary had been stolen, or that someone had broken into her house while she slept.

***

Julia walked into Meredith's home almost exactly fifteen minutes later. She wore a pair of brown trousers and a tan blouse. Even though the day had already grown warm, she looked as cool as ever—though there was deep concern in her gray eyes.

"Meredith." She took Meredith's hand and squeezed it. "How are you doing?"

"I'm a little shaken up."

"How long have the police been here?"

"They came about twenty minutes ago." Meredith motioned toward the back of the house. "They just went into the courtyard to look for clues."

Julia studied Meredith from head to toe, and Meredith realized she was still in her pajamas.

"Go take a look around while I change," Meredith told her friend. "There are muddy footprints leading into the study."

"And the diary is really gone?" Julia shook her head. "What a shame."

Meredith went upstairs and changed into a pair of fitted khaki pants and a navy blue shirt and jacket combination. She slipped on a pair of flats and went back downstairs. She found Julia coming out of the kitchen.

"I fed GK," Julia said. "He was meowing and rubbing up against my legs, so I used my amazing detective skills to deduce that he was hungry."

Meredith smiled, thankful for Julia's sense of humor. "Oh, good. I forgot to feed him in all the fuss."

"I thought so."

"Did you get a chance to look at the shoe prints?"

"Yes—and they're definitely men's shoes."

Meredith crossed her arms and tried not to shiver. She hated to think about the man who had worn those shoes. "Can you tell what kind of shoes they were? Loafers, sneakers, sandals?"

Julia shrugged. "From what I can tell, they just look like a pair of casual shoes. No special markings." She held up her phone. "I took several pictures."

"The officers think it must have been one of the people who were here yesterday." Meredith put her hands up to her cheeks and shook her head. "But I can't imagine any of them breaking into my house—especially Beatrice. If those are men's shoes, we can rule her out."

Julia lifted her eyebrows. "Can we?"

"Of course we can."

"Maybe she hired someone."

"Julia, I know Beatrice is a lot of things, but I don't think she's a thief."

"Who knows what lengths she'd go to for something she wants." Julia wasn't a fan of Beatrice and was a little more vocal about it than Meredith. "After all, she's spent her entire time in Savannah trying to climb the social ladder, and her Southern persona is hardly genuine."

"I don't know." Meredith put her hand on the back of a dining room chair. "I still think it's Ron's look-alike, whoever he is."

"But why? Who is he? How would he know about the diary?"

"Just like everyone else, I suppose, from the newspapers."

"I suppose—but while we're trying to find out who he is, we can't rule out the others. Even Beatrice."

Meredith couldn't disagree.

"I'll go to the office and let Carmen know what's happened," Julia said. "I'll have her start researching each of the suspects, and I'll make a few calls as well."

"After the officers leave, I'll head to the office. I can talk to Ron's sister and see if she can help identify the look-alike." Meredith was ready to tackle another mystery. "We need to know who he is, so we can find him."

Julia shook her head. "You need to stay home today, Mere. Take care of yourself."

"I'll do no such thing." She couldn't imagine sitting at home all day when there was an active investigation at hand—especially one that involved the Bellefontaine family diary and a break-in at her home.

"What about the broken lock? Don't you need to take care of that?" Julia asked.

"I already texted Arnold to come over and fix the back door." Meredith would need to call her boys and let them know what happened, though she hated to think what they'd both say. They had been encouraging her to get an alarm system since Ron's death, but she hadn't gotten around to it. "I'm also going to call a home security company and have someone come by as soon as possible to put in a system."

"It's about time," Julia teased, though Meredith knew her friend was also relieved.

It wasn't that Meredith hadn't wanted a system, but there was a part of her that was reluctant to admit she was weak or vulnerable. She hated to acknowledge it now.

"All right then," Julia said. "I'll head over to the agency and start working. You take your time coming."

"I'll wait until Arnold arrives to fix the door. He said he could be here this morning."

Julia turned suddenly. "You know what this means, don't you?"

Meredith could think of several things, but didn't know which one Julia had in mind. "No, what?"

"This is our first case that isn't a missing person case." She smiled wryly. "I didn't want to say anything at the time, but I was a bit apprehensive that people were going to think we only accept cold cases involving missing children."

Meredith smiled back at her. "Well, this should put those apprehensions to rest."

Julia put her hand on Meredith's forearm. "Just remember, if you decide not to come in today, I'll completely understand."

Meredith appreciated Julia's concern, but she wasn't about to sit by and let her friend do all the work. They had a mystery to solve, and Meredith intended to solve it.

Chapter Four

It was well past ten when Meredith finally arrived at Magnolia Investigations. Thankfully, Arnold had been free to come by and fix the back door. Meredith still hadn't called her sons, but she knew she needed to before they heard about the break-in from someone else. Already, word had started to spread about the theft, and Meredith had been forced to turn off the ringer on her phone.

Magnolia Investigations was housed in a beautiful antebellum home facing Forsyth Park in the historic district of Savannah. It had previously been Ron's office, but shortly after his death, an electrical fire had destroyed much of the interior. When Meredith and Julia decided to reopen the agency, they had hired Arnold Mains to remodel the space. Julia's and Meredith's offices had been finished first so they could get to work. All that was left was Ron's old office and the kitchen. They were going to turn Ron's office into a conference room once it was completed.

There was no parking on the street, so Meredith pulled into one of the spots in the back of the house and entered the building using the rear entrance. She stepped into the long hall and walked to the front where the receptionist's desk was situated in the parlor. It was near the front door so she could greet people when they first entered.

"Meredith!" Carmen Lopez looked up from her computer and spoke with both surprise and chastisement in her voice. "*¿Estás loco?* You should be at home. Why are you here?"

"I'm not crazy," Meredith said with a playful roll of her eyes. "And I'm here because I work here." She was familiar with Carmen's mothering. "Do I have any messages?"

Carmen shook her head, muttering in a mixture of Spanish and English. "You should be home, with your feet up, drinking a cup of tea. You have your heart to think about, you know." She lifted a pile of pink slips out of Meredith's in-box. "Several newspaper reporters have called, requesting interviews. They want to know what's in the diary. I didn't tell them anything about this morning."

"Good." Meredith took the slips of paper and noticed Beatrice Enterline's name on the top of the stack.

"I just got off the phone with Beatrice." Carmen tightened her mouth in disapproval. "She was practically hyperventilating about the diary."

Meredith sighed. "If any more reporters call, please tell them I'm unavailable for comment."

"Will do, boss."

Meredith walked toward her office just across the hall, glancing though the pile of pink notes.

"Meredith?" Julia poked her head out of her office just past Meredith's. "Got a minute?"

Nodding, Meredith redirected her steps toward Julia's office. The room was bright. It faced the back courtyard and had been a dining room at one point in the early history of the home. A large white fireplace dominated one wall with a gilded mirror hanging above the mantel.

"What do you need?" Meredith asked.

Julia turned her laptop toward Meredith. On the screen were listed links to an apparent Google search.

"What is it?" Meredith asked.

"I typed in Conner Pearlman, antiques appraiser, Atlanta, in every conceivable combination I can think of, and there's no record of him anywhere. Nothing. It's like he doesn't exist."

Frowning, Meredith moved closer to the screen, setting her pink slips on Julia's desk. She scanned the list for a couple of seconds. "But Chase recognized him from his work at the college library."

Julia shrugged. "I can't seem to find him anywhere. Do you have his business card?"

Meredith grimaced. "I gave his card to the police officers this morning and didn't bother to copy down his number. Are you sure he doesn't have a website? Did you check the online Yellow Pages?"

"Yes, and I can't find a number, a website, a Facebook page, or anything else, for that matter."

"That's strange. Hopefully Mr. Stone can give us his number. I'll add him to the list of people I need to call." Meredith shook her head, ashamed to admit the truth to her friend. "I still haven't called my boys. I'm almost afraid to tell them what happened. They'll probably force me to move out of my house by the end of the day."

Julia turned her laptop around again and gave Meredith a reassuring smile. "They're concerned because they love you."

"I know." Meredith picked up her pink slips and started toward Julia's door. "But they need to trust me when I tell them I know what's best for me."

The bell over the front door jingled, signaling a visitor. "I hope that's not a reporter," Meredith said with another sigh. "I don't have time to talk to them."

Carmen's voice was faint as it trailed to them from the drawing room. "Hello, Miss Maggie Lu. How are you this fine morning?"

"I've had better days, Carmen. Better days indeed. But the Lord is good, and I'm still here."

Meredith met Julia's gaze and smiled. They had grown to love Maggie Lu since connecting with her on their very first case. She had helped them solve the mystery of Harlowe Green's missing brother as well, and was a wealth of Savannah history no Google search could provide.

Meredith and Julia stepped out of the office and met Maggie Lu in the entry. She greeted them with big hugs. "How are my two favorite private eyes this morning?" she asked.

Meredith caught Julia's subtle question in her eyes and nodded permission for Maggie Lu to be brought up to speed.

"Oh, Meredith, I'm so sorry," Maggie Lu said after Julia told her of the theft. "I should have talked to you about that diary before you took it home, but I was visiting Delyse at the nursing home." She shook her head, sadness weighing down her dark brown eyes. "If I had talked to you, I would have told you to leave it right where you found it."

Meredith frowned. "What do you know about the diary?"

"More than a body should." She shook her head, her lips pursed in unhappiness. "And it hasn't brought anyone any good since the day it was written."

"You two go on into Meredith's office," Julia said to Meredith and Maggie Lu. "I'll bring some coffee, and we can talk about that diary."

Meredith's office was housed in the old music room with a fireplace almost identical to the one in Julia's office. Large windows filled one wall from floor to ceiling, giving her a spectacular view of Forsyth Park. Her desk sat in the corner of the room, but a comfortable floral sofa and two wingback chairs were in the center, in front of the cold fireplace.

"Have a seat, Maggie Lu." Meredith pointed to the sofa. She wanted to ask her about the diary but didn't want to start talking about it until Julia appeared. "How's Charlene?" she asked instead.

Maggie Lu's daughter, Charlene, ran the Downhome Diner, one of the newest and most popular diners in Savannah's historic district. Two months ago, Meredith and Julia had met Charlene when she came to Magnolia Investigations to ask for help in finding her mother. They had not only found Maggie Lu but had made new friends as well.

"She's good. Busy, but good." Maggie Lu nodded, contentment on her face. "Thanks to you and Julia, we're both a lot happier these days." She clasped her hands and leaned back into the sofa. "And how is that lawyer friend of yours, Mr. Crowley?"

Despite being a grown woman with two sons and two grandchildren, Meredith found herself blushing at the mention of

Quin Crowley, the man she had met while investigating Maggie Lu's disappearance. They had become friends, but their careers kept both of them busy—at least, that's what Meredith told herself whenever she thought about the handsome lawyer. She had kept Quin at a comfortable distance these past couple of months, unsure how to categorize their relationship. He was friendly and had invited her to attend two different events with him, but both times she'd had to say no. He hadn't called or texted in a couple of weeks, and she was afraid he had taken her refusal as a rejection. She wasn't sure how to mend that—or even if she wanted to.

"Here we are." Julia appeared with a tray and three cups of steaming coffee.

Meredith was thankful she wouldn't have to answer Maggie Lu's question. She rose from her chair to help Julia with the tray.

"I've got it," Julia said, shooing Meredith away. "Sit back down."

The look on Maggie Lu's face told Meredith that she hadn't forgotten the question and probably wouldn't let it lie—but for now, they had more important things to discuss.

"No cream or sugar for Maggie Lu," Julia said, handing her the cup of coffee. "And cream, no sugar, for Meredith."

Meredith wrapped her fingers around the hot cup and settled back in her chair. "Maggie Lu, what do you know about Anna Coles's diary?"

A range of emotions passed over Maggie Lu's face as she shook her head. "That book caused a lot of trouble for Miss Temperance back in the late fifties."

"Oh, that's right." Meredith leaned forward. "I forgot you told me you worked for Aunt Temperance when you were a teenager."

"Only for one summer, when I was fifteen. I was still getting used to being called Louvenia." Maggie Lu took a sip of her coffee and then lowered the cup. "It was the craziest summer of my life. That diary held some kind of power over Savannah, and it forced Miss Temperance to go into hiding, in her very own home."

Meredith met Julia's wide-eyed gaze.

"How did we never hear about this?" Julia asked Maggie Lu.

"Because I promised Miss Temperance I'd never talk about that diary again, or that summer, and I haven't—not until now."

"Why are you talking about it now?" Meredith asked.

"It gave Miss Temperance a world of trouble, and I should have warned you about it too."

"Did you read it?" Meredith had only read the first few entries, and now that it was gone, she wished she had read the whole thing. Why would someone want to steal it? Did it really reveal where Blackbeard's treasure was buried? There were so many unanswered questions. And now that the diary was gone, Meredith would have to find the answers some other way.

"Miss Temperance guarded that book like it was the most precious thing in the world. She never let it out of her sight, but she had a hard time reading it, so she asked me to read it to her."

Excitement made Meredith lean forward. "Do you remember what it said?"

"I tried to forget everything about that summer, and that's the honest truth. I read almost the whole thing to her, but it's been over sixty years, and a lot of living has happened since," Maggie Lu admitted. "I don't remember what the diary said, but I do remember what happened that summer. I've heard of gold fever before, but the only time I ever saw it was in 1959. All of Savannah had the fever, and I watched Miss Temperance fight it too. I was never so scared for a body in my life."

***

The feather duster in Louvenia's hand dangled precariously as she leaned toward the voices in the hall.

"No, sir," Franklin said in a stern voice. "Miss Temperance is not seeing visitors."

"But I'm here about the diary," the man outside the front door said, his voice tight with desperation. "I need to see it. My wife is sick, and I've been out of work for months. If nothing changes, we'll lose everything, for sure. I just want one little peek—"

A scuffle ensued, and Louvenia's pulse escalated. She dropped the duster and almost toppled off the step stool.

"I said no," Franklin told the man. "You need to leave, please, sir."

Louvenia scrambled down the stool and peeked around the corner of the dining room and into the front hall. Franklin, Miss Temperance's butler, was a tall man, with broad shoulders and thick arms—but he was old, and the man at the door was young and spry.

"I need that diary!" the man said, trying to push past Franklin.

Thankfully, Miss Temperance had put all the staff on alert, and the gardener appeared on the front porch.

"No, you don't," Robbie said as he helped Franklin remove the man from the premises.

Shaking, Louvenia retrieved the duster, her white cap falling over her eyes as she bent forward.

"Louvenia," Miss Temperance said in her slow, even voice from the top of the stairs. "Please close the front door."

"Yes, ma'am." Louvenia couldn't see her employer, but Miss Temperance seemed to know exactly where Louvenia was at all times. Granny Luv had warned her when she took the job with Miss Temperance Bellefontaine that the woman would be watching her carefully, especially in the beginning. Granny Luv had worked for rich women almost all her life and had years of experience. If Louvenia listened and obeyed, she should have no trouble.

"And be quick about it," Miss Temperance called. "I don't want anyone else to slip in while Franklin and Robbie are otherwise occupied."

Louvenia pushed her cap up, ran to the front door, and closed it tight against the outside world.

When she turned, she saw Miss Temperance standing at the top of the stairs in a wool pencil skirt and matching green jacket with a wide collar. She wasn't an old woman, probably in her midthirties, but she was stern and old-fashioned, her hair pulled back into a tight knot. Both her parents had died when she was a teenager, and she had raised her two younger brothers, who were now married and raising families of their own. Miss Temperance had never married, though Louvenia had heard rumors about several suitors she'd turned away because she thought they were only after her money.

Now she was old beyond her years, and lonely. Her brothers rarely visited her, and she hardly left her home.

Louvenia dropped her gaze and started to move back into the dining room when Miss Temperance stopped her.

"They've come for the diary, you know."

Louvenia paused in the middle of the foyer. Miss Temperance could only be speaking to her, because she was the only help left in the house on this Saturday morning.

"They think it contains information about a buried treasure." Miss Temperance walked down the straight, open staircase, one slender hand gliding on the rail while she clutched the diary close to her chest in the other. "What do you think, Louvenia?"

Panic tightened Louvenia's chest as she looked right and left, feeling like a cornered mouse. Granny Luv had told her to get her work done as quietly and efficiently as possible, without drawing unwanted attention.

"Don't be afraid," Miss Temperance said, her light blue eyes looking directly at Louvenia. "Do you think there's a buried treasure in Savannah?"

"I don't know, Miss Temperance."

"What do you know about pirate history?"

"Only what I learned in school."

"Is it true you want to be a schoolteacher, Louvenia?"

It was Louvenia's greatest dream to be a teacher. She loved learning and wished she could spend her whole day with her nose buried in a book. Memories of sitting with her friend, Harriet Bessett, reading Little Women *in stolen moments under the magnolia trees at the Bessett Plantation filled her with bittersweet feelings. It was best if she didn't think too long on Harriet.*

"Yes, ma'am. I want to be a teacher."

"Then I shall tell you about pirates." Miss Temperance walked purposefully toward the back of the hall and paused to motion Louvenia to follow her.

Louvenia swallowed as she gripped the duster. Should she follow Miss Temperance? Granny Luv never told her how to handle a situation like this.

"I won't bite," Miss Temperance said. "I want to show you something in the library."

Louvenia quietly followed Miss Temperance. She had been in the library several times to dust and polish, though it was hardly ever used and didn't need to be cleaned often.

The shades had been drawn in the room, just like the others on the main floor of the old plantation home, making the room dark. Miss Temperance had told Louvenia to keep the shades drawn, since she didn't want treasure hunters looking in on her through the windows.

While still clutching the diary, Miss Temperance turned on the lights. She took a long stick with a metal hook and pulled a large wall map down from a roll near the ceiling. It was a map of the United States of America. She used the stick to point to Georgia.

"There were many factors that led to piracy in colonial America," Miss Temperance began. "Poor working and living conditions in Europe, the rise of legal privateers hired by different countries during times of war to overtake and raid enemy ships, and the increased trade between the old world and new."

Louvenia stood as still as a statue listening to Miss Temperance, unsure what to say or do.

"Some believe there were over five thousand active pirates on the ocean during the golden age of piracy in colonial times." Miss Temperance ran the pointer along the eastern seaboard, stopping on Georgia again. "Blackbeard, one of the most feared of the pirates during his

lifetime, was rumored to have hidden a vast treasure before he was killed in battle. He said that only he and the devil knew where he had buried it."

Louvenia swallowed hard as a shiver ran up her spine. She knew enough about Blackbeard to know that he was a fearless man. It was rumored that he went into battle with lit fuses under his hat to scare off his enemies. His real name was Edward Teach, but he'd gained the nickname Blackbeard because of his thick, dark beard. He was also unusually tall and fierce.

"He was only active for two years before his death," Miss Temperance continued. "But in that time, he was relentless in his pursuit of riches. He died in 1718, fifteen years before Anna Coles came to Georgia with her husband, Joseph, in the first wave of colonial settlers to Savannah."

Louvenia felt a little bolder as she listened to her employer with avid interest. "Did you read all that in the diary, Miss Temperance?"

"No. That's common knowledge." She pointed to Savannah on the coast of Georgia. "There is an island not too far away from here where it's rumored that Blackbeard hid with his men in the creeks and inlets—and some people believe he buried his treasure there. It's called Blackbeard's Island, and it's over five thousand acres in size."

"Why do people think the diary will tell them where the treasure is buried?"

Miss Temperance held up the old book. "That's what I'm trying to learn. Rumors have followed this diary since it was written by Anna Coles in the 1730s, but she chose to keep it hidden. Every person who has inherited it since then has done the same." She tucked the book back into her protective grasp. "I recently discovered that my mother had inherited the diary from her grandmother, but kept it in a safe at the bank with Anna's writing desk all these years and never once spoke to me about it. I heard rumors about a pirate diary from my classmates, but I had no idea it really existed or that it was in my family's possession."

Louvenia had heard lots of rumors about a pirate diary growing up as well, but like all the pirate tales in Savannah, it was hard to know which ones were real and which were just imagined.

"Apparently, my mother didn't want me to know about it until I reached thirty-five. She didn't think I'd be mature enough to handle it before that. Her lawyer told me about it just this week, after my birthday, and that's when I retrieved the diary and desk." Miss Temperance pointed at a small, portable writing desk open on the table next to her.

Louvenia remembered the day Miss Temperance had gone to the bank and come home with the writing desk and diary. From that day, until this one, people had been coming to her home both night and day, either asking to see the diary or offering to buy it. There had been a few attempts at a break-in, so Franklin and several of the others had kept vigil around the clock to protect Miss Temperance and the book.

"Does it say where the treasure is buried?" Excitement bubbled up in Louvenia's chest, despite the fact that the treasure wouldn't be hers, even if she knew where it might be located.

Miss Temperance shook her head, and a frown marred her stern brow. Something akin to regret, or embarrassment, passed over her face before she cleared her expression. "The lettering is small, and my eyes are weak, so I haven't been able to read it." She paused for only a moment and then went on, "Do you read well, Louvenia?"

Louvenia lifted her shoulders with pride. She was the best reader in her class. "Yes, ma'am."

"Do you think—perhaps, after your chores are done—that you might read to me from this diary?"

The request took Louvenia off guard. Her mouth slipped open, and she stared. "Me?"

"As I said, my eyesight is poor, and I can't seem to make out the words on my own. It was written over two hundred years ago, and the ink has faded."

A different sort of excitement welled up in Louvenia. She'd never read a book so old, or so mysterious.

"But," Miss Temperance warned, her jaw tight, "whatever you read in this book must stay between us, do you understand? You must not whisper a word of it to anyone, not even your grandmother." She leaned forward, the pupils of her eyes growing smaller as she narrowed her gaze on Louvenia. "If we uncover the treasure, I will share one-tenth of it with you—but if you ever breathe a word of this to anyone, I will not give you a dime, and I will make sure you and your family cannot find work in all of Georgia. Do you hear?"

Louvenia's heart pounded, and her palms started to sweat. If she helped Miss Temperance find the treasure, Granny Luv and Louvenia's older brother, Benny, would never have to work again. It was worth keeping her mouth quiet—something she'd already learned to do after Miss Harriet went missing.

"Yes, ma'am," Louvenia said quietly.

"You'll help me read the diary?"

"I will."

"Good. We'll get started after you've finished dusting."

Louvenia turned and left the library as quickly as she could, driven by both fear and anticipation. As soon as she finished dusting, she'd have permission to hold and read one of the most interesting books she'd ever seen.

And, more than that, she might learn where Blackbeard buried his treasure.

Chapter Five

NOT LONG AFTER MAGGIE LU left Magnolia Investigations, Julia sat across from Meredith in Meredith's office, their coffee cold and forgotten.

"I have a feeling," Julia said as she rose and lifted both cups off the coffee table between them, "if we knew more about Anna Coles, we might have a better clue as to why her diary is so important."

"She was one of the first women to live in Savannah," Meredith said. "That, in itself, makes her important."

"I know." Julia held up the cups. "I'm going to get us some fresh coffee." She continued to talk to Meredith, since the coffeemaker was on a cart in the hall between their offices. "I mean, who was she, and why have people linked her to Blackbeard's treasure? Doesn't that seem like a big jump?"

Meredith had never stopped to wonder why rumors had always circulated about the treasure being connected to Anna.

"All we know is her name and that she came to Savannah in 1733." Julia reappeared with the steaming cups.

"We know she's an ancestor to the Bellefontaines."

"That's a start." Julia handed a cup to Meredith. "You've spent years researching your family genealogy. Do you know who her parents were or where she came from?"

"I've researched my side of the family," Meredith corrected. "I haven't spent much time on Ron's side. I thought I'd get around to it one day, if my children or my grandchildren ever expressed interest."

"Maybe now's the time." Julia didn't sit down but held her coffee and looked contemplative. "And, if you do some research on Ron's family, maybe you'll find out who the look-alike is." She nodded her head toward the door. "I'm going to keep looking for information on Conner Pearlman."

Meredith also stood. "I'll call Ron's sister Gwyn and see if she knows who the look-alike is and ask her how far back she's researched the Bellefontaine family. Maybe she knows about Anna."

"Sounds good." Julia took her coffee and left Meredith's office.

Meredith had set her purse on her desk and went to it now to get her cell phone. She'd missed ten calls, all of them from people wanting to know if the diary mentioned the treasure.

After she listened to a few of them, she found Gwyn's number on her phone and placed the call.

"Hello, Meredith," Gwyn said on the other end. She was a busy grandma who took care of her grandchildren two days a week. From the commotion in the background, Meredith guessed that today was one of those days.

"Sounds like you have your hands full. Should I call back at a different time?"

"Of course not." There was a slight pause, and then the noise died down considerably. "Is that better?" Gwyn asked.

"How'd you do that?"

"I stepped into the pantry and closed the door." Gwyn laughed. "They can fend for themselves for a couple of minutes. They're playing with Play-Doh at my kitchen counter." She let out a long breath. "How are you? I've been thinking about you today. I know you got the diary out of the safe, and I've been dying to know what you've discovered."

Gwyn had recently delved into Bellefontaine family history. Meredith had assumed Aunt Temperance would leave the diary to Gwyn or Barb, since they were Bellefontaines by birth, but the will had stipulated Meredith as the recipient. The two sisters hadn't been upset, since they assumed they'd get a chance to read the diary one way or the other and knew Meredith loved history as much as they did.

"Unfortunately, someone broke into my house last night and took the diary out of my safe."

"What?" Gwyn's voice raised a notch. Meredith could imagine Gwyn, her shoulder-length gray hair tied back in a loose ponytail as she stood in her pantry, her favorite apron fastened around her front. "Meredith, that's horrible. Are you okay?"

"I'm fine, and Julia and I are already on the case." Meredith refused to give in to the fear that she'd never see the diary again. "We're fairly certain we've narrowed the thief down to four people who knew where the safe was. I know who three of them are, but the fourth is a mystery. That's why I'm calling you—at least, that's one of the reasons I'm calling."

"I'll tell you everything I know."

"Yesterday Chase and I saw a man on the sidewalk in front of my house. When we went after him, he disappeared."

"Who was he?"

"That's the thing. I don't know—but he looked exactly like Ron. They could have been twins."

"Seriously?"

"Yes. I was hoping you might know who it could be." Meredith closed her eyes, hoping and praying Gwyn would have some answers. "I know it's a long shot, but did Ron have a relative that looked like him? Someone I might not know?"

Gwyn paused for a moment. "There is someone who comes to mind."

Meredith took a seat behind her desk, eagerly listening for Gwyn to keep talking.

"As you know, Aunt Temperance had two brothers, Nicholas and Albert. Nicholas was mine and Barb and Ron's father and Uncle Albert had one son, James."

"I didn't know you all had a cousin."

Gwyn sighed. "That's because the family disowned him when he was eighteen, a few years before you met Ron. From what I remember, he was a scoundrel. He used Aunt Temperance for her money when it was convenient for him and got into a lot of trouble with the law. Once he was disowned, we weren't allowed to talk about him again and, to be honest, I have no idea what happened to him. I heard he moved to California or Washington, or somewhere on the West Coast."

"And did he look like Ron?"

Gwyn paused again. "They could have been brothers. The resemblance was uncanny. Some people actually thought they were twins."

"How old would he be?"

"He was a couple of years older than Ron, so he'd be about sixty-eight, I think."

The man outside Meredith's home had to be close to that age.

"Do you think you saw James?" Gwyn asked.

"I do." Meredith hated to ask the next question, but she had no choice. "Do you think he's capable of breaking into my home and stealing the diary?"

"I don't know, Meredith. It's been decades since I saw him last."

At least knowing his name was a start. "I'll see if I can learn more about him on my own," Meredith said.

"Please let me know what you find out."

"I will."

"Is there anything else I can help you with?"

Meredith leaned back in her chair as she fiddled with a paperclip on her desk. "I was hoping you'd know more than I do about Anna Coles. Do you know where she came from or who her parents might be?"

"I actually did some research on her when I learned that you inherited the diary a couple of weeks ago." Gwyn's voice raised with excitement. "Every time I researched her in the past, I hit a brick wall when it came to her parents. So, this time, I decided to research her husband, Joseph, and I discovered the most amazing thing."

Meredith held her breath as she waited for Gwyn to continue.

"Joseph worked for a man named Daniel Defoe."

"Daniel Defoe?" Meredith sat up a little straighter. "As in the author of *Robinson Crusoe*?"

"The very one! But it gets better. The research I did said that Joseph married Daniel Defoe's youngest daughter—"

Meredith squeezed the paperclip so hard that it popped out of her fingers and flew across the room.

"Her name was Anna." Gwyn could barely contain her excitement. "I did a little more research into Daniel Defoe, just to make sure I was on the right track, and the dates for Anna Coles's birth are the exact same as Daniel Defoe's youngest daughter, Anna. Both records show that they were born in London. I'm convinced it's the same person."

"You think Anna Coles was Daniel Defoe's daughter?"

"I can almost guarantee it. Daniel Defoe has an unbelievable history in England. He was not only an author, but he was also a merchant, a trader, a pamphleteer, and a spy. He wrote under at least a hundred and ninety-eight pen names."

"What?" Meredith could hardly believe her ears. How had this history been lost to the family?

"And Joseph Coles was one of his last assistants before Daniel died in 1731, just a couple of years before Joseph and Anna came to Georgia." Gwyn released a shriek followed by a gale of laughter. "I've been found," she said to Meredith.

"It sounds like you have your hands full." Meredith laughed, missing her own grandchildren, Kaden and Kinsley. "I'll let you go, but thanks for all the information."

"I'll email you everything I found, if you think that would be helpful."

"Definitely. That would be great." Meredith said goodbye and ended the call. She then left her office and poked her head into Julia's.

Julia looked up from her computer screen and removed her readers before giving Meredith her full attention. "I can tell by the look on your face you found something interesting."

"Two things." Meredith rested her forearms on the back of a wingback chair in front of Julia's fireplace. "Ron has a cousin named James Bellefontaine who could have been his twin. He was disowned by the family back in the seventies, and the last Gwyn heard, he was living out west. According to her, he was unscrupulous and got into trouble with the law. I plan to look into that as soon as I can."

"I know a former police detective who can look into that for us. I'll give him a call." Julia leaned forward with anticipation. "Now, what's the other thing?"

Meredith came around the chair and took a seat on the edge. "Gwyn thinks Anna Coles is Daniel Defoe's daughter."

"The author?"

"Yes, and she thinks Joseph, Anna's husband, was Daniel's last assistant before Daniel died in 1731."

"What else do you know about Daniel Defoe?"

"Not a whole lot. He wrote *Robinson Crusoe* and *Moll Flanders*, among other things."

Julia frowned and then tapped the track pad on her laptop and began to type.

Meredith went to stand behind Julia. "What are you doing?"

"I think I remember something else about Daniel Defoe." She had typed his name into the Google search bar. "Aha! I'm right."

"What?"

Julia read from the screen. "'It's believed that Daniel Defoe also wrote *A General History of the Pyrates*, though it's never been proven true or false. Defoe used so many pen names, many scholars believe not all of his work has been accredited to him, but *A General History of the Pyrates* was written in the right time frame and has many of the hallmarks of his work. It was published under the name Captain Charles Johnson.'"

Meredith glanced at the article on the screen. *A General History of the Pyrates* was apparently a tell-all about the lives and times of real pirates. Several pirates had become angry when the book was published, because it revealed information about them that was previously unknown.

"It looks like he wrote other pirate and seafaring novels," Julia said. "So he must have had some knowledge of pirates." She looked up at Meredith. "And Joseph Coles was his assistant?"

"That's what Gwyn thinks."

"Maybe that's why rumors always circulated about Anna and her diary. If people suspected that she and Joseph had some kind of insider knowledge of pirating activity in the area, and she was a writer, like her father, they might think her diaries contained pertinent information."

"That seems like a stretch." Meredith nibbled on her thumbnail. "I think there's some connection here, but it has to be stronger than Anna simply being Daniel Defoe's daughter. Something else must have happened to lead people to believe she knew where the treasure was."

"Do you think she wrote about it in her diary?"

"Maybe—but we won't know for sure unless we find it."

And now that Meredith had a name for the mysterious man lurking around her house yesterday, she was one step closer.

***

By the time Meredith arrived home that evening, she was exhausted and ready for a light supper before bed. Thankfully, Arnold had fixed the back door and added a second deadbolt for more protection. Meredith had called a home security company, but they couldn't come until Monday morning to give her an estimate. She had called two other companies, and the wait was even longer.

Julia had invited Meredith to stay with her and her husband, Beau, for the weekend, but Meredith was certain that whoever broke into her house had taken what they wanted and wouldn't bother her anymore. It was pretty clear they knew exactly where to find the diary and would be long gone by now. She had thanked Julia, but politely refused.

"I think I've put off calling Chase and Carter for too long," Meredith told GK when she walked into the kitchen to feed him. "What do you think?"

GK rubbed up against Meredith's leg and purred.

As she set out GK's dish of food, she found Carter's number first and placed the call. He didn't disappoint her and told her all the reasons why she should either take a roommate or move into a secure apartment building. When she told him she had finally set up an appointment for a home security system to be installed, he eased his ranting, but told her she should have taken Julia up on the offer to stay at her house. Meredith assured him she would be fine and would sleep with his old baseball bat next to her in bed that night.

After she got off the phone with Carter, she called Chase.

"Hey, Mom." Chase answered almost immediately. "Have you had a chance to read Anna's diary?"

"About that." Meredith pulled bread and sandwich fixings from the refrigerator. "Someone broke into the house last night and stole the diary."

There was a pause on the other end. "You're joking, right?"

"I wish I was. Julia and I are already on the case, so you can rest assured that we'll find the diary *and* the person who stole it before the police do." She tried to make her voice sound light and confident.

"Are you being serious with me?"

She sighed. "Whoever broke in knew right where to look for the diary."

"And you're at the house now? Alone?" His voice started to sound more and more like Carter's.

"Yes, but I have a home security company coming on Monday—"

"I'm coming to stay the weekend with you."

"That's ridiculous. I'm fine." A movement near Troup Square caught Meredith's eye, just like it had the night before. A man stood in exactly the same spot, under the same tree. This time, there was just enough light out to get a better look at him.

Moving carefully, so as not to draw attention, Meredith went to a different window to get a better look at him.

"Mom?"

"Just a second, Chase."

"What's going on?"

Sweat began to trickle down Meredith's back as she recognized the same man she saw yesterday. He looked just like Ron. Was it James Bellefontaine? And, if it was, why was he standing outside in the square? Was he the one who broke into her house last night? If he did, why was he back?

Meredith knew if she told Chase who was standing in the square, looking at her house, he'd call the police and come immediately.

A part of her wanted him to—but another part was curious why this man continued to come back. If the police came, they'd scare him off again, wouldn't they? What if she stayed where she was and watched him? She could stay up all night if need be. If he approached the house, she could call the police then. Right now, he was simply standing in the square.

"Mom, I'm coming, and I won't take no for an answer."

"Don't be silly."

"Why are you whispering?"

Had she whispered?

"That's it. I'm on my way—"

"What are you doing?" a voice asked right behind Meredith.

Meredith jumped and screamed, her heart pounding hard against her chest. She dropped her phone and pressed against the wall.

Carmen stood behind her, a backpack slung over her shoulder, a grocery bag in hand, and an eyebrow cocked.

"You almost scared me to death." Meredith placed her hand over her chest and slumped against the wall. "What are *you* doing?"

"Mom? Mom?" Chase yelled into the phone.

Meredith picked it up again. "Calm down, Chase. It's just Carmen."

Chase grew quiet. "Carmen's there?"

"Apparently."

Carmen held up the spare set of keys Meredith had given her to use whenever she wanted to cook in Meredith's kitchen. It was an open invitation, and Carmen had come often—which was how she'd ended up scaring Chase a few weeks back.

"I decided you shouldn't be alone." Carmen placed the bag of groceries on the counter. "I'm staying the weekend with you."

"Is she staying with you?" Chase asked.

Relief washed over Meredith, though she would never admit to Chase—or Carmen—that she appreciated having the company.

"I guess I don't have a choice," Meredith said, feigning annoyance.

"Good," Chase said. "I'm happy you won't be alone." After a brief hesitation, he asked, "Can I talk to Carmen?"

Meredith held out her cell phone to Carmen. "It's Chase."

A brief smile crossed Carmen's lips and something softened around her eyes before she turned away with Meredith's phone. "*Hola.*"

Meredith couldn't hear what Chase was saying, but Carmen nodded several times and said *sí* more than once.

"I will." Carmen turned, enough for Meredith to see her face, and she found a shy smile on the young woman's lips. "See you then."

When Carmen met Meredith's gaze, she masked her emotions and handed the phone back.

Chase had already hung up.

"Well?" Meredith looked expectantly at Carmen.

Carmen's sassy eyebrows rose to matching heights. "We have everything under control."

"You do?"

"Sí, *señora.*" She set her backpack on the floor and started to pull the groceries out of the bag on the counter. "I'll stay the night with you, and then Chase will come tomorrow to make sure everything is okay."

Carmen began to hum softly as she made herself comfortable in Meredith's kitchen, and Meredith couldn't help but admit that she felt much better knowing Carmen was there.

When she glanced out at Troup Square, James Bellefontaine—if that's who it was—had disappeared once again.

Meredith would get to the bottom of this mystery, and she was thankful she had friends like Carmen who were there to help.

Chapter Six

THE DOWNHOME DINER HAD QUICKLY become Meredith and Julia's favorite place to eat in downtown, historic Savannah. Bright and cheery, with yellow walls and large vintage photos, it always made Meredith smile. Red vinyl stools lined the sparkling counter, and comfortable booths wrapped around the outside of the room.

Meredith sat in one of the booths, waiting for Julia on Saturday at lunchtime. She had invited Carmen to come, but Carmen had chosen to stay at Meredith's house to prepare an authentic Guatemalan meal for supper. She wouldn't tell Meredith what she was making, but from the groceries she had pulled out the night before, Meredith was almost certain chiles rellenos were on the menu.

Chase was due to arrive sometime in the afternoon, and Meredith wasn't sure if she should be home when he got there, or if he and Carmen would rather she make herself scarce. She wasn't exactly certain what was going on between them, but then again, she wasn't sure if they knew either.

"Sorry I'm late," Julia said as she entered the diner and joined Meredith at their booth. "I didn't sleep well last night, and that messed up everything this morning."

"I'm sorry you didn't sleep well." Meredith had already drunk half of her coffee, and it had begun to cool. When Charlene caught her eye and lifted the pot of coffee with a questioning look, Meredith nodded.

Julia looked more sad than tired, in Meredith's opinion. "Are you feeling okay?" she asked her friend.

Julia sighed. "I'm fine—but I'm worried about Beau."

Charlene approached the table with a fresh pot of coffee and a cup for Julia. She glanced at the clock over the counter and smiled. "I can officially wish you a good afternoon."

"Hi, Charlene," Julia said with a half-hearted smile.

"What can I get y'all?" Charlene asked after she refilled Meredith's coffee cup. "Shrimp and Grits, Pot Likker Noodle Bowl?"

"I'll have the biscuits and gravy on your specials board," Meredith said, not needing to look at a menu.

"And for you, Miss Julia?" Charlene asked.

"I'll just have the coffee, thanks."

Something was definitely wrong.

"Let me know if you change your mind." Charlene winked and left them to talk.

"What's going on, Julia?" Meredith leaned forward. "You never pass up a meal here."

Julia wrapped her hands around her coffee cup, staring into the dark liquid. "I think Beau is cheating on me."

Meredith blinked several times before Julia's words even made sense. "What?"

"It started last week." Julia finally looked up at Meredith, grief filling her eyes. "At first, I thought he was golfing late, but it happened twice last week and twice this week. I tried calling him last night, after I thought he should be home, but he didn't answer. I called his golfing buddies, but they weren't with him. And when he came home, and I asked where he'd been, he kept changing the subject. He never did tell me."

"That's strange." Meredith shook her head. "But I really doubt he's cheating on you. Beau's the last person I can imagine doing that."

"That's what I thought too." Julia bit her bottom lip and looked out the window.

Meredith reached across the table and squeezed Julia's hand. "I'm sure there's a good explanation. Try not to worry."

Julia let out a long, low breath. "You're right. Beau's been faithful all these years. Why would he start seeing someone else now?" She nodded. "Let's not talk about it anymore, okay?"

Meredith leaned back in her seat, finding a subject that would make Julia smile. "Chase is coming into town this afternoon, and Carmen is at my house cooking up a Mexican storm."

The comment had the intended effect, and Julia lifted her eyebrows. "You don't say?"

"Chase called last night and talked with her for a little while, and then they texted after that into the evening." Meredith shrugged. "I don't know if they're just becoming friends or if it's something deeper."

The door opened, and a familiar woman entered the diner.

"Don't look now," Meredith whispered to Julia. "But Beatrice just walked—"

"Meredith! Julia!" Beatrice zeroed in on the ladies. "I've been looking for you two."

Meredith closed her eyes briefly and then fixed a smile on her face.

"Meredith." Beatrice glided over to their booth, her pink sundress trailing with ribbons. "I am positively devastated, darling. How are you?"

"I'm fine—"

"Bless your heart. I can't stop thinking about your precious diary." She slid into the booth next to Meredith—much too close for comfort—and put her hand on Meredith's. "Do the police have any clues?"

"Beatrice," Julia said, "how did you hear about the diary?"

"I just bawled and bawled when I heard the news," Beatrice said to Meredith, ignoring Julia. "Y'all must be beside yourselves."

Meredith scooted back on the bench, but Beatrice inched closer.

"I'm really okay," Meredith answered. "The investigation is keeping me busy."

"The police said the thief broke into your house." Her eyes grew wide as she looked to Julia. "In the middle of the night." She looked back at Meredith. "While you were in your bed."

"That about sums it up," Julia said dryly.

"You must be terrified to be home alone." Beatrice put one hand on her chest and fanned her face with the other. "I'd be terrified."

"I'm not alone." Meredith smiled. "Chase is coming home for the night."

"Oh, I'm so glad to hear it, honey." Beatrice patted Meredith's hand.

"Why were you looking for us?" Julia asked as she crossed her arms.

"I was going to suggest that we have a big unveiling of the diary at the annual membership meeting of the Savannah Historical Society." Beatrice's eyes glowed with her plans. "And I thought we could encourage everyone to come dressed in clothing from the early eighteenth century for the gala that evening. The theme will be Colonial Savannah." She moved her hand in the air, as if seeing the words up in lights.

The Savannah Historical Society hosted a formal midsummer gala in conjunction with their annual membership meeting at the end of July. The gala was used as a fundraiser and a reason for people to gather together and socialize. Meredith used to preside over the prestigious affair, but now it was in Beatrice's hands.

"What if we can't find the diary before then?" Meredith asked.

Beatrice's eyes dimmed. "We can still celebrate Savannah's colonial days, though the diary would have been the crown jewel in my magical night." She sat up straighter. "And the police told me they hope to recover the diary soon."

"So that's how you know," Julia said, her arms still crossed. "The police have questioned you, haven't they?"

Beatrice lifted her nose and didn't meet Julia's or Meredith's curious gazes. "They have."

"And?" Julia asked.

Beatrice stood and ran her hands down the front of her dress. "I was appalled to be interrogated as if I were a common criminal."

"You were one of the last people to see the diary," Meredith said gently. "They simply wanted to know what you remembered about the afternoon."

"They were very intrusive," Beatrice said, as if she was insulted. "They wanted to know where I was the night the diary was stolen."

"Where were you?" Julia asked, matter-of-factly.

Beatrice's mouth dropped open. "Are you suggesting *I* took the diary?"

"Of course not," Meredith said quickly. "We just need to know about everyone who was there."

"The police planned to call Conner Pearlman and Anthony Stone as well," Julia said. "Not just you."

Meredith suddenly remembered that Conner Pearlman had handed Beatrice his card when she'd asked him about appraising her diary collection. "By the way," she said, "do you still have Pearlman's business card?"

Beatrice frowned and looked inside her purse. She rummaged around for several moments and then produced the card. "Here." She handed it to Meredith. "I don't plan to call him any time soon. He had shifty eyes and was a little too eager to get his hands on that diary, if you ask me."

"Several people were," Julia said, "if I remember correctly."

Meredith set the card on the table next to her coffee cup. "We'll keep that in mind when we talk to him. Thanks for the card."

"I should be getting along." Beatrice snapped her purse shut. "Let me know the minute you find that diary, so we can start planning the unveiling at the gala." She walked to the door and waved goodbye as she slipped outside.

"Beatrice!" Julia called after her.

Beatrice didn't hear—or, she pretended not to hear—as the door closed behind her.

Julia settled back into the booth. "She never did tell us where she was the night the diary was stolen."

"No." Meredith lifted the card. "But she did give us Conner Pearlman's number."

"I think she's hiding something."

"I think she's just insulted."

"Either way, she was there right before the diary was stolen, so until I know otherwise"—Julia pulled her coffee cup up to her lips—"she's still a suspect in my book."

Meredith glanced down at the business card. "Hopefully we can learn more about the appraiser and strike him off our list too."

"Do you want me to call him?"

"No." Meredith shook her head. "I'll call him when I get home."

It was Saturday, but she didn't think the appraiser would mind if she had a few questions for him.

***

On the short ride home from the Downhome Diner, Meredith found herself looking intently at men walking along the streets, searching for Ron's look-alike. It wasn't easy, since hundreds of tourists filled the old squares and milled around the attractions, restaurants, and stores in downtown Savannah.

Forcing herself to loosen her shoulders and focus on the road, she tried to enjoy the beautiful Saturday afternoon, marveling in the dappled sunlight and horse-drawn carriages.

Chase's car was parked in one of Meredith's two parking spots behind her house when she pulled up. Meredith raised her eyebrows, surprised that he'd already arrived. She wasn't expecting him for a couple more hours.

"Hello," she called out when she entered the back of her house. The last thing she wanted to do was alarm Chase and Carmen by her sudden presence. "I'm home."

"Hey, Mom." Chase opened the door into the back entry, a big smile on his face.

She returned the smile, so happy to see him again. "You're here earlier than I anticipated."

"I hope that's okay."

"Of course it is."

"I was able to cancel my plans this morning and thought I'd come sooner to help Carmen make supper." He looked more and more like his father the older he got. "She's teaching me how to make chiles rellenos."

"You don't even like Tex-Mex food." She walked up the steps and gave him a quick hug.

"It's growing on me." He placed a kiss on her cheek. "Carmen has convinced me to give it another try. She claims I don't like it because I've never had *her* Tex-Mex—except it's Guatemalan, of course."

Meredith smiled to herself as she followed Chase into the kitchen. Carmen was there, pots steaming on the stove, ingredients spread out over the countertops, salsa music playing from the Bluetooth speaker on the shelf.

"Hola, boss." Carmen grinned as she wiped crumbs off the countertop. "Did you have a good lunch with Julia?"

"I did." Though she wished Julia hadn't been worried about Beau. "How are things going here?" Meredith glanced between Carmen and Chase, her eyebrows raised in question.

Chase and Carmen smiled at each other.

"Couldn't be better," Chase said. "But I wish Carmen would let me do more of the cooking."

Carmen lifted a shoulder and winked at Chase. "I cannot share my secret family recipes with just anyone."

Meredith's cell phone rang in her purse, and she lifted it to look at the display screen.

QUIN CROWLEY.

Warmth filled Meredith's cheeks, and she couldn't stop her heart from fluttering a little.

"Another newspaper reporter?" Carmen asked.

"No." Meredith shook her head. "It's Quin Crowley."

"The lawyer?" Chase frowned.

Meredith could only nod as the phone continued to ring.

"Well?" Carmen asked. "Aren't you going to answer it?"

"What does he want?" Meredith asked. "Why is he calling?"

Chase laughed. "You won't know until you answer."

Taking a deep breath, Meredith finally pressed the green button. "Hello?"

"Hi, Meredith." Quin's voice was strong and steady, just like him. "Is this a good time to chat?"

Meredith turned away from Chase's and Carmen's curious glances and set her purse on the kitchen table. "It's a great time. What can I do for you?"

"Nothing." Was he smiling on the other end? It sounded like he was smiling. "I just heard about the diary and wanted to call and make sure you're okay."

"Oh." That was all? For some reason she had expected him to invite her out again—was that why she felt a little disappointed? "Boy, it doesn't take long for bad news to spread, that's for sure. I'm doing fine. Julia and I are already on the case, and my son Chase is here with my friend Carmen to keep me company."

"Invite him to supper," Carmen whispered loudly. "We have plenty."

Meredith waved away her suggestion.

"Do you have any significant leads?" Quin asked.

"We've narrowed it down to four suspects, but one of them is someone we don't know."

"Is there anything I can do to help?" he asked.

"Go ahead, Mom," Chase said. "Ask him to join us."

Meredith tried to ignore Chase and Carmen, but neither one was going back to their cooking.

"I appreciate the offer," Meredith said to Quin. "I don't think there's anything you can do right now."

"Except for come over," Carmen said in the same loud whisper.

"Don't hesitate to ask if there is something." Quin paused. "I've missed seeing you, Meredith. I was hoping we could get together some time to catch up."

"Is he asking you out?" Carmen asked, her eyes aglow.

Meredith waved her away again.

"I'd like that," Meredith said to Quin.

"Just ask him," Chase urged Meredith. "What do you have to lose?"

"Actually," Meredith said into the phone, her heart pounding a little harder, "are you busy this evening? Carmen is making an authentic Guatemalan meal, and she insists she has enough for another guest."

"Yes!" Carmen waved a spatula in the air. "Good job, Meredith."

Meredith wanted to roll her eyes. Instead, she smiled and said to Quin, "Would you like to join us?"

Quin paused on the other end of the phone. "Are you sure?"

Even though she'd been pressured by Carmen and Chase, she was happy she'd asked him. "Yes. I'd love to catch up and introduce you to one of my sons."

"I'd like that too."

"Come whenever you'd like. Carmen should have supper ready by six, but if you come early, we can enjoy some appetizers on the back deck."

"I'll be there as soon as I wrap up a project I started here at the house."

"See you then."

"Bye, Meredith."

She pulled the phone away and stared at the dark screen. Had she just invited an eligible bachelor over to her house for supper?

"Don't look so shocked." Chase laughed. "I knew you had it in you."

"*Eres bonita cuando tus mejillas son rosas,*" Carmen said with a smile.

"What did you say?" Chase asked her.

"I told your mother she's pretty when her cheeks are pink."

Meredith put her hands to her warm cheeks and shook her head. "I have some work to do before Quin gets here. I'll leave you two to your matchmaking ways and go into the study."

Their laughter followed her down the back steps and into the basement.

She needed to call Conner Pearlman and wanted to look over the writing desk again, in case she missed a clue.

But, more than that, she needed a little space to process her invitation to Quin.

The writing desk sat exactly where she'd left it on her large oak desk in the study. She'd only opened it the one time at the bank but hadn't looked over it very carefully. After all these years, she doubted there would be anything left in it from Anna, besides the diary that had been stolen, but it was worth a shot.

With great care, Meredith unhooked the metal latch and slowly opened the box. It lay down flat, with one side slanted and the other side perfectly square. The slanted side had a solid, smooth writing surface. On the top right-hand corner, the initials *AMC* were carved in beautiful script. They must be Anna's initials. Meredith ran her fingers over the engraving, remembering that Anna had said the desk and diary were a gift from her father on her wedding day.

Meredith lifted the writing surface and glanced underneath where the diary had been and where someone might store extra paper. There was nothing in the container, so Meredith lowered the slab of wood and looked in the boxes on the other side where someone might have stored pens or pencils, as well as ink bottles. Again, it was empty.

Nothing.

A pang of disappointment passed through her as she looked down at the writing desk—but what had she hoped to find?

Instead of dwelling on her disappointment, she pulled the business card out of her back pocket and dialed Pearlman's number into her phone.

The phone rang twice, and then a woman answered. "Hello?" she said.

"Hello, this is Meredith Bellefontaine. Is Conner Pearlman available?"

"Who?"

"Conner Pearlman."

"I'm sorry. I think you have the wrong number."

Meredith frowned as she looked at the card again. "Isn't this the number for Conner Pearlman, the antiques appraiser?"

"No. I don't know who Conner Pearlman is. I've never heard of him."

"Whose phone number is this?"

"Mine."

"And who are you?" Meredith set the card down on her desk.

"Um, I'm not comfortable giving my name out to strangers."

Perhaps Conner Pearlman had a new phone, and this woman received his old number. "How long have you had this phone number?"

"At least five or six years."

"And you've never heard of Conner Pearlman?"

"No, I haven't." The woman paused. "Goodbye."

The connection went dead, and Meredith pulled her phone away from her ear. She checked the card again and compared it to the number she had dialed. It was the same.

Why would Conner Pearlman give them a wrong number? Maybe it was a typo—perhaps one of the numbers was off—but didn't people check those things before they had their cards printed?

Meredith was more confused now than ever before. She and Julia couldn't find a record of Conner Pearlman anywhere online, and now the number he'd given them was wrong as well.

Maybe he wasn't an antiques appraiser after all. Anthony Stone had been the one who introduced them. He said he and Conner Pearlman were old friends—so was Mr. Stone lying too?

Meredith had a lot of unanswered questions, ones that needed answers soon.

But for now she had a guest coming, and she needed to get ready.

Chapter Seven

THE FRONT DOORBELL RANG, AND Meredith hoped Chase would answer for her. She was still in her bedroom, standing in front of the full-length mirror, putting the last touches on her outfit.

She'd spent far too much time on her appearance, fussing about what to wear. She had already tried on four different outfits. Carmen had come up at one point to see what was taking her so long, but a timer had gone off in the kitchen, and she didn't trust Chase to leave her beans and rice alone.

"Mom," Chase called up the stairs. "Mr. Crowley's here."

Meredith looked at her appearance one more time, turning this way and that to check every angle. She'd settled on a pair of blue jean capris with a white button-down shirt, tucked in with a brown belt. She had touched up her makeup and put on her favorite earrings and then slipped on a pair of comfortable yet stylish sandals. She didn't want to look like she was trying too hard—but she didn't want to look uninterested either.

"Ugh." She shook her head at her reflection. She hadn't been this silly about a man since her first date with Ron.

Taking a deep breath, she put on a smile, remembering what her mother had told her about a woman who smiles. She had said that no matter what a woman wore, if she didn't wear a smile, her outfit wasn't complete.

Chase stood in the front entry with Quin, chatting comfortably as Meredith walked down the steps.

Quin glanced up when she appeared, and he grinned. "Hello, Meredith."

"Hi, Quin." She wasn't sure how to greet him. Should they shake hands, give a quick hug, do nothing at all?

Before she could decide, he leaned in and gave her a brief hug. "It's good to see you again," he said. "You look great."

"Thank you. So do you." He smelled as good as he looked too.

He was a handsome man in his early sixties with silver hair and the most unique eyes Meredith had ever seen. One was blue and one was brown.

"I see you've already met Chase." Meredith smiled at her son.

"Yes," Quin said. "We were just talking about his work in Atlanta. Sounds like he took after his mother in the history field."

"Mom was the person who introduced me to history and showed me how to appreciate people and events from the past," Chase said. "It's been a really rewarding job."

Meredith squeezed Chase's arm, a little pride in her heart. "He's far surpassed any of my accomplishments."

"And Mr. Crowley tells me he's a corporate lawyer," Chase said, changing the subject. He usually did when Meredith shined a light on his success.

"I am." Quin nodded but turned his attention on Meredith. "But it's not nearly as exciting as owning an investigation agency. You've solved some pretty amazing cases, Meredith."

"I don't solve them on my own. I couldn't do what I do without Julia and Carmen."

"Speaking of..." Chase motioned toward the back of the house. "Why don't we join Carmen in the kitchen? I think she's about ready for a little break from cooking, and we can sit out on the back deck."

"That sounds good to me." Quin indicated that Meredith should lead the way.

Meredith's nerves had started to settle a little. She was thankful for Chase's calming presence as they walked into the kitchen. It didn't even look like Carmen had been cooking there just an hour before. Everything looked tidy again.

"Hola," Carmen said to Quin. "It's nice to see you again, Mr. Crowley."

"And you too, Carmen." He looked at her and then at Chase. "And please, call me Quin."

"Shall we step outside, Quin?" Chase asked. "Carmen and I set the appetizers and drinks out there. We'll bring out the main course in a bit."

"I should have you two over more often," Meredith teased. "I could get used to this."

Carmen opened the glass door that led onto the back deck from the kitchen. It was a large deck with comfortable furniture, several potted plants, and a magnificent view of Troup Square.

The heat had let up a little and was bearable as they took their seats.

Carmen and Chase sat on one couch and Meredith and Quin sat on the other, facing them. Between the couches, a low coffee table boasted refreshing sweet tea and platters with guacamole, spiced mango, nachos, and fresh tortilla chips.

They enjoyed small talk, commenting on the beautiful square and the warm weather. They praised Carmen for her delicious food, and Chase even declared how much he liked it. Finally, the conversation turned to the diary.

"The weirdest thing happened this afternoon," Meredith said as she set her plate of appetizers on her lap. "I called the phone number on Conner Pearlman's business card, but it was the wrong number. A woman answered and said she had never heard of him."

Chase frowned. "That is weird."

"Not to mention that Julia and I can't find anything online about him or his appraisal company."

"Really?" Chase continued to frown. "I wonder if someone at the university has a number for him."

"Are you certain you remember seeing him at the university?" Meredith asked, recalling that Chase had recognized Conner the day they'd met.

"I thought so," Chase said. "He looks really familiar, but if he hadn't told me his line of work, I don't know if I would have placed him."

"So, you're not sure if you recognize him from the university?" Meredith leaned forward. "You might know him from somewhere else?"

"I don't think I *know* him," Chase said slowly. "Just recognize him. Like I've seen him somewhere."

"Maybe at a different job?" Quin offered. "Somewhere you go often. A store or restaurant, or something like that?"

"Maybe." Chase set his iced tea on a coaster and shook his head. "It's more like I've seen him in an advertisement, or something like that. His face looks familiar."

Everyone was quiet for a minute as Chase stared down at his plate of appetizers.

"I feel like I've seen him in a suit and tie, his big, toothy grin staring at me." Chase shook his head. "Does that even make sense?"

Carmen shrugged. "Maybe he's on a billboard or—"

"That's it!" Chase pulled his cell phone out of his pocket. "I know exactly where I've seen him before. His picture is plastered on bus billboards all over Atlanta." He typed something into his phone.

Meredith looked at Quin, who smiled.

"Here." Chase turned the phone around for Meredith to see. "He's the president of the Atlanta Savings and Loan. His name isn't Conner Pearlman, it's Troy LeBlanc."

Meredith took the phone and stared down at the man who had introduced himself as Conner Pearlman. There was no question it was the same person.

"What in the world?" Meredith handed the phone back to Quin. "Why would he tell us his name is Conner Pearlman and he's an appraiser?"

Sunshine gleamed off Chase's glass of iced tea as he lifted it to his lips and took a drink. Condensation dripped from the glass onto his lap. "Maybe it's time to visit Anthony Stone. Isn't he the one who hired Conner Pearl—I mean, Troy LeBlanc?"

"I think it's time to talk to both of them," Meredith said. "I'll call Atlanta Savings and Loan on Monday and ask to speak to Troy LeBlanc."

"Do you know Anthony Stone?" Carmen asked Quin. "Both of you are lawyers, no?"

"I don't know him," Quin said to Carmen. He turned to Meredith. "But I'd be happy to visit him with you, if you'd like."

Meredith was sitting close to Quin, and when she looked at him, she was reminded how close. He made her feel emotions she'd buried almost two years ago and thought she'd never resurrect again. But here she was, enjoying his company and wondering if she wanted more of it. Did she want him to visit Anthony Stone with her? It was something she could do on her own—but it wouldn't hurt to have another lawyer present when she confronted the man, would it?

"I would appreciate that very much," she said to him.

Quin smiled and nodded. "Would Monday morning work for you?"

Meredith nodded. "That would be just fine."

Chase and Carmen were quiet as they sat across from Meredith and Quin, and when Meredith turned back to them, they were both grinning.

She felt like scolding them, as if they were mischievous children. Instead, she gave them a warning look and went back to enjoying her refreshments.

In Troup Square, the Saturday foot traffic was especially high, and Meredith's gaze landed on the spot she'd seen Ron's look-alike two nights in a row. Would he be there again tonight?

A shiver ran up her spine, despite the heat, and Meredith was happy Chase would be spending the night.

First thing on Monday, Meredith would talk to Julia and see if she had a contact at the police department who could run a background check on James Bellefontaine. She'd also talk to Officer Clemmons and Officer Ellis and see if they'd made progress on the investigation. Then she'd call on Anthony Stone and get to the bottom of Troy LeBlanc's true identity and why he had lied.

It would be a full week. She just hoped that by the end of it she'd have Anna's diary back in hand.

***

On Monday morning Quin opened the heavy oak door into the law offices of Anthony Stone and allowed Meredith to enter before him. As one of the oldest lawyers in Savannah, Mr. Stone's offices were in a historic building in the heart of downtown with thick Greek Revival columns out front. Inside, marble flooring and heavy woodwork greeted Meredith as they stepped into the reception hall.

Her shoes clicked on the polished floor, echoing off the high ceilings. "Is Mr. Stone available?" she asked the young receptionist sitting at the front desk.

"Do you have an appointment?" The woman's bright red lips were vibrant against her white teeth.

"No, but please tell him Meredith Bellefontaine is here to see him."

The receptionist lifted a phone and pressed a few buttons. Her long red nails made a tapping noise that was far louder than necessary.

Quin stood beside Meredith, his gaze roaming over the beautiful room.

The rich details were incredible. Meredith had never been in the building before, but it was another fine example of pre-Civil War architecture. If she had to guess, she'd date it between 1830 and 1855.

"Mr. Stone," the receptionist said into the phone. "There's a Meredith Bellefontaine and guest to see you."

"Are you sure we shouldn't have made an appointment?" Meredith whispered to Quin.

"Better to take him off guard, if we want to get the truth out of him," Quin said back, just as quietly.

Hanging up the phone, the receptionist pointed at the wingback chairs in the waiting area near a massive fireplace. "Mr. Stone will be out to receive you in a moment."

Meredith and Quin went to the chairs she indicated and took a seat. They were hard and cold, covered in dark brown leather and shiny brass tacks. The fireplace dominated one wall, though it was empty and lifeless at the moment. Above it, a painting of Anthony Stone looked down on them with an unsmiling face.

Unease slithered through Meredith's spine, and she forced herself to look away from the painting.

She met Quin's warm gaze.

"Thank you for coming with me," she said quietly. "I appreciate having someone who can approach this situation from a nonpersonal point of view."

His eyes were disarming as he smiled. "I hope it's a little personal."

Meredith caught her breath, uncertain what he meant by his statement. "I—I just mean, the diary is very important to the Bellefontaine family. I had hoped to pass it on to my children and grandchildren someday. I'm feeling a little too close to the situation to be objective right now."

"I know what you meant, Meredith." He spoke gently. "I just want you to know I'm not here for professional reasons. I'm here because I'm your friend, and I want to help."

She looked down at her purse, which she'd set on her lap. "I guess that is personal."

His voice was even lower. "I'd like to think so."

The grandfather clock stood on the other side of the room, its steady *ticktock* suddenly very loud in the quiet space.

"Mrs. Bellefontaine, what a pleasant surprise." Mr. Stone appeared at the opening leading into the office area. He stood tall and proud, his white mustache and hair perfectly trimmed and styled. He wore another three-piece suit, pressed and spotless.

Meredith and Quin rose and met him under the arch. Meredith extended her hand to the lawyer and then introduced Quin. "This is my friend, Mr. Quin Crowley."

"Anthony Stone," Mr. Stone said to Quin. "It's nice to meet you." He paused and frowned. "I feel like I've heard your name before."

"I'm also a lawyer," Quin said. "Corporate attorney."

"Ah, yes. That's why it sounds familiar." He motioned toward a door down a long hall. "Won't you step into my office?"

They followed Mr. Stone through the door and into a stunning room. Rich, dark trim dominated the space. Three of the four walls were covered in floor-to-ceiling bookcases with beautiful leather-bound books. The fourth wall had floor-to-ceiling windows with deep burgundy curtains. Leather wingback chairs sat across from Mr. Stone's desk.

"Won't you have a seat?" Mr. Stone shut his door and then took his own seat. "I must confess, I'm surprised to see you,

Mrs. Bellefontaine—especially with your lawyer friend. To what do I owe this visit?"

Meredith settled into her chair and straightened her back. "I'm here about the missing diary. I was hoping you could answer a few of my questions."

"Missing diary?" Mr. Stone frowned, his white bushy eyebrows turning into a *V* on his forehead. "What missing diary?"

Quin glanced briefly at Meredith, his own frown marring his handsome face.

Was it possible Mr. Stone hadn't heard?

"Anna Coles's diary was stolen out of my home the very same day I retrieved it from the bank." She tilted her head. "Haven't you heard?"

Mr. Stone looked from Meredith to Quin, shock and horror on his face. "You must be joking with me. The diary was stolen?"

"I'm afraid I'm very serious." Meredith leaned forward. "Haven't the police contacted you?"

"No. I haven't heard a word from anyone about the diary."

"It's been in all the local papers," Quin said to Mr. Stone. "Everyone has been talking about it."

"I try not to read the papers." Mr. Stone shrugged. "Nothing but garbage and propaganda."

"The police asked me who was at my house the day it was stolen." Meredith played with the snap on her purse. "They said they would call you and the others."

"I haven't received a call. At least, not that I know of."

It seemed almost ludicrous that Mr. Stone had not heard about the missing diary, making Meredith even more suspicious.

"Do you have any idea who might want the diary?" Meredith asked him.

"No." Mr. Stone shook his head. "I don't know of anyone who wants it—but I'm sure there are a lot of people out there who do."

"Where were you on Thursday evening?" Quin asked him.

"Am I a suspect?" Mr. Stone stared at Quin.

Meredith didn't want him to become defensive. They probably wouldn't get anything out of him then. "The diary was stolen from my safe. There were only four people, besides my son and my colleague, who knew where I put it. You are one of those people. We're not accusing you. We're simply trying to get to the bottom of this mystery."

"And, hopefully, find the diary," Quin added. "If you're innocent, then we can anticipate your cooperation, correct?"

Mr. Stone looked at both of them for several heartbeats before he nodded. "Of course you can."

"Wonderful." Meredith let out a breath she hadn't realized she was holding. "Could you tell us where you were the night the diary was stolen?"

The leather seat beneath Meredith creaked as she shifted positions and waited for Mr. Stone to recall Thursday evening.

"I believe I ate dinner with my wife and my appraiser friend, Mr.—" He paused, and then went on. "Mr. Pearlman. After we dropped him off at his hotel, we went home and were there for the rest of the night."

"And your wife can verify your alibi?" Quin asked.

"Most definitely."

"About Mr. Pearlman." Meredith waded in carefully, knowing Mr. Stone was lying to her about his friend—and could possibly be lying about everything else as well. "I tried calling the number on his card, but it was a wrong number. And when Julia tried finding him on the internet, she wasn't able to locate a Conner Pearlman from Atlanta—at least, not one that's an antiques appraiser."

Mr. Stone stiffened and didn't meet Meredith's gaze.

"Is it possible," Meredith continued, "that Conner Pearlman is not an antiques appraiser, but a bank president named Troy LeBlanc?"

Sweat glistened on Mr. Stone's brow, and he lifted his hand to fiddle with a stack of papers on his desk.

"We know who Troy LeBlanc is," Quin said to Mr. Stone. "We just hoped you'd help us find him."

"And tell us why he said he was an appraiser," Meredith added.

"I, um…" Mr. Stone cleared his throat. "It's complicated."

"Are you longtime friends?" Meredith asked. "As you said? Or did you just meet him?"

Mr. Stone rose from his chair and walked to the window. He looked out toward Whitaker Street, his arms crossed. It took several moments before he answered. "It's true that Troy and I have been friends for years. We met a good fifteen years ago or more."

"Why did he say his name was Conner Pearlman?" Quin asked.

"It was his idea." Mr. Stone returned to his desk but didn't sit down. "It was all meant in good fun. If I had known the diary would go missing, I would never have agreed to the charade. I never imagined I'd be questioned. This most definitely puts us in a bad light."

More than he realized.

"What kind of game?" Meredith asked. "I'm confused."

Mr. Stone waved his hand as if it was inconsequential. "Right after Miss Temperance passed away, I was having supper with Troy, and I mentioned the diary. He's somewhat of an amateur treasure hunter. Where some men go to Africa and hunt big game, Troy travels the world in search of pirate treasure on his vacations." Mr. Stone put his hand on the back of his chair. "He's donated much of what he's found to the pirate museum in St. Augustine—you're more than welcome to verify that information. He doesn't do it to become rich. He just does it for fun."

Meredith had visited the pirate museum with Ron on a vacation a few years back. It had been fascinating to see all the treasure that had been recovered over the years.

"I thought he might find the diary interesting," Mr. Stone said, "given his pastime. So, when I said it was being inherited by you, he told me he'd love to peek inside the diary to see if it actually had information about Blackbeard's Treasure. I didn't think you'd let just anyone look at the diary, so I suggested he could pretend to be an antiques appraiser. It was his idea to change his name." Mr. Stone lifted his hands and shrugged. "That's all there is to it. He made up the fake business cards to go along with the ruse."

"Didn't he think I'd try calling him?" Meredith asked.

"We assumed he'd have a chance to look at the diary and then we'd be on our way. We didn't anticipate getting interrupted that day—or for the diary to be stolen."

Meredith met Mr. Stone's gaze and studied him for a moment, trying to weigh the honesty in his words. There were no telltale signs of lying, though it was evident he was uncomfortable. "My husband's aunt trusted you, Mr. Stone. You were a confidant and lifelong friend. What you and Troy LeBlanc did was very immature and unprofessional."

Mr. Stone's gaze hardened, and he pursed his lips. "Perhaps your dear aunt should have seen fit to leave me a little something in her will for all my troubles."

Silence filled the room as they stared at one another.

"You allowed LeBlanc to act out this ruse in retribution?" Quin asked.

Turning his gaze on Quin, Mr. Stone said, "Troy is an accomplished treasure hunter. He told me if he was able to get access to the information, and he found the treasure, he'd split the profits with me. I felt that was more than adequate for everything I did for Temperance through the years. She was not an easy woman to deal with."

Meredith stood, and Quin followed.

"What you've done is very unprofessional," Meredith said again.

"No harm was done." Mr. Stone's gaze softened again, and he became contrite, his voice dripping with Southern gentility. "I do hope you'll accept my apology, Mrs. Bellefontaine. Neither of us meant any ill will toward you or the diary, and we'll do whatever possible to help you recover it."

"Where is LeBlanc now?" Quin asked. "Did he return to Atlanta?"

"I believe so. He came to the house for brunch on Saturday morning and said he planned to visit some of the sights in Savannah before heading home."

"Do you have his phone number?" Meredith asked. "I'd like to talk to him personally."

"Yes, of course. My secretary should be able to give you the number on your way out."

Mr. Stone moved around his desk and opened his door. "And, if there's anything else I can do to help you, please don't hesitate to ask. I'm horrified about what's happened."

They left his office, and Meredith was given a slip of paper with Troy LeBlanc's real phone number.

"Thank you for your time," Meredith said to Mr. Stone.

Quin opened the exterior door, and he and Meredith exited the office building.

For a moment, they stood outside in the sweltering heat, and Meredith could only stare at the cars parked in front of the building. She felt duped and foolish. She'd allowed Mr. Stone and LeBlanc into her house under false pretenses. And they'd almost gotten away with their plan.

"I'm sorry, Meredith." Quin put his hand on the small of her back and directed her toward his car, which was parked down the block. "That man should be reported to the bar association."

"I'd rather not—at least for now." Meredith walked close beside him. "Until we're certain who took the diary, I'd like his cooperation. If we report him, he'll only cause us trouble."

"I'm surprised he admitted the truth to us." Quin took his keys from his pocket and unlocked the door with the fob.

"I'm not certain he told us the truth—at least, not the whole truth." Meredith didn't like the feeling she had concerning Mr. Stone and Troy LeBlanc. There had to be something else the lawyer hadn't told them. "I think he admitted all those things to us so we'd assume he was telling us everything. I think he's still hiding something."

"You might be right." He opened the door for Meredith. "Did you have a chance to run a background check on James Bellefontaine?"

"Julia's taking care of that today."

"And the other suspect?"

"Beatrice Enterline." Meredith got in the car, and Quin closed the door. She couldn't even say Beatrice's name without sighing.

Quin opened his door and got into the vehicle. "Does she have an alibi?" he asked.

"Not that I know of. I'd like to talk to her again."

"And what about the police investigation? Have they made any progress?"

"I called to speak to the officers in charge of the investigation, and they were very evasive, telling me it had been a busy weekend at the precinct." She shook her head. "I think they haven't done much, to be honest."

"It might be up to you and Julia."

"I'm not afraid to do the hard work. I just want the diary back."

A few minutes later, they pulled up to the back of Magnolia Investigations where he'd picked her up earlier.

When he came to a stop, he didn't make a move to get out of the car. "What's your next step?"

Meredith glanced out at the beautiful antebellum home that had been Ron's offices for years. It was still strange to know she'd followed in his footsteps and taken over the work he couldn't finish. "I plan to make a trip to the library and learn more about Anna Coles and her father, Daniel Defoe. If I can find the connection between them and Blackbeard, maybe that would give me a clue why the diary has always had so many rumors connected to it."

"Please let me know if I can help," Quin said. "I've really enjoyed spending time with you again."

"So have I." She smiled and put her hand on the door handle.

"Let me." He jumped out of the car and went around to open the door for her.

Meredith stepped out and clutched her purse. "Thanks again."

"My pleasure." He put his hand on her arm. "Don't be a stranger."

"I won't."

But as she walked inside Magnolia Investigations and was met with the sights and sounds so deeply connected to Ron, she wondered if it was a good idea to continue her friendship with Quin. She wasn't sure if she was ready.

Chapter Eight

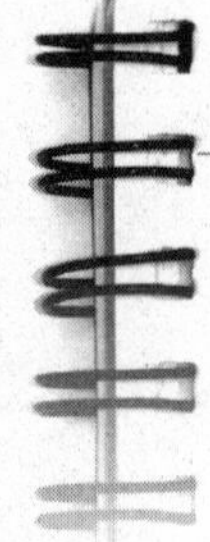

August 13, 1733
Colony of Georgia

The heat has become unbearable. I have retreated to the shade of my small home with my traveling desk to write in my diary this morning. But even here, the air is thick and moist, hanging heavy like the moss on the large oak trees. Not a single breeze eases our discomfort, nor does a storm remove the humidity. It is like this both day and night, and I feel as if I might suffocate from the effects of it. Ann has gone to retrieve our daily water, and we hope to get our wash done before the sun reaches its zenith.

My heart longs for the coolness and comforts of England, and I am not the only one. Already, there have been several families who have abandoned this colony. General Oglethorpe tried to stop them, to promise that these hardships are fleeting and temporary, but it is difficult to believe. He reminded us that we received free passage to come to Georgia and that we signed a contract—more accurately that our husbands signed them—but the families stole away in the middle of the night, and I can only imagine they have gone north to more established and cooler colonies. I, myself, long to go north and then to one day return to my beloved England when I might afford the passage. I do not want my dear Ann to marry one of these colonists and make her life here, but I fear she will marry John Gready and do just that. I do not disapprove of Mr. Gready. I just want a better life for Ann. I fear this colony will never amount to anything and will be nothing but toil and trouble for my dear girl.

I have tried to discuss my fears and my longings with Joseph, but he does not want to listen to me. He is far too preoccupied with whatever takes him away from the colony. We are like two strangers, living side by side, with two very different dreams. There is a rumor that more than one man has secretly taken possession of lands outside Savannah to grow and cultivate his own fields, to work for his own good and not the good of the others. One of these men is Noble Jones. He works harder than anyone I have ever met, yet he leaves the colony for days on end, just like Joseph. The only difference is, I do not believe Joseph is building his own plantation. I do not believe he is capable of this, nor does he have the desire to do so. Instead, I have my own suspicions about Joseph, and it all centers around a book he never lets out of his sight.

He has owned this book for years and has spent every available moment poring over it. It is a book very similar to the one I'm writing in now. Any time I have ever tried to look over his shoulder to see what the book contains, he becomes angry with me and slams the cover closed. I have asked him what the book holds, but he refuses to answer. When I have gone to look for the book while he is sleeping, I can never find it. And, when he leaves on his trips, he always takes it with him. I know the book is handwritten, and I've often suspected it is my father's handwriting, but I cannot examine it closely enough to learn the truth.

Joseph worked for my father for several years, and when my father died, many of his possessions were divided between me and my seven siblings. My father was a prolific writer and had at least a hundred manuscripts published. Joseph helped him on many of those projects toward the end of my father's life, and he was the one who went through my father's things to divide his writings among my siblings. I often wondered what, if anything, Joseph kept for himself, and now I am starting to suspect he took this particular book. I also have my suspicions about which book it is, but only time will tell. I must get a better look at it before I share my suspicions in this diary.

Regardless which book it is, if my father wrote it, I would like to read it. I do not think that is too much to ask. All the other things I inherited from him I was forced to leave in England when we made this trip. I long for a connection to my home and my family, and if Joseph's book is that connection, I will do whatever I can to read it.

I can see Ann returning from the well with the aid of Mr. Gready. I will put my diary away for now, but I will not rest until I know what Joseph's book contains. It may answer many of my questions—though I fear what the answers may be.

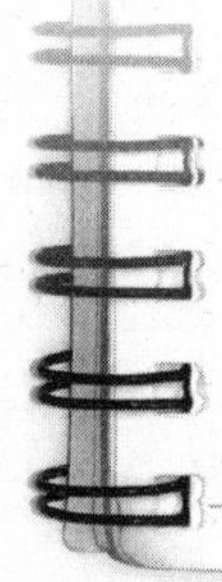

Meredith and Julia met at the Carnegie Library on East Henry Street late Monday afternoon. The brown brick building, with its square corners and clean lines, was the only prairie-style architecture in all of Savannah. Inside, the arts and crafts style was prominent in square pillars, half walls, and thick wood trim. It had become one of Meredith's and Julia's favorite places to visit while investigating, because it was home to their very helpful friend, Rebecca Thompson. They had met Rebecca while trying to uncover the truth behind Harriet Besset's disappearance in May. Rebecca had also proven to be indispensable when they worked on the case of Harlowe Green's missing brother.

If anyone could answer their questions about Daniel Defoe or Blackbeard's Island, it would be Rebecca.

"Hello," Rebecca said to the ladies when she spotted them walking toward the circulation desk in the large main room of the library. "Meredith, I've been meaning to call and ask how you're doing. I heard about the diary."

Meredith rested her arms on the high desk and smiled at her friend. "Julia and I are working hard to find the diary. That's why we've come here today."

"I'm happy to help." Rebecca stood and gave Meredith and Julia her full attention. "What would you like to know?"

It took a few minutes to fill Rebecca in on everything the ladies had already uncovered, but the look of complete concentration on Rebecca's face told Meredith she was following every twist and turn.

"So," Meredith said, "we're here to learn everything we can about Daniel Defoe and Blackbeard's Island."

"You've come to the right place!" Rebecca's calm and confident demeanor was exactly what Meredith needed at that moment.

"That's what we hoped to hear," Julia said with a grin.

"Why don't y'all move to a table while I get the files we have on Blackbeard's Island?" Rebecca motioned to one of the tables along the outside of the room near a large window. "We can use my laptop and do a little research on Daniel Defoe as well. I have a few resources in mind that might help."

Meredith and Julia did as Rebecca suggested and found a table. There were a handful of other patrons in the room, but most were sitting in front of laptops with earbuds in their ears. A woman stood near a bookshelf, glancing at titles, while an elderly gentleman sat in an armchair with a newspaper in hand. The room was quiet, except for the occasional laughter coming from the children's section.

"Did you hear back from your police friend?" Meredith asked Julia.

"No. He didn't think he could pull the information until this afternoon. Hopefully we'll know more when we get back to the office."

"I'm anxious to know if the look-alike is Ron's cousin." Meredith hadn't seen him since the night Carmen had surprised her, but that didn't mean he wasn't still lurking around.

"Do you really think he's the one who broke in and took the diary?"

Meredith set her purse on the table. "I'm not so sure anymore. Now that I know that Anthony Stone and Tony LeBlanc lied to me, I'm having a hard time trusting them."

"And don't forget about Beatrice." Julia lifted an eyebrow.

"I haven't. I plan to talk to her again soon, and hopefully not in a public place. She might be more willing to open up if it's one-on-one."

"What about Troy LeBlanc?" Julia asked. "Have you had a chance to call his number?"

"I did, but it was his work number, and his assistant told me he would be out of the office on vacation all week."

"Oh, really?" Julia raised both eyebrows this time. "Did the assistant say where?"

"He wouldn't give me any information—not even his cell phone number."

"So, we're back to square one with him?"

"At least we know his real name."

"I suppose that's a start."

"I'll call Mr. Stone again and ask if he has LeBlanc's cell number or if he knows where LeBlanc might be reached."

"Didn't Mr. Stone say that LeBlanc had brunch on Saturday and then planned to see some of the sights in Savannah before heading home?"

Meredith nodded.

"Perhaps he's still here." Julia clasped her hands on the table in front of her. "When you talk to Mr. Stone, ask him where Troy was staying. Maybe we could pay him a visit."

Rebecca walked toward them with a gray, acid-free file folder box. On the outside was marked BLACKBEARD'S ISLAND. She also had her laptop bag slung over her shoulder.

But it was the smile on her face that made Meredith the most excited. Rebecca was a wealth of information, and Meredith loved spending time with her, gleaning knowledge and facts about her beloved city. Rebecca's husband, Kelvin, was known as the "Voice of Savannah" and led boat excursions up and down the Savannah River. Both he and Rebecca were fascinating individuals with an incredible grasp of Savannah history.

"Here's a good place to start," Rebecca said to the ladies as she set the file box on the table. "But I'd like to talk to Kelvin about the island and see what he knows. The folder doesn't contain much information."

Meredith opened the box and glanced at the folder headings. PIRATE ACTIVITY & LORE, GOVERNMENT USE, PRIVATE USE, AND WILDLIFE PRESERVE.

"The island was known as Blackbeard's Island since at least 1760, when it was written on a map," Rebecca said as she set her laptop bag on the table. "In 1800 it was sold to the US Navy and used as a federal timber reserve for a couple of decades, but then it wasn't used again until 1880, when it became the largest federal marine quarantine station on the south Atlantic coast."

Meredith removed the PIRATE ACTIVITY & LORE file from the box as Rebecca talked. It wasn't very thick and only held a few copied newspaper articles.

"The quarantine station was deactivated by 1909 when vaccines for yellow fever were developed," Rebecca continued, "and in 1914 President Woodrow Wilson turned the island into a wildlife preserve, which it remains to this day."

"What about the pirates?" Julia asked. "Why is it named after Blackbeard?"

"It's named Blackbeard Island because of the rumors that have swirled around it for centuries." Rebecca took a seat and opened her laptop. "I'd like to ask Kelvin more about the legends associated with the island, but from what I know, Edward Teach, also known as Blackbeard, was rumored to spend time on the island between 1716 and 1718 when he needed to hide. Somewhere along the line, people believed he buried his treasure there."

"Has there ever been a hunt?" Meredith asked.

"In the 1880s, a group of people launched a search on the north side of the island, but nothing was ever found." Rebecca typed something into her computer and then glanced up at Meredith and Julia. "I don't know how someone determined the treasure was supposed to be there, but much of the north side of the island was eroded by that time."

"And there hasn't been a search since?" Julia asked.

"No authorized search." Rebecca shrugged. "Visitors still try to hunt for it today, but it's a federal violation."

"You said it was known as Blackbeard's Island since at least 1760?" Julia asked. "I wonder when and why the rumors started to circulate about that particular island. Weren't there a lot of places Blackbeard frequented?"

"I'm sure there were," Rebecca conceded. "But like I said, I don't know much about the pirate legends associated with the island. If Kelvin knows more, I'll have him give one of you a call when I talk to him later."

Meredith glanced over the newspaper articles concerning pirate activity. The first two were full of the same information Rebecca had told them, highlighting the legends of buried treasure. But it was the third one that caught her eye.

"Listen to this," she said to the other two, her heart rate picking up speed. "This article was written in 1959 and mentions both Temperance Bellefontaine and Anna Coles."

"What does it say?" Julia asked, leaning forward.

Meredith read it aloud. "'Since the original colonists founded Savannah in 1733, the rumors of pirate's treasure on Blackbeard's Island has been closely linked to the diary of Mrs. Anna Coles. It's believed the diary has clues hidden throughout indicating where the treasure is buried, though it's not clear how Mrs. Coles acquired that information.'" Meredith paused and felt her eyes grow wider. She looked up at Rebecca and Julia. "Do you really think the clues are hidden within her diary?"

Julia shrugged impatiently. "Keep reading!"

"'The diary has passed from one member of Mrs. Coles's family to another since her death in 1790,'" Meredith read, "'but has not been made public. As late as 1886, members of the family have used the diary to search for the buried treasure, but several accidents and mishaps through the years have forced each owner to keep the diary in hiding. Apparently, the diary not only holds clues about where the treasure might be buried, but the family also believes that the book is cursed, and only trouble and misfortune follow the owner.'"

"That doesn't sound promising." Julia grimaced.

"There's more," Meredith said, pointing to the rest of the article. "'Recently,'" she read, "'Miss Temperance Bellefontaine inherited Anna Coles's diary from her mother, and from her aunt before her. Only time will tell if the rumors about the curse or the treasure are true.'"

Meredith finished the article and turned the page to see if anything had been printed on the back.

"Is there anything else about Temperance owning the diary?" Julia asked.

There were no other articles in the folder. Meredith shook her head.

"Who wrote the article?" Rebecca asked.

"Robert Wilson." Meredith didn't recognize the name.

"He wrote for the *Savannah Tribune* for years," Rebecca said. "Let's just say, his articles were somewhere between fact and fiction. His writing was purely meant to sell copies."

"Is he still alive?" Julia asked. "Could we question him about this article or see where he found his information?"

"He passed away in the late 1980s." Rebecca shook her head. "I don't know of any family members in the area either."

"Could I get a copy of this article?" Meredith asked.

"Of course. I'll copy it before you leave." Rebecca motioned to her laptop. "As far as Daniel Defoe is concerned, I'm familiar with his work, and I actually recall something that may be helpful." She typed on her keyboard as Meredith passed the article to Julia so her friend could see it for herself.

"Here it is." Rebecca turned the laptop for them to see. "There's a Daniel Defoe library in London. They've spent years gathering Defoe's manuscripts and writings. Apparently, they were distributed between his descendants upon his death. There are still many missing."

Meredith glanced at the website briefly before Rebecca turned it back around and typed a few more things. Her face was serious as she scrolled for a moment. "Ah! I found it. There's a contact form."

"Wonderful." Meredith leaned forward. "We can ask them if they have information on Anna and her husband. If so, maybe they might know why Anna is connected to Blackbeard's treasure."

"I'll send the message," Rebecca said. "But I'll put your name and email on the form, Meredith. Hopefully they'll respond to you in a day or so."

"That sounds perfect." Meredith was eager to know more about Anna and her family. It was still amazing to think Ron was descended from Daniel Defoe.

A few minutes later, while Meredith and Julia looked through the Blackbeard Island box, Rebecca asked Meredith for her email address. "There," she said as she finished typing. "The question has been submitted."

Closing the laptop, she smiled at Meredith and Julia. "Is there anything else I can help with?"

Julia met Meredith's gaze. "I can't think of anything right now."

"Neither can I," Meredith said. "But I do know where I need to make my next stop."

Julia smiled. "Maggie Lu?"

"I have a feeling she knows more about the diary than she's letting on." Meredith took her purse and stood. "And now that I know about the supposed family curse on the diary, I'm almost certain she was sworn to secrecy because of Aunt Temperance's superstition."

Julia and Rebecca also stood.

"I'll make a copy of the article for you," Rebecca said. "And you can be on your way."

"Thank you." Meredith followed Rebecca back to the circulation desk. She put a few dollars on the counter for the copy and to donate to the library.

"Since it's getting late," Julia said to Meredith, "I'll call Maggie Lu when we get back to the agency and see if we can stop by tomorrow to visit with her."

Meredith glanced at her watch. It was only three o'clock. "Don't you think there's enough time left today?"

"I need to go shopping," Julia explained to Meredith with a twinkle in her eye. "It's our wedding anniversary Thursday, and I'm making some special plans to surprise Beau."

"I forgot to ask how things are going between you," Meredith said quietly, sorry she hadn't remembered until now.

The twinkle dimmed from Julia's eyes, and she looked down at her hands. "Still the same." She spoke just as quietly, though Rebecca had turned on the copier, and she wouldn't be able to hear them. "He hasn't told me where he was."

Meredith put her hand on Julia's arm and gave it a little squeeze. "I still don't think you have anything to worry about."

"I just wish he'd tell me." She lifted her shoulders and smiled at Meredith. "But I'm choosing to trust him, and I won't let it ruin our anniversary dinner. In fact, maybe it's some kind of surprise for our anniversary."

"I'm sure that's what it is." Meredith let go of her arm.

"Here you go." Rebecca took the copy out of the machine and handed it to Meredith. "I'm here if you need anything else, and I'll be sure to have Kelvin call if he knows more about Blackbeard's Island."

Meredith folded the copy in half and smiled at Rebecca. "Thanks again."

"My pleasure."

Meredith and Julia walked out of the library.

"I'll see you back at the agency," Meredith said. "I'm eager to see if any information came in on James Bellefontaine."

"Okay, I'll see you there."

They parted ways, and Meredith got into her car. She was thankful for learning more about Anna Coles and her diary, but she wasn't any closer to knowing who took it from her home.

Chapter Nine

The ride back to Magnolia Investigations gave Meredith a few minutes to digest all the information they'd just learned at the library. When she stepped into her office, she set her purse on her desk and then went to check in with Carmen.

"Any messages for me?" she asked.

"No, boss," Carmen said with a smile. "But I made a fresh pot of coffee just a few minutes ago. Nice and dark, just how you like it."

"Thank you."

"*No problema.*"

Meredith stopped at the cart in the hall and filled a cup with the steaming hot liquid for Julia. The aroma wafted up and filled her nose as she walked to her friend's office. Just smelling it, she felt refreshed and energized. "Got a minute?"

"Of course. I'm just checking my email to see if Captain Villeneuve got back to me."

Julia's office was neat and orderly, just like her. Meredith set the cup of coffee down on Julia's desk and took a seat on one of the chairs across from her. Sunshine streamed through the window, and just outside, in the courtyard, the Spanish moss swayed in the gentle breeze.

"It'll be just a minute," Julia said absently as she typed a few things into her laptop and then scrolled for a second. "Ah!" She smiled at the computer screen. "He did get back to me."

Nerves bubbled in Meredith's stomach as she tried hard to be patient.

Julia scanned the report for a minute, her eyes growing wider and wider.

"What?" Meredith asked, leaning forward, her elbows on the desk to get a better look at the computer. "What does it say?"

Julia finally met her gaze, concern wrinkling the corners of her eyes. "This guy has quite a rap sheet. He's been convicted of identity theft, burglary, embezzlement, and petty theft."

"Really?" Meredith grimaced. "Is there a picture?"

Julia clicked on a link and sighed deeply. "It looks like he's our guy."

She turned the computer for Meredith to see a recent mug shot.

Dread filled Meredith's gut. "It's him. James Bellefontaine." There was no denying it. "That's the same man I saw outside my house."

Julia frowned. "Why did he suddenly show up, after all these years? Do you think it's because of the diary?"

"It has to be." Meredith settled back in her chair, though her heart felt anything but settled. "It's too coincidental that he'd come on the very same day the diary arrived."

"But why did he come back?" Julia asked. "You said you saw him two more times, standing in Troup Square watching your house. If he had the diary, why didn't he move on?"

"I have no idea." It didn't make sense to Meredith either. "Maybe there's something else he wants."

"I can't imagine what. If he did take the diary, why is he hanging around, increasing his chances of getting caught?"

"I haven't seen him for a couple of days. Maybe he did leave. Where does it say he lives?"

Julia scanned the report again. "Los Angeles."

"He's a long way from home."

The hall clock ticked in a steady rhythm as Meredith processed all the information.

"What do you want to do?" Julia asked.

"I think we should definitely share this information with Officers Jackson and Ellis. They should be on the lookout for James if he's still in Savannah."

"And if he's not?"

"My gut tells me that if he took the diary, then he's going to use it to try to find the treasure on Blackbeard's Island." Meredith rubbed the back of her neck, which was starting to feel tense. "So I doubt he returned to California."

"Maybe we should also warn the staff at the wildlife preserve on Blackbeard's Island to be on the lookout for him," Julia suggested.

"The island is over five thousand acres, and there are no active staff members on duty," Meredith reminded her. "They patrol several barrier islands up and down the coast. I think it's easier said than done."

"Right." Julia turned the computer back around to face herself. "But it wouldn't hurt."

"I'll call Officer Clemmons, if you want to call the wildlife preserve offices." Meredith stood to leave the room.

"How do you feel about being alone at home, now that you know more about James Bellefontaine?"

"I met with the home security company today." She had stopped at home before going to the library. "They gave me an estimate and put me on the schedule."

"When will they install the system?"

Meredith sighed. It wasn't soon enough. "Next week."

"What will you do until then?"

Meredith shook her head. "Pray that no one tries to break in again—and keep my cell phone close."

"I'd feel better if you came and stayed with Beau and me."

"I wouldn't dream of—"

"You won't have to stay alone, boss." Carmen popped her head into the office. "I'll stay with you until your system is set up."

"I can't ask you to do—"

"You didn't." Carmen grinned and left the room as quickly as she'd entered, calling behind her, "I'll be there with supper later today."

Meredith met Julia's smiling face.

"I'm happy she'll be there, Mere," Julia said. "It'll help me sleep a little easier."

It would make Meredith more comfortable as well. And she might get to see Chase again, sooner than she expected. The only thing she didn't like was that this whole ordeal made her feel vulnerable and helpless.

Julia closed her laptop and stood. "I'm heading out early to get my shopping done. Let me know if you get ahold of Maggie Lu and we can meet with her tomorrow."

"I plan to call her right after I call Officer Clemmons."

"Okay," Julia said absently as she put her laptop in her bag. A little sigh escaped her lips when she picked up her cell phone and glanced at the screen.

"Everything okay?" Meredith asked.

Julia lifted a shoulder and smiled. "It's nothing." But the smile didn't quite reach her eyes.

"Beau?"

"I'm just worried. He's usually so quick to answer my texts or calls, but I called him over an hour ago, and he still hasn't responded."

Meredith walked across the room and gave her friend a hug. "Things will be just fine," she said in her most reassuring voice.

"I'm not usually so mistrusting," Julia said with shaky laughter. "Maybe it's working with all these family mysteries we've had. It's making me feel a little insecure." She pulled out of Meredith's embrace. "I'm sure that's it."

"I'm sure too." Meredith smiled at her friend. "Call me if you need anything."

"I will."

They walked out of Julia's office together, and Meredith grabbed a cup of coffee to take back to her office to make a few phone calls.

"Rebecca from the library called to talk to you," Carmen said as she brought a pink slip to Meredith. "She said she talked to her husband, and he reminded her of something they had at the library that might help you. You don't need to call her back, but she said you'd want to see what she found."

Meredith took the slip of paper from Carmen. "At the library?"

"Yes. She said she'll be there until five today, and then she'll be there tomorrow from eight to four."

It was only four o'clock. If Meredith left now, she could still get to the library before Rebecca left. She didn't want to wait until tomorrow to see what she had found.

"I'll go now." Meredith emptied her coffee cup into a to-go container. "I can make my other phone calls from home later."

"Okay," Carmen said. "I'll see you around six at your house."

Meredith smiled at Carmen, truly thankful to know she wouldn't have to be alone tonight. "Okay, but don't sneak up on me this time."

Carmen winked at her and returned to her desk.

***

It didn't take her long to return to the pretty brown-brick building that housed the Carnegie Library. The library had been organized by the Colored Library Association of Savannah in 1906, and the building was built and dedicated in 1914. Recently it was chosen as one of the ten most beautiful libraries in Georgia by the Georgia Public Library Service.

Meredith pushed open the door and took in the familiar scent of ancient ink and paper. It was a smell that never grew old to her.

Rebecca stood at her usual place behind the circulation desk, helping a gentleman whose back was toward Meredith. She caught Meredith's eye and smiled in acknowledgment and then returned her focus to the man in front of her.

Trying to be patient, but wanting to know what Rebecca had found, Meredith sighed to herself and got in line.

"It's very interesting that you should ask about Blackbeard's Island," Rebecca said to the man in front of Meredith—a little louder than necessary. "I know right where to find the box."

Blackbeard's Island? Meredith looked closer at the man standing before her. He was about medium height, with dark brown hair. He wore a pair of khaki pants and a blue polo shirt.

Rebecca caught Meredith's eye again, communicating something Meredith didn't understand, and then looked back at the man. "If you'll just fill out this research form, Mr. Nelson"—she grabbed a pencil and a form and set it on the desk—"I'll go get that box for you."

"Thank you. There's no hurry." Mr. Nelson took the form and then glanced over his shoulder. "I'll let you help the next—"

Meredith's eyes grew wide as she met the gaze of Troy LeBlanc.

He also stared at her, recognition dawning on his face.

"Mrs. Bellefontaine," he said. "What a pleasant surprise."

Rebecca gave her a questioning glance and then turned and left the desk to retrieve the box.

"Troy LeBlanc." It took Meredith a moment to collect her thoughts. "I was hoping to get an opportunity to talk to you again."

"Troy LeBlanc?" he asked, his eyebrows raised.

"There's no use pretending," Meredith said, feeling a little more confident with each passing second. This man had tried to dupe her and had come into her home under false pretenses. If anyone should feel uncomfortable, it should be him—not her. "I've already spoken to Mr. Stone, and I know exactly who you are."

"Ah, yes." LeBlanc smiled and set his pencil on the desk. "Anthony told me you stopped by his office."

"I tried getting ahold of you at your bank," she continued, "but they said you were on vacation for the week. I was going to ask Mr. Stone for your cell phone number so I could chat with you too."

LeBlanc held up his hands, as if in surrender. "You've caught me now. What would you like to know?"

Meredith didn't want to discuss this in front of everyone, and already, there were more than a few curious glances sent their way. "Shall we continue this conversation at one of the tables?" she asked.

"Of course."

When they were both settled, Meredith didn't waste a moment. "Mr. LeBlanc, why did you lie to me?"

LeBlanc shook his head, a smile on his handsome face. "I'm very sorry, Mrs. Bellefontaine. Anthony and I never imagined things would play out the way they have. We never meant any trouble for you or the diary. I spent years hearing the legends about the diary from my father and grandfather, and the lure of finally seeing Anna Coles's writing for myself was too great. When Anthony told me the diary was coming out of hiding after so long, I couldn't let this once-in-a-lifetime opportunity pass. Again, I am deeply sorry."

Meredith didn't know what to make of him. He seemed genuine—but it didn't change the fact that he had lied.

"Why are you here researching Blackbeard's Island—and why did you tell Rebecca that your name is Mr. Nelson?"

He shrugged. "I thought I'd get a little more time to look through the diary, so I took the week off from work to do some amateur treasure hunting." He set his clasped hands on the table. "Since I'm here,

I thought I'd make the most of it and find out what I can about the island from the library. Maybe I'll find something that will aid my search." A half smile tilted his mouth. "I doubt I'll find anything, but the thrill of the hunt is almost as good as the discovery."

"And the fake last name?"

LeBlanc shrugged again. "I usually don't use my real name when I'm treasure hunting. I like to keep my personal and professional lives separate. For whatever reason, people don't trust treasure hunters, so I need to keep my reputation intact for my bank job."

"You do know it's a federal violation to hunt for treasure on the island."

LeBlanc shook his head. "It's actually not a violation to hunt—only to remove relics from the island."

Meredith frowned. If that was true, then why bother to hunt?

"It's not the treasure I'm after, Mrs. Bellefontaine," LeBlanc said, as if reading her thoughts. "But the thrill of the adventure." He leaned forward, a gleam in his eyes, and said in a conspiratorial voice, "I like to think that if I'd lived three hundred years ago, I'd have been a naval privateer. This is the closest I can ever get. I've found several other treasures, most of which I've donated to the pirate museum in St. Augustine."

"Yes, Mr. Stone told me." Meredith appreciated his quest for adventure, though she didn't feel he should lie to achieve his goals. "My biggest concern, though, is returning the diary to my family, where it belongs. I will do whatever I can to retrieve it."

"I wish you well," he said. "And if I happen to come across anything suspicious while I'm poking around Savannah, I'll be sure to let you know."

"I appreciate your offer."

"Perhaps," LeBlanc said, "if you do find the diary, I could coerce you into showing it to me?"

Meredith wasn't so sure about that. It was like rewarding a child for being disobedient.

Rebecca appeared on the other side of the room, saving Meredith the trouble of answering. The Blackbeard Island box was in one hand and a rolled-up piece of paper in the other. The look she gave Meredith was filled with both questions and concerns.

Meredith smiled at her, trying to reassure her that everything was fine—though she wasn't quite sure what to make of Troy LeBlanc aka Conner Pearlman aka Mr. Nelson.

"I have the box," Rebecca said to him. "And my husband Kelvin reminded me of something else that might be of interest to both of you."

She set the box on the table, and then she set the paper down and started to unroll it and flatten it onto the table.

It was a handwritten map, yellowed with age, with a few dirt marks and wrinkles.

Meredith and LeBlanc stood to get a better look.

"What is it?" Meredith asked.

Rebecca pointed to the corner where the name MARKUS WHEATON was written with the date JULY 15, 1886 underneath.

"I talked to Kelvin after you left, Meredith." Rebecca set a book on each corner to keep the map from rolling up again. "He said there isn't much known about Blackbeard's Island or the supposed treasure, just a lot of unsubstantiated rumors. But he did remind me about this map. It was stored with several other maps we have in our collections room. If I'm correct, it's the map made for the 1886 exploration of the island."

A series of landmarks, notations, and directions all pointed toward the northern end of the island, near a burial ground.

LeBlanc crossed his arms and moved restlessly from one foot to the next. "Do you know who Markus Wheaton is, or where he got this information?"

Both he and Rebecca looked to Meredith, who shook her head. "I've never heard of him before."

"Didn't the article mention that Anna Coles's descendants made the last official search for the treasure in 1886?" Rebecca asked.

Meredith opened the Blackbeard's Island box and found the article in question. "It does."

"Maybe the author of the article was aware of this map," Rebecca said, "and knew Mr. Wheaton was a descendent."

"I know who I could ask." Meredith pulled her cell phone out of her purse and found Gwyn's number. She pressed the green TALK button and waited for Gwyn to pick up.

"Hi, Meredith," Gwyn said on the other end.

"Hi, Gwyn." Meredith took a seat, her legs a little unsteady with the new discovery. "I have a quick question I hope you can answer."

"Go ahead."

"Do you recognize the name Markus Wheaton from your family tree?"

"I do. He was my fifth or sixth great-grandfather, if I remember correctly." She paused. "Hold on a second, I was just working on our family tree last night and have the information on the dining room table."

Meredith put her hand over the phone and spoke to Rebecca and LeBlanc. “My sister-in-law is checking on Markus Wheaton right now.”

They waited for less than a minute before Gwyn responded. “I found him.”

Meredith waited anxiously for her to continue.

“It looks like he was born in 1851 and died”—she paused for a second—“in July of 1886.”

“He died in July of 1886?” Meredith felt her eyes grow wide.

“Yes, July 16, 1886.”

Meredith met Rebecca’s shocked gaze.

“Does it say how he died?” Meredith asked.

“Um.” Gwyn didn’t say anything for a couple of seconds. “The source I have says he fell off a cliff and drowned.”

“Really.” It was more of a comment than a question. “That’s remarkable.”

“What’s this about?” Gwyn asked.

Meredith told her where she was and what she was looking at.

“Do you think this has anything to do with the diary?” Gwyn asked.

“I think it confirms why the diary has been hidden away. The family is afraid of it—they think it’s cursed.”

“That’s just poppycock.”

“I know, but there has to be a reason the family has kept the diary under lock and key for so long. Aunt Temperance refused to talk about it all those years.”

“Well,” Gwyn said. “I think it’s silly—but then again, look what happened the day it came into your possession. I just hope you can find it again.”

"So do I. Thanks for your help, Gwyn."

"Anytime."

Meredith said goodbye and ended the call.

"For whatever it's worth," Rebecca said to Meredith, "I'd be happy to make a copy of the map for you to have for your own records."

"I'd appreciate it," Meredith said.

"Would it be any trouble to make a copy for me?" LeBlanc asked sheepishly. "I might just head on out to Blackbeard's Island and take a look around myself."

"Of course not."

Meredith wasn't sure what to think about Troy LeBlanc, but the map was part of the library's collection, and anyone had a right to it. Maybe he would find something helpful—then again, maybe he wouldn't. No one else ever had.

Chapter Ten

CLOUDS FILLED THE SKY AS Meredith pulled into the Downhome Diner's parking lot the next morning. Maggie Lu had suggested they meet for breakfast at Charlene's restaurant, and Meredith was only too happy to oblige. Carmen had gone to the office to open Magnolia Investigations for the day, and Julia should be arriving any minute. Meredith had called Julia the night before to tell her when to meet and to fill her in on what had happened at the library.

Through the window, Meredith could see that Maggie Lu was already seated at one of the booths. She met Meredith's gaze and waved. Meredith waved back, glad to see her friendly face.

Another car had pulled into the parking lot just ahead of Meredith. And when the woman got out, Meredith realized it was Beatrice. She exited her car and readjusted the jacket of her dress suit. It was surprisingly simple, compared to the extravagant outfits she usually wore. But the large floppy hat on her head, which was the exact same color as her outfit, put her appearance over the edge.

Meredith stepped out of her car and walked toward the diner. "Hello, Beatrice," she said as they arrived at the door.

"Oh, Meredith, my goodness." Beatrice's hand fluttered near her chest. "I didn't see you there."

Meredith was surprised she could see anything out from under that hat.

Instead of opening the door and entering the restaurant, Beatrice took a step away, as if she planned to leave. "I just remembered something—will you excuse me?"

"Wait." Meredith put her hand out to stop Beatrice. "I was hoping to talk about the diary with you. I had planned to call you later today to see if we could meet."

"Oh…well." Beatrice looked toward her car, as if searching for an escape route. "Now isn't a good time. I—I forgot about a meeting I have this morning."

"Is there a better time?"

Beatrice started to walk away from Meredith. "I'll be sure to call and let you know."

"How about later today?" Meredith asked.

"Yes, yes, we'll make something work. Ta-ta, Meredith." Beatrice bounded away, her hat flopping as she rushed to her car. Within seconds, she pulled out of the parking lot, passing Julia, who was coming in.

"Was that Beatrice?" Julia asked, stepping out of her car a moment later.

"The one and only."

"Where was she off to in such a hurry?"

"I mentioned I wanted to talk to her about the diary."

Julia pinched her lips together. "Just as I suspected. She's hiding something." She opened the restaurant door and motioned for Meredith to enter. "Did you schedule a time to meet with her?"

"I tried to, but she didn't commit."

"I'll call her if you want."

"I'll call her." Meredith gave Julia a sidelong glance. "I might go a little easier on her than you."

Julia smiled. "She can handle me. Besides, we'll see her at the historical society luncheon on Friday."

"Oh, about that," Meredith said. "I talked to Carter this morning, and he's really worried about me. He wouldn't stop fussing until I agreed to go to Charleston for a couple of days to set his mind at ease." She waved to Maggie Lu again. "He didn't have to twist my arm too much. I've been missing Kaden and Kinsley. I'll be back on Friday morning in time to go to the luncheon."

"That sounds good to me," said Julia. "It'll give me more time to make our anniversary dinner extra special."

"Well, look here," Maggie Lu said to the ladies when they approached her table. "Two of my favorite detective ladies."

"Hello, Maggie Lu." Meredith slid into the seat across from Maggie Lu, and Julia slid in after her. "Thank you for agreeing to meet with us."

"I had a feeling y'all would be calling me again." Maggie Lu leaned back in her seat, her forearms resting one on top of the other, and shook her head, looking between both ladies. "This is about that diary again, isn't it?"

Meredith and Julia exchanged a look, and then Julia nodded. "You were a little quiet about it last time. We were hoping you had remembered more and would tell us."

"I told you ladies, I tried to forget about that time in my life, for many reasons."

"Now, Mama." Charlene arrived at the table with three empty coffee cups in one hand and a pot of steaming coffee in the other. "Your memory is still sharp. I'm sure you could tell Meredith and Julia more than they ever wanted to know."

Maggie Lu laughed and took Charlene's hand in hers after Charlene set the cups down. She smiled up at her daughter, pure love and joy in her expression. "I can't argue with my baby," she said, patting the top of Charlene's hand. "No, ma'am, I can't."

Charlene poured coffee for each of them and took their orders. When she walked away, Meredith met Maggie Lu's gaze. "I know you remember more than you're letting on, Maggie Lu. It would be a big help if you could share some of your memories with us. More than anything, I'd like to get the diary back."

"You only need to share the memories you want to share," Julia assured her. "The last thing we want is to cause you discomfort."

"My, my, my," Maggie Lu said as she looked down at her coffee mug, shaking her head. "That was a long time ago. Things were much different then. I wouldn't even know where to start."

"You mentioned that you read the diary out loud to Aunt Temperance. Do you remember anything specific about what you read?" Meredith asked.

"A few things, though to my fifteen-year-old mind, it wasn't all that interesting, if I remember correctly."

"Really?" Meredith asked, surprised by her admission. "There wasn't anything in there about a pirate treasure?"

"Now, let me see." Maggie Lu squinted her eyes, as if deep in thought. "I don't recall the diary saying anything about where the treasure might be, but it did say that Anna Coles was mighty afraid of some book her husband guarded with his life. I do remember that."

"What about a curse?" Julia asked. "We've found some mention of family members claiming Anna's diary was cursed. Did you witness anything like that?"

"Did I ever."

***

The morning sun had not yet crested the horizon as Louvenia walked through the tall grass, wet with dew, toward the back of Miss Temperance's home. She only came to the house three mornings a week, but each time she came, after her chores were done, she and Miss Temperance sat in the fancy parlor, on one of the hard, slippery sofas, and Louvenia read aloud from the old diary.

At first, things had been new and exciting, with the prospect of finding clues about the treasure still fresh on Louvenia's mind. But as the days had turned to weeks, and there was nothing but whining and complaining from Anna Coles in the pages of the diary, Louvenia began to get bored. It was still interesting to learn about the early colonists, and Louvenia wondered if young Ann would marry her suitor, or why Mr. Coles was always running away from his wife, but she didn't think the diary had anything about pirates or treasures.

The back door was locked, and Louvenia rapped on it with three quick taps, a pause, and then two more taps before Robbie opened it with a smile.

"Morning, Miss Louvenia," he said in his congenial voice, his handsome face shining for her, despite the big bags lining his eyes and

the exhaustion marks creasing his mouth. "How are you this beautiful morning?"

"I'm doing just fine, Robbie," she answered. "Any news to share?"

Robbie stretched his arms and let out a huge yawn. "I'm just going off the night shift. Franklin'll be up soon. Nothin' interesting happened last night, though there's been some powerful strange things happening around the place since that diary came here."

"What kind of things?" Louvenia liked to keep to herself when she came to work at the big house. She tried not to gossip or pay too much attention to anyone else. Granny Luv told her to mind her manners and her own business. Nothing good came from getting into all the goings-on with the help—but the way Robbie talked about strange things, she couldn't help but ask now.

"Just little things, you know?" Robbie said. "Strange accidents that don't make sense, things lying around that don't belong places, a big branch crashing out of a tree with no warning, stuff falling off shelves."

Louvenia took an apron off a hook on the wall in the back entrance and tied it around her waist. "Can't those things be explained? Maybe someone's being careless."

"It's different somehow."

Louvenia wasn't superstitious, nor was she easy to scare. "I better be getting to work."

She moved into the large kitchen at the back of the house. The room was warm and filled with the aroma of fresh coffee. The cook, Betty, was already making a mess of pancakes on the large black griddle.

"Morning, Louvenia," Betty said. "The tray's made up for the missus, though I doubt she'll eat a thing." Betty shook her head, her

lips puckered in disapproval. "Mm, mm, if she doesn't eat something soon, she'll blow away on the next wind. You heard it from me first."

Louvenia picked up the tray on the counter, inhaling the scent of coffee, pancakes, and scrambled eggs. "I don't know how she can turn this food away, Betty. It all looks delicious."

"Thanks, honey. There'll be some waiting for you when you have a minute to spare."

Holding the tray in both hands, Louvenia pushed the swinging door open with her backside and started the trek to Miss Temperance's room. It was in the opposite corner of the house, on the second floor.

The house was darker than usual with the cloud cover outside. All the shades were pulled, the doors and windows locked, and the air was stale. A chill ran up Louvenia's back as she climbed the stairs, thinking about what Robbie had said, though she reminded herself she didn't believe in such nonsense.

Nothing moved in the house, and this far away from the activity of the kitchen, all was quiet.

With a light knock, Louvenia balanced the tray with one hand and opened Miss Temperance's bedroom door with the other. Usually, Miss Temperance was still in bed when Louvenia arrived, but this time, she was sitting in the corner of her room on a rocking chair. She gripped the diary in both hands as she rocked, back and forth, staring at the far wall. She was dressed already, but Louvenia had a sneaking suspicion that she had worn the outfit the day before. It was wrinkled, and her hair, which was usually smoothed back in a bun, had wisps sticking out in disarray. She didn't seem to notice Louvenia when she entered.

"Morning, Miss Temperance," Louvenia said with more cheer than she felt in the dreary room. "I've brought up your breakfast."

"Take it back," Miss Temperance said. "I'm not hungry."

"Oh now, Miss Temperance. You've got to eat something." Louvenia set the tray on a table and went to the window to open the shades. This high up, among the branches of the magnolia trees, no one could see into her room.

"Leave them be," Miss Temperance said. She rocked harder, her eyes bright with fear. "There are prowlers everywhere. They want my book. They'll climb those trees to see me in here."

Louvenia didn't know what to say to her employer. Miss Temperance hadn't been this upset a couple of days ago when Louvenia had read to her, though she'd become increasingly skittish and fearful.

"Are you all right, ma'am?" Louvenia asked, walking toward her.

Miss Temperance finally looked at Louvenia, as if seeing her for the first time. "Oh, it's just you, Louvenia."

"Yes, ma'am. It's just me."

"Have you read any more of the diary?" Miss Temperance asked, and then shook her head, as if clearing it. "No, that's right. You can only read it while you're here, and you haven't been here for a few days, have you?"

"Are you feeling all right, ma'am?" Louvenia asked again. She knelt by Miss Temperance's feet. "Did you sleep last night?"

Miss Temperance looked over at her bed and shook her head. "If I sleep, someone will come in here and take my book."

"Robbie and Franklin are taking care of you. They won't let anyone come into the house."

"What if someone bribes them?"

"They're trustworthy, ma'am." Louvenia smiled as brightly as she could. "No one will let anything happen."

"What about you?" Miss Temperance asked. "Have you been keeping to yourself about what you're reading to me?"

"Yes, ma'am." Louvenia would never breathe a word of what she'd read in the diary—besides, there wasn't much to tell, in her opinion.

Miss Temperance reached out her thin hand and placed it on Louvenia's cheek in a rare show of affection. "I know I can trust you." Peace seemed to settle over her face. "Will you stay by my side while I sleep, and guard the diary?"

"What about my chores?"

"Let them go for today." Miss Temperance's shoulders sagged, and her head lulled to the side.

Louvenia stood and helped Miss Temperance to her feet. "I'll help you get into bed."

She found a nightgown and helped Miss Temperance change, and then she held the covers back while Miss Temperance climbed into bed, never letting the book out of her grasp. When she set her head on the pillow, she was asleep within a moment, passed out from exhaustion, no doubt.

Louvenia stared at the book in her employer's hands and wondered if she should leave it there or if she should hold it while the woman slept.

With hours of nothing but sitting ahead of her, Louvenia decided to take the diary from Miss Temperance. She then pulled the rocking chair up to the window. Opening the shade just a crack, enough for a little daylight to shine into the room and give her some light to read, Louvenia bypassed the section she'd been reading to Miss Temperance about the latest case of yellow fever and the endless list of chores that consumed Anna Coles's life, and found a new passage that looked promising. Anna talked about her father's writings and how she suspected that her husband had taken one of her father's books but was keeping it hidden from her.

Louvenia read on, suddenly curious about the book Anna's husband hid from her. What was in the book? If it was handwritten, was it a diary, like the one Louvenia was reading? Or was it an instruction book, something Anna's husband was following? But what kind of instructions would Anna's father have written that her husband chose to follow?

She read for quite a while, wading through endless details, when a call arose from the lower level of the house.

"Fire! Fire!"

Fire?

Louvenia lifted her head and sniffed the air, but could not smell any smoke. Was there really a fire?

Not wanting to wake Miss Temperance if it wasn't necessary, Louvenia clutched the book to her chest and opened the door.

"Fire!" Betty yelled as she plodded up the steps, her wide girth preventing her from moving fast. "Fire, Miss Temperance!"

"Fire?" Louvenia asked. "Where?"

"In the back of the house! We've got to get Miss Temperance out of here."

"She's sleeping really hard," Louvenia said. "I don't know if we can."

"Come, child." Betty passed Louvenia and went to Miss Temperance. "Wake up, ma'am, wake up!"

The faint smell of smoke wafted up the stairs and hit Louvenia's nose.

"Who's tending to the fire?" she asked.

"Franklin and Robbie. I called the fire department, and they're coming, but we can't leave Miss Temperance inside." Betty shook their employer. "Wake up, Miss Temperance."

Miss Temperance woke with a start. "My diary." She frantically felt the bed, her eyes wild with fear.

"I have it, ma'am," Louvenia said, rushing to her side, putting it into her hand. "It's here."

"There's a fire in the back of the house," Betty said much more calmly than before. "We've got to get you out of here."

"A fire?" Miss Temperance stared at Betty. "What happened?"

"There's no time for all of that right now." She tried to take Miss Temperance's hand, to pull her from the bed, but Miss Temperance wouldn't move.

"I demand to know."

"I don't rightly know how it started, ma'am. I just smelled the smoke and alarmed Franklin and Robbie."

The smoke was now pouring into the room, and there was no more time for questions.

Louvenia helped Betty get Miss Temperance out of the bed, and then she grabbed a robe and put it on Miss Temperance's shoulders.

"We need to hurry," Betty said. "It's burning fast."

Outside, Louvenia steered Miss Temperance to stand under the protection of a live oak tree as they waited for the fire department to arrive.

"It's the curse," Miss Temperance said under her breath as the flames licked the back side of the house, near the kitchen. "That's why my mama kept the diary in hiding all these years, to protect me."

Louvenia frowned. "Curse?"

"My great-aunt heard about the diary and sent me a letter," Miss Temperance explained. "She warned me to put the diary back in its safe, or I'd suffer the consequences—but I didn't listen, and now look. She said family members have died, suffered great injuries and loss, and been badly hurt while in possession of the book."

"I don't believe in curses," Louvenia said. "God is bigger than all that."

Miss Temperance held the diary away from her for a moment and looked at it, shaking her head. "I can't put it back until I know what it says—until I know where the treasure is hidden."

As Louvenia watched the firefighters work to put out the flames, their red trucks pumping water against the pretty white siding of Miss Temperance's big old house, she couldn't help but think the diary wasn't worth all this.

Chapter Eleven

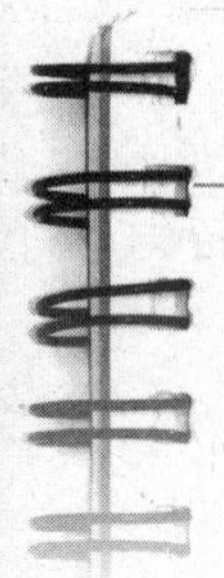

December 15, 1733
Colony of Georgia

Today is the first day in a new chapter of my life. Yesterday, my dear, sweet Ann was married to Mr. Gready in the small chapel on Johnson Square. On her fourteenth birthday, Mr. Gready approached Joseph and asked for Ann's hand in marriage. I adamantly opposed my husband's decision, though I was but one of four voices in the matter, and I could see my girl was set on having her way.

The wedding took place just one short week later, and was a bright spot in an otherwise gloomy existence for myself and many of the other colonists. But now I am alone, with no other companion save this diary to fill my long days and nights. My hope and prayer is that Mr. Gready will be a good husband and will serve alongside Ann with a steadfast and faithful heart. Mr. Gready's home, which looks much like ours, is not so far away, so I will console my lonely heart with the knowledge that I can see Ann whenever I desire.

Now that the excitement of the wedding has come and gone, I find myself staring at the winter months with dread.

I miss my family in England more and more with each passing day, and I cherish the letters I receive from them. Now that Ann will stay in America with her husband, though, my desire to return to England has become torn. I cannot imagine leaving her here—yet the thought of never seeing my homeland again fills me with an ache I cannot explain. I will pray that God directs my paths, and, if it be His will that I stay in Savannah for the rest of my days, I pray I will find peace and contentment with my lot in life.

My pen hovers over the page as I contemplate whether or not I should write these next words. I fear if I touch ink to paper and share what has transpired, it will make it real, and there will be a permanent record, when all I want to do is forget it happened. But I fear if I keep this inside, it will eat away at me like a cancer, and I will grow even more bitter and angry.

This Sunday last, while we were making final preparations for Ann's wedding, and Ann was away at one of her friend's homes, Joseph was in the jolliest mood I've ever seen him. He was almost giddy as we were preparing to give our daughter away, and I suspected he was eager to be done with the care and feeding of her. My heart was not as light, nor as joyful, and I was moping about, tears ever present and ready to fall. I do believe Joseph had broken one of General Oglethorpe's rules and had imbibed in alcohol. I began to suspect that mayhap Joseph was smuggling it into the colony from Charles Town and that was what took him away from Savannah so often. In my state of unhappiness, I could no longer keep my mouth closed, so I accused him of smuggling. At first he just laughed, his spirits so high, but then he saw that I was serious, and his mood began to sour.

The floodgates of my lips were opened, and with all the anger and angst I have kept so close to my heart all these months, I began to attack him with my words, and the more I attacked, the angrier he became. I could see in his eyes he was about to strike me, but I did not care. My heart hurt so that I thought I might lose my mind. As I hurled accusations, he hurled them back at me, calling me ungrateful and unworthy. He said he had married me out of pity and as a favor to my father. I was an old maid when he met me, ugly and unwanted. He told me my father begged him to take me off his hands and promised Joseph he would compensate him for his troubles. But shortly after we married, my father went bankrupt and returned to debtor's prison. My husband said he found himself with a wife he did not want nor desire, and no fortune to console his disappointment.

I wept as my husband told me these things with no empathy or love. I could see then that he hated me—had probably always hated me—and had only married me because he thought he would gain something for his troubles. I had long suspected as much, but to hear the ugly truth cut me deeper than anything before.

But my husband was not finished. I do not know if it was the alcohol speaking, or the fact that he had finally told me the truth. He said when my father died, Joseph took the only thing of value my father possessed, a journal he kept while interviewing pirates for his novels. Joseph went to his bag and retrieved the book he kept so close to his person at all times. He held it up and asked if I knew what the book was, but did not wait for me to answer. He said, "This book is my payment for marrying you, though there is no fortune large enough to compensate for that sacrifice. It is the only hope I have of wealth in this lifetime."

My heart was breaking as he spoke to me, but I could see that he did not care. He had not married me out of love or even affection but in the hopes of getting rich. I no longer cared what was in the book but only that I finally knew the truth I had tried so hard not to see.

"I believe this book contains the location of Blackbeard's treasure," Joseph finally admitted to me. "It is on a barrier island not far from here. If you want to know why I leave, it is to find the treasure."

Could it be true? Did the book truly contain that information?

"If I find it, you and I will not want for anything, and we can return to England." He looked at me with disgust. "But I imagine that will not be good enough for you either, and you will continue to be ungrateful for all I have done for you."

I finally knew why we had come to Savannah and why Joseph had chosen me for his wife. It was all about money.

Now, as I sit here, days later, tears still stream from my eyes and my heart is still raw from the truth. But I also feel free for the first time in years, though it is hard to understand

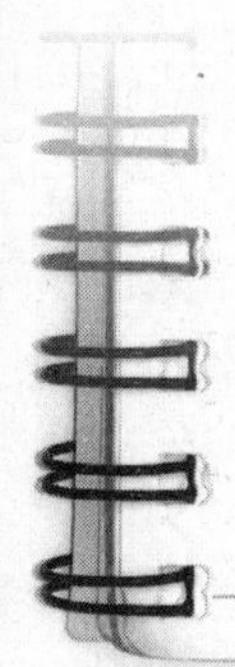

why. Mayhap it is because I no longer care if Joseph loves me or not. I have accepted that there is nothing I can do to earn his love or make him like me. He is a man driven by a need for wealth, and that is his one and only love. There is not enough room in his heart for both that and me.

He is gone again, and this time, I do not care if he returns.

White, puffy clouds drifted lazily overhead as Meredith waited on the front porch of Magnolia Investigations for Julia Friday morning. The historical society luncheon was scheduled for that day in the beautifully renovated Mansion on Forsyth Park, which was situated directly across the park from where Magnolia Investigations was located. From where Meredith stood, she could glimpse parts of the large redbrick and terra-cotta Victorian Romanesque mansion that housed the hotel. The ornate details and craftsmanship made it a fantastic piece of architecture and a must-see building in Savannah. It was on the trolley route, and Meredith had pointed it out to visitors countless times while giving tours of the city.

Since there was no parking on the street in front of Magnolia Investigations, Julia approached in her car and had to go around the block to park behind the old house. It took her several minutes to join Meredith on the porch.

Julia had texted Meredith to say she would meet her at the agency. They had agreed to walk to the luncheon together, through Forsyth Park, so Meredith waited on the porch, checking her phone to make sure they still had enough time.

She hated to be late for society events.

Julia was looking at her phone as she stepped out onto the porch. She let the door close behind her but didn't glance up to greet Meredith.

It wasn't like Julia to be so distracted.

She wore a pretty silver blouse and a black pantsuit with black flats. Her earrings and necklace were elegant yet bold, and her hair was perfectly styled. But there was something missing from Julia's demeanor that usually set her apart from other women. The joy she so effortlessly radiated was absent today.

"Are you ready?" Meredith asked.

Julia finally glanced up and blinked a couple of times before she nodded. "How was your time with the grandkids?"

"It was wonderful, as always," Meredith said. "Kaden told me all about the *Titanic*, and Kinsley braided my hair every time I sat down." She grinned. "And Carter let me come home, so mission accomplished."

They crossed Whitaker Street and entered Forsyth Park. Straight ahead and to their left was the large, famous fountain, one of the most photographed and iconic structures in Savannah. Meredith marveled at how well it had withstood the test of time, since it was over a hundred and sixty years old. Though it was iconic, it wasn't unique to Savannah, because it had been ordered from a catalog. Several other similar fountains dotted American cities across the country. Not only was it a famous place for proposals, pictures, and visitors, but every year during the week of St. Patrick's Day, the water in Forsyth Park fountain, as well as in all the other fountains in Savannah, was dyed green to celebrate the holiday.

Families played in the park while some people lounged, read books, or sat on benches with their lunches. Dozens of people strolled the paths, walked their dogs, or jogged. It was a beautiful day to enjoy being outside, though Meredith suspected Julia wasn't paying attention to any of it.

"How did your anniversary dinner go?" she asked.

Julia walked for a few feet before she answered Meredith. "I made a really elaborate supper last night for Beau, and even sent him a reminder text to let him know to be home by six." She crossed her arms and looked straight ahead on the path. "In forty-three years, he's never missed one of our anniversaries until yesterday."

"Oh, Julia." Meredith stopped walking and faced her friend. "I'm so sorry."

"I waited up until nine and then left dinner on the table and went to bed." An uncharacteristic tear slipped down her cheek. "He came to bed when he got home about fifteen minutes later and didn't even bother to see if I was still awake. He just got into bed and fell asleep."

"What happened this morning when you woke up?"

"I was so angry and hurt, I got up before him and cleaned up the dining room and kitchen." She wiped the tear impatiently. "When he came downstairs, he was whistling and happy, as if nothing had happened. He gave me a quick peck on the cheek and said he had an early tee time with his golfing buddies. He said he'd grab breakfast when he got to the clubhouse, and then he left."

Meredith frowned. Beau was usually so conscientious and thoughtful when it came to Julia. Why was he being so thoughtless now?

"You don't know where he was last night?" she asked Julia.

"I have no idea. I've asked him several times now, but he changes the subject or evades the question. I feel foolish questioning his buddies again, so I don't even know how to find out." She shook her head, determination on her brow. "I'm not going to give up without a fight, though. I love my husband, and I've known him for a long time. I have to believe he's not intentionally hurting me, so I'm going to give him the benefit of the doubt."

Meredith admired her friend for her positive attitude and her faith in her husband.

"We should hurry," Julia said, "or we'll be late for the luncheon."

They walked through the park, beside the café and pavilion, and across Drayton Street to the large, beautiful hotel. When they entered the ornate lobby, they were greeted by one of the historical society board members.

"We'll be enjoying our luncheon in the Viennese Ballroom," she said.

Meredith had been in the hotel several times and had actually hosted many events there with the historical society. The building was home to a spa, a fantastic restaurant and cooking school, and a hundred and twenty-five guest suites. The owner, Mr. Kessler, had amassed an impressive art collection, which was on display throughout the property. He had also commissioned a hat exhibit, showing a hundred years' worth of women's hats. The remarkable collection was housed within glass showcases, and each time Meredith looked at it, she found new details to enjoy.

They entered the ballroom, which was small and intimate. Ten round tables had been set up within the gilded room, long white linen and elegant fresh floral centerpieces decorating each one. Beatrice stood near the entrance to the ballroom, presiding over the affair. She wore a floor-length gown, with blue floral print from top to bottom. Pinned to her chest was a large blue corsage, and her pixie-styled haircut was meticulously arranged. Diamond earrings, necklace, and bracelet shimmered under the chandeliers.

"Compared to Beatrice, I feel like I'm dressed for a funeral," Julia said under her breath.

"To be fair," Meredith said, just as quietly, "I've seen her wear something just as bright and floral to a funeral once."

Beatrice greeted each new arrival with a brief handshake and a kiss on each cheek. She took a few seconds with each member to comment on their appearance, ask about their family, and generally remark about the beauty of the room.

But when she caught sight of Meredith and Julia, she suddenly became concerned about a group of ladies on the opposite side of the room. She waved at the group and nodded with a smile plastered to her face, though they didn't even seem to notice her.

"Will you excuse me?" Beatrice asked the woman in front of Meredith. "Please have a seat. I'm needed elsewhere." She floated across the room, the hem of her gown trailing after her.

"I suppose there is some benefit to Beatrice avoiding us," Julia said wryly.

"Oh, Julia." Meredith shook her head.

"It's really starting to bother me though." Julia crossed her arms and held her chin in one hand as she watched Beatrice for a second, her gaze calculating. "Why doesn't she want us to question her? I know it has something to do with the diary."

"I'll corner her a bit later and see if I can get the answer out of her," Meredith promised. "Or at least schedule a time to finally have that talk."

"Look," Julia said to Meredith, tilting her head toward the back corner of the room. "Nicole Stone is here today."

The lawyer's wife was a longtime member of the Savannah Historical Society, though she rarely attended the functions. She was a quiet, reserved woman. Meredith had never had more than a passing conversation with her before.

"I see a couple of places open at her table," Meredith said. "Shall we sit there?"

"That could be beneficial to our investigation, though there's a reason no one is sitting next to her." Julia let out a sigh. "If I remember correctly, she's very difficult to talk to."

"Not everyone is as outgoing as Beatrice." Meredith enjoyed seeing Julia smile again.

They walked across the room, the delectable aroma of lunch seeping into the ballroom. Meredith's stomach growled, though Carmen had made a large breakfast of huevos rancheros just that morning.

"Any idea when your home security system will be installed?" Julia asked.

"Hopefully on Monday." And it couldn't be soon enough.

"How's it going with Carmen at your house?"

"I love having her there." Meredith not only enjoyed Carmen's cooking but loved the companionship and energy she brought with her. "Chase is coming today and relieving her of her duties." Meredith smiled. "He told Carmen *he's* making supper for *her* tonight. He's making fried chicken, collard greens, mashed potatoes, and corn bread. Carmen said she's had all those foods before, but he said she hasn't had *his* recipes."

"It sounds like they really enjoy each other."

Meredith nodded. "They're becoming good friends."

"And maybe more?" Julia asked with a smile.

"Only time will tell, I suppose."

They approached the table and found Nicole Stone watching the activity in the room with mild interest. Two empty seats were to her left, and to her right, three ladies chatted in a steady stream of conversation.

"May we join you?" Meredith asked.

Mrs. Stone glanced up, recognition dawning on her face. "Of course."

She was a tall, thin woman, with long, elegant hands. Her white hair was styled in a twist at the back of her head and she wore simple, tasteful jewelry. She rose to greet them, her back and shoulders stiff with good manners.

"I'm Meredith—"

"Yes," Mrs. Stone said. "I am quite familiar with you, Mrs. Bellefontaine. You presided over the historical society for years, if I'm correct."

Meredith shook her hand and nodded. "Please, call me Meredith. And this is my friend and colleague, Julia Foley."

Julia extended her hand. "It's so nice to meet you, Mrs. Stone. And please, call me Julia."

"It's a pleasure to meet you, Julia," Mrs. Stone said. "And I hope you both will call me Nicole. Won't you have a seat?"

They sat down, and a waiter immediately appeared at their table to fill their glasses with ice water.

"I recently had the opportunity to meet your husband," Meredith said to Nicole. "He was a lifelong friend and attorney to my husband's aunt."

"Oh, how nice." Nicole took a sip of her water.

An awkward silence filled the space, and Meredith met Julia's glance.

"He introduced me to a friend of his," Meredith continued, unwilling to be deterred. "Mr. Troy LeBlanc."

"Yes. Anthony and Troy have been friends for several years."

Again. Silence.

"I ran into Mr. LeBlanc at the library the other day." Meredith tried again. "He mentioned that he had brunch with you and your husband last Saturday."

"Did he?"

"Yes." Meredith smiled. "Apparently, he's an amateur treasure hunter and plans to spend some time in Savannah looking for Blackbeard's long-lost treasure."

"How nice."

"Did he mention anything about the treasure to you or your husband?" Meredith tried to sound nonchalant, but she waited eagerly for Nicole's response.

Nicole's face was without expression as she regarded Meredith. "I vaguely remember some mention of Troy's hobby, though I have very little interest in such things."

Meredith realized if she wasn't straightforward with the woman, she would get nowhere. "Your husband and Mr. LeBlanc also visited my home last week when I came into possession of Anna Coles's diary." She smiled to lessen the intensity of her comment. "Mr. LeBlanc lied about who he was, hoping to read the diary to look for clues about the treasure." Her smiled faded. "But that very same evening, the diary was stolen, and there were only a few people who knew where I was storing it. Your husband and Mr. LeBlanc were two of those people."

Finally, there was a crack in Nicole's façade as her mouth slipped open and she glanced at the women on her other side to see if they were listening. She leaned toward Meredith and whispered, "Are you suggesting my husband and Troy stole your diary?"

"No." Meredith shook her head. "But, unfortunately, I haven't been able to rule them out as suspects."

If Meredith knew anything about Nicole Stone and women like her, she knew that appearances meant everything.

"Of course, I would like to think the best of them," Meredith continued. "However, they did come to my house under false pretenses." She glanced at Julia for affirmation and then back at Nicole. "And it makes them look very suspicious."

Nicole straightened her back and turned toward Meredith and Julia, as if trying to shield the conversation from the other women. She spoke through tight lips. "What would it take to rule them out as suspects? I'd be happy to answer any of your questions."

It was the response Meredith had hoped for.

"Did your husband or Mr. LeBlanc discuss the diary or the treasure with you?"

"They didn't speak about the treasure or the diary with me. I heard them mention something in passing about it, but I didn't pay any attention."

"How many times have you seen Troy LeBlanc since a week ago yesterday?" Julia asked.

"We had supper with him at the Olde Harbour Inn where he was staying on Thursday evening, and he came to brunch at our home on Saturday."

It was the same information Mr. Stone had told Meredith when she and Quin had visited him at his office.

"Did you see Mr. LeBlanc any other time this past week?" Julia asked. "Or did your husband mention him?"

Nicole thought for a moment. "No, I don't believe so."

"And do you recall where your husband was last Thursday evening?" Meredith asked. "After supper at the hotel?"

Again, the older woman thought for a moment. "At home. With me. We went to bed almost as soon as we arrived home from the hotel."

"And he stayed home all night?" Julia asked.

Nicole's eyes grew wide. "Of course he did." She leaned even closer. "I'm a light sleeper and wake up several times throughout the night. He never left our bed."

Meredith knew she had pushed Nicole as far as she would go without becoming angry, so she smiled. "I've spoken to your husband, and your story matches his exactly. I'm certain he's not the one who took the diary." But she wasn't certain whether or not he and LeBlanc had a hand in its disappearance.

"If you think of something else about Mr. LeBlanc, or your time with him..." Julia took a business card out of her purse and handed it to Nicole. "Please don't hesitate to call us."

Beatrice stood at the front of the ballroom and clinked a glass with a piece of silverware. "Ladies, may I please have your attention? I'd like to offer grace, and then we'll begin our meal."

As Beatrice prayed for the food, Meredith closed her eyes, mentally checking Mr. Stone off her suspects list.

Chapter Twelve

The walk back to the office was a little less rushed as Meredith and Julia compared notes about the case. It was clear Mr. Stone wasn't the man who had broken into Meredith's home to steal the diary, but that still left Troy LeBlanc, James Bellefontaine, and Beatrice as suspects. Since it was a man's footprints found in Meredith's home, they knew it couldn't be Beatrice, though whether or not she had someone steal the diary for her was another matter. Meredith had her doubts about Beatrice being the culprit, but until they knew why she was avoiding them, Meredith had to keep her on the list.

The spinach quiche and croissants from the luncheon had been delicious, but Meredith was eager to get back to the office for a cup of Carmen's coffee.

"At least we know Mr. Stone wasn't lying about his interactions with LeBlanc," Julia said to Meredith. "Have you heard any more from him or about him since you ran into him at the library?"

"Nothing," Meredith said. "I wonder if he's on the island looking for the treasure even now."

"I called the DNR yesterday," Julia said. "They're aware that someone is out there. They said that if he finds anything, he's not allowed to remove artifacts from the island."

"What would happen if he did find something?" Meredith asked.

"The man I spoke to said they would bring in a professional archeologist to excavate the site if something is found."

Dark clouds rolled across the sky, suddenly obscuring the sun. Both Meredith and Julia glanced up.

"Looks like we might be in for a storm," Meredith mused. She loved storms, as long as she was safely tucked inside a building.

As they crossed Whitaker Street, Meredith noticed a man standing on the porch outside Magnolia Investigations.

It was James Bellefontaine.

Meredith's heart rate started to race as she reached the bottom of the steps.

Julia inhaled a sharp breath and froze beside Meredith.

The resemblance to Ron was so striking, Meredith's knees became weak, and she had to grip the handrail for strength.

"Hello," James said as he walked to the top of the stairs. "Your secretary told me I could wait for you out here. I hope it's not a problem."

Julia looked to Meredith, as if ascertaining what Meredith wanted her to do—but Meredith didn't know. She couldn't think straight.

"Wh-why are you here?" Meredith finally asked.

James wore a pair of jeans and a button-down shirt. His full head of hair was dark with gray at the temples, and he had stunning blue eyes. It was hard to imagine that this man was guilty of so many crimes, especially because when Meredith looked at him, all she could think about was her kind, honorable, and generous husband.

"I'm not here to cause you any trouble," James said as he started down the stairs toward them.

Meredith and Julia backed onto the sidewalk as he approached. A crack of thunder reverberated overhead, but the rain held off.

"Why have you been lurking around Meredith's house?" Julia asked. "We saw you last Thursday, and Meredith said she's seen you a couple of times since then."

James looked up at the menacing clouds and then back toward the offices. "Should we step inside so we can talk?"

"I think Meredith and I would like answers now," Julia said in her no-nonsense tone. As a criminal court judge, she'd gained a tough exterior and could hold her own with anyone.

"I apologize for scaring you," James said to Meredith. "It wasn't my intention."

"Who are you?" Meredith asked, though she knew full well. She wanted to hear it from him.

"I'm your husband's cousin, James Bellefontaine."

"Why have you come after all this time?" Meredith asked. "Ron's sister, Gwyn, told me she hasn't seen you for over forty years."

James ran his hand over the stubble on his chin. "It's true. My family disowned me when I came of age, and I haven't been back to Savannah since then."

Another burst of thunder rumbled overhead, and he winced. "I recently heard that Aunt Temperance passed away, and it made me realize how foolish I've been to let things come between me and my family."

Meredith and Julia listened to him quietly, though neither made a move to welcome him into their offices.

"I came back to see if I could reconnect with Ron and Gwyn and Barb and salvage something of our relationship, but then I learned that Ron had also passed away." He shook his head, regret lining his features. "I found his address—your address—and just thought I'd walk past your house to picture the life he led. But then I saw you, and your son, who looks so much like Ron, and I couldn't face the past. I tried to return several times but couldn't get up the courage to knock on your front door."

Had he broken in the back door instead?

Meredith couldn't stop the unkind thought from forming. His story seemed very heartfelt and genuine, but doubt niggled at the back of her mind. This man had appeared out of nowhere on the very day she inherited the diary—and then it went missing. The coincidence seemed too unlikely.

"What gives you the courage to face her now?" Julia asked, her tough exterior revealing none of her thoughts regarding this man.

James met Meredith's gaze. "I have to leave Savannah in a few days, and I don't think I'll ever get a chance to return. I decided to come here, to Ron's offices, to learn more about him, and that's when I discovered that you reopened his agency. It made me realize that the best way to get to know Ron was to meet his wife. So that's what I'm doing."

"I think it's important that you know we did a background check on you after you scared Meredith the other day," Julia said. "We know all about your criminal past."

James lifted his chin but didn't say anything.

"And we find it very interesting that you suddenly showed up on the very same day that Meredith received an inheritance from your aunt."

"The diary?" James asked. "I read in the newspaper that it was stolen."

Meredith studied his face, looking for any telltale signs that would give away his involvement—but saw none. Had he perfected lying over all these years?

"Yes," Julia said. "It was stolen just hours after you showed up."

James's eyes grew wide. "You don't think I stole it, do you?"

"Actually," Meredith said, "you are one of our prime suspects."

"I've put crime behind me," he said. "I'm a new man."

His voice seemed genuine, but Meredith had to remind herself that he was an identity thief and embezzler. Could he really be trusted? Weren't men like him masters of manipulation and charm?

"I was hoping to see a few other places from my childhood," James said. "Is Aunt Temperance's plantation home still in the family? I'd hate to intrude on strangers if the place was sold."

"It was sold years ago when she went into assisted living." Meredith wasn't sure how much she should tell him.

"And all her things?" he asked. "I'm assuming they were divided among the family?"

"For the most part."

"And the diary," he said. "How did it end up going to you? Shouldn't it have gone to Gwyn or Barb?"

"Mr. Bellefontaine." Julia's voice was stern. "The only person who should be questioned right now is you. Meredith owes you no explanations."

"I don't mean to intrude." He put up his hands. "I'm just here trying to reconnect with my past. It's been so long, I'm just curious." He moved around Meredith and Julia toward the sidewalk. "I can see now that my presence here is only making you more uncomfortable, so I'll go." He nodded at both of them. "I hope you find the diary."

And, with that, James Bellefontaine walked away.

"What do you make of that?" Julia asked Meredith after a few moments.

"I have no idea."

Raindrops began to fall around them, so they scurried up the steps and onto the porch. From where they stood, they watched James cross Whitaker Street and enter Forsyth Park. He disappeared behind a row of live oaks and was finally out of sight.

"Do you still think he's the guy?" Julia asked. "I looked at his feet while he was talking, and he was wearing casual shoes. I can't be sure, but they look pretty consistent with the size and shape of the footprints found in your house."

"There's no way of knowing for sure. It's definitely not enough of a clue to go on."

"I wish we would have asked him where he's staying while he's in town," Julia said, "or at least gotten a phone number."

"I wonder if he'll try to contact Gwyn." Meredith hugged her arms around her middle. "I'll call her right away and tell her we saw him. She'll let me know if he contacts her." She reached for the door handle. "I'm not going to call Barb about it. I'll find out from Gwyn if he's gotten in touch with either of them." A conversation with Ron's other sister—the snooty and very untactful one—wasn't anything she had the mental energy for right now.

"I still think it's a strange coincidence that he showed up the very day you inherited the diary—yet why would he approach you now if he has it?"

"Maybe it's like you suggested. Maybe he's looking for something else from me. He did ask a lot of questions—but I don't know what he would still want."

"I find it hard to believe he's reformed, but I suppose it's not impossible."

"I don't know." Meredith sighed and shook her head. "It's all so strange. I wonder if he really is leaving Savannah in a few days or if that was just a lie."

"I have a feeling we'll be seeing James Bellefontaine again. If he didn't get the information out of you that he came to get, he'll probably be back."

Meredith hoped Julia was wrong, but experience told her otherwise.

***

The rain did not let up for the rest of the afternoon, and it was still pouring when Meredith and Carmen parked behind Meredith's house later that evening. Chase's car was already in Meredith's second parking spot, and Carmen had parked down the street, then jumped into Meredith's car for the ride to her house. They laughed as they ran through the rain and into the courtyard. Meredith fumbled with the keys while Carmen held the umbrella, and when they finally entered the house, it smelled divine.

"*Delicioso,*" Carmen said. "It smells like Chase has been cooking."

The aroma of fried chicken wafted on the air as they set their wet things in the back entry and climbed the short flight of stairs to the hall above. In the kitchen, Chase had country music playing, and GK was lying on his bed near the window.

Chase had his back to them, line dancing to "My Achy Breaky Heart." Around his middle he wore one of Meredith's old, frilly pink aprons to cover his button-down shirt and slacks.

Meredith began to giggle at the sight, trying to hide the sound behind her hand—but Carmen was not so tactful. Her laughter caused Chase to turn and pause in the middle of his dance. He grinned, his face turning three shades of pink before he had a chance to turn down the music and remove his apron.

The kitchen was a mess. There wasn't a clean spot on any counter. Half a dozen dirty pots and pans were in the sink, and all the ingredients he'd used were strewn about the room. Melted butter dripped down a cabinet, and grease was splattered all over the stove.

"What have you done to my kitchen?" Meredith asked, her eyes wide. "It looks like you've been in a battle, and I'm not sure who won."

"When you eat my fried chicken, you'll know who won." Chase's grin was so handsome, and so like his father's, it made Meredith's heart ache with loneliness for Ron.

"Aye yai yai." Carmen went to the sink and looked at the dishes, shaking her head in disapproval. "If I didn't know better, I'd think you were raised by a pack of wolves."

Chase's grin turned into something softer and sweeter when he looked at Carmen. "Hello," he said.

Her disapproval vanished, and her face also softened. "*Hola, amigo. ¿Cómo estás?*"

"I'm good," Chase said. "Better now that you're here."

Meredith suddenly felt like an intruder in her own home. She wasn't sure what to do, so she started to clean up the mess her son had made.

"No, *señora*," Carmen said, taking the bag of flour out of Meredith's hand. "Chase will clean after we eat. Maybe he'll learn not to make such a mess."

"Hey, I thought the rule was that we clean together," Chase said in mock surprise. "I helped you clean up after you cooked last week."

"*I* didn't make such a mess," she reminded him.

"I suppose you're right." His smile was warm and gentle. "But will you keep me company while I clean?"

The smile she offered in return could have lit up a dark room. "Sí, I will keep you company."

Chase laughed as he surveyed the room around him. "I did make a mess. Frying chicken isn't as easy as it looks."

The food was on the counter. Steaming mashed potatoes with melting butter, creamy collard greens, crispy fried chicken, and more.

"Should I help you move this to the dining room?" Meredith asked. "I see you've already set the table."

"Yes, thanks, Mom."

They moved the food to the table, and Chase changed the music to a gentle, classical station. It had been a few weeks since Meredith had enjoyed a meal around her dining room table with her family, and she was thankful for this time. She wished the diary hadn't been stolen and her home hadn't been broken into, but as the rain continued to pour outside, splashing against the windowpanes, and she enjoyed the delicious meal her son had cooked, she couldn't help but be thankful that God had brought blessings out of the trial.

"We had an interesting visitor to the agency today," Carmen said to Chase, while glancing at Meredith with a pointed look, as if threatening to tell him if she didn't.

"Who was that?" Chase asked, looking from Carmen to Meredith.

Meredith set her fork down and sighed. "James Bellefontaine."

"Dad's doppelganger?" Chase's eyebrows rose.

"Yes." Meredith needed to tell him the whole truth, though he wouldn't like it. "Julia had a background check done on him, and we learned he has quite a criminal record."

Chase lowered his fork and stared at Meredith. "What kind of record?"

"Theft, embezzlement, burglary."

"Does he seem dangerous?"

"I don't know what to make of him," Meredith told her son. "He said he was here to reconnect with his past, and he seemed genuine."

"You can't trust him, Mom." Chase clasped his hands together. "He's a conman. He told you what you wanted to hear."

"I don't trust him," Meredith said. "I called your aunt Gwyn and told her to keep her eyes open for him and to tell your aunt Barb to do the same. I'll watch for him as well. In the meantime, I'm trying to find out more about him. I'd like to know where he's staying and possibly talk to him again. I didn't get a chance to ask him where he was the night the diary was stolen."

"I'd stay as far away from him as possible," Chase advised. "If the family disowned him, they must have had good reason."

"Well..." Meredith picked up her fork again and took a scoop of the creamy potatoes. "Aunt Temperance was a little paranoid and hard to please, but I'll take your recommendation to heart. I'll only seek him out if I know it's safe and it will help our case."

"She's not going to listen to you," Carmen said to Chase. "You know she won't."

"I know."

Meredith shook her head and ignored them.

"When will the security system be installed?" Chase asked.

"Hopefully on Monday."

"Why the delay?" he asked. "This is ridiculous. Why don't you call a different company?"

"I'm already this far into the process with this one, I don't want to start over. Besides, you'll be here with me."

"Until Sunday."

"I'll come back Sunday night," Carmen said to both of them.

"We can't keep asking you to do that," Chase told her.

"It's not difficult." Carmen pointed at her plate and then at the beautiful room around her. "I'm truly enjoying myself."

"Don't feel obligated," Chase said. "If I need to take a day off work to stay here with Mom, I will."

"No, you won't." Meredith spoke with authority. "I'm a grown woman and will be just fine on my own."

"Don't worry, *amiga bonita*." Carmen set her hand on Meredith's. "I'll be here."

Meredith doubted she'd have any more trouble from the thief, whoever he was, but it would be nice to enjoy Carmen's company for a couple more days.

Chapter Thirteen

After a rainy weekend playing board games with Chase and Carmen, watching old black-and-white movies in her family room, talking to her grandchildren on their weekly Snapchat conversation, and baking pecan pies and cookies with Carmen, Meredith felt refreshed and ready to tackle another week.

Monday morning dawned bright and warm, and Meredith woke with a bounce in her step. She was eager to return to the office and get back to work. She and Carmen enjoyed a breakfast of fresh caramel rolls, and then they took their separate cars to work. The home security company had called and delayed their arrival by two more days, promising to be there bright and early Wednesday. Meredith warned them that if they did not install it then, she would call another company, though she didn't want to start the process all over again.

Julia had not arrived yet when Carmen unlocked the back door and they entered their offices. Carmen hummed a happy tune while she walked to the coffeemaker and started to make a fresh pot of their favorite beverage.

Meredith entered her office and set her purse on the desk. She turned on her laptop and took a seat.

It took a few moments for the computer to boot up, but before long she was looking at the emails she'd missed over the weekend.

The first one to catch her eye was from the Daniel Defoe Library in London.

Wishing Julia was there to share the email with her, she clicked on the message and began to read.

Dear Mrs. Bellefontaine,

We were overjoyed to receive your message last week. It isn't every day that we are contacted by a family member of Mr. Defoe. We took your query to several of our docents and volunteers and are sending you all the information we have gathered. Attached please find this information and let us know if there is anything more we can do to help.

Regarding your inquiry about Mr. Defoe's youngest daughter, Anna. We have confirmed that she married Mr. Joseph Coles on 7th June, 1718, and left for America on the ship Anne *in 1732 with General Oglethorpe. She settled in the colony of Georgia and lived to the age of 86.*

As to your inquiry about Mr. Defoe's work on A General History of the Pyrates, *there have been many disputes as to whether or not he wrote the book, but it is our educated guess that he did. We have done extensive research into his writings and believe he kept a diary or journal while meeting with pirates both in and out of prison for his research. There are some rumours that he may have pinpointed the location of several different treasures through the years, the most famous of which is Blackbeard's treasure, and written that information in his diary as well. However, the diary in question has long since been lost to history. You might find it interesting to note that the book was nicknamed* The Devil *by the pirates, since all of their secrets were recorded within. When Edward Teach so famously said "Only the devil and I know the whereabouts of my treasure, and the one of us who lives the longest shall take it all!" some think he meant Mr. Defoe.*

We hope these answers satisfy your questions, but we are available should others present themselves. If we can be of further assistance, do not hesitate to contact me personally.

Yours respectfully,

Mr. Matthew Foxgrove

President of the Daniel Defoe Library

Meredith stared at the screen for several moments, absorbing the information she'd just read. It matched up with what Maggie Lu had told them in the Downhome Diner. Daniel Defoe had kept a diary of the pirates' deepest and darkest secrets, and that was probably the book Joseph said he'd taken from Daniel's collection after he died. What she wouldn't give to see that diary! She couldn't even begin to imagine what stories it could tell. It was a shame that the book was lost to history, as Mr. Foxgrove had so elegantly stated.

"Good morning, Julia," Carmen said in the front foyer.

"Hello, Carmen."

Julia appeared at Meredith's door. "Good morning."

Meredith turned the computer for Julia to see what she'd just read. "We received a response from the Daniel Defoe Library. They confirmed that Anna Coles is Daniel's daughter. They also shared some interesting information about Daniel's connection to the pirates and possibly to Blackbeard's treasure."

Julia took a seat across from Meredith in one of the designer chairs Meredith had purchased from a SCAD store in downtown Savannah. The Savannah College of Art & Design was spread out over forty historic buildings they had purchased and remodeled. They were a dominating presence in town and had done amazing work to revitalize the area. Meredith had used several of their students to redesign her home and loved supporting them by purchasing their products, like the chair.

"That's amazing, Meredith." Julia leaned back after she finished reading the email. The smile she plastered on her lips did not reach her eyes.

"What's the matter, Julia?" Meredith closed the laptop and pushed it to the side. "Beau again?"

"I don't know what's going on." Julia's shoulders slumped. "I'm trying to be patient and understanding, but I can't reason away what happened last night."

Meredith left her chair and went around her desk to sit in the chair next to Julia. "What happened?"

"He felt bad about missing our anniversary the other day," Julia began, "so he asked me if I'd like to go out on the town Saturday night. We ate on the riverfront, went to a show at the Historic Savannah Theater, and afterward we had ice cream at Leopold's. It was as if nothing had happened and we were having a wonderful time, just enjoying each other's company."

Meredith listened and nodded empathetically.

"But while we were in Leopold's, a very flashy woman approached. Someone I'd never met before. She wore bright makeup and tight leggings. She greeted Beau as if they were friends." Julia shook her head. "It's not uncommon for Beau to know people I don't know, but then she said, 'I'll see you on Thursday night, honey.'" She swallowed, hard. "He just smiled and went back to his ice cream. I waited for him to explain, but he didn't. When I asked him who she was, he said he couldn't remember her name and then said he wanted to go home. I waited all night for him to tell me who the woman was, but he didn't."

"That is strange," Meredith conceded. "Who do you think she was?"

"I have no idea!" Julia threw her arms up in frustration.

"And he won't tell you?"

"No." She lifted an exasperated shoulder. "It's maddening. I'm considering following him, though I've always detested paranoid wives. I never thought I'd be one."

"You're not being paranoid, Julia. You're concerned and confused. There's a big difference."

"Well, I don't know about that. What I do know is that if he doesn't tell me what he's up to soon, I think I might hire a private investigator." She looked pointedly at Meredith.

Meredith opened her eyes wide. "Me?"

"Why not?"

"I'm not going to follow—"

A woman's voice interrupted their conversation, saving Meredith from Julia's request.

"Hello, Carmen, darling. Are Mere and Jules in today?"

"Beatrice," Julia mouthed the name to Meredith and shook her head. "I don't want to see her right now."

Meredith shrugged. It was probably too late. Julia couldn't get from Meredith's office to her own without encountering Beatrice in the hall. "Don't you want to question her?"

Julia grimaced.

"They're in Meredith's office," Carmen said.

"Don't bother to get up, honey," Beatrice said. "I'll let myself in."

Within seconds, Beatrice stood in Meredith's office. The perfume she wore was so overpowering, it made Meredith's eyes water. The pattern on her one-piece jumper was multicolored stripes from shoulders to toes and reminded Meredith of a circus.

"I'm so happy to find you both together," Beatrice said as she glided into the room and stood before them. "I had the most wonderful idea come to me, and I can't imagine why I didn't think of it before."

Meredith rose and indicated the couch and chairs in the middle of the room. "Would you like some coffee?"

"Oh no, I don't have time for a social visit. This is all business, dear." She took the seat Meredith suggested, and Julia sat across from her. Meredith sat next to Beatrice.

"I'm glad you're here," Meredith said. "I've been wanting to talk to—"

"Yes, yes, that can wait." She put her hand on Meredith's knee to silence her. "I want to tell you my idea before I forget."

Julia kept her mouth shut, but she looked at Meredith with a hint of impatience.

"I've decided to offer a substantial reward to the person who recovers your diary, Meredith. Not only is it a vital piece of Savannah history, it's a vital piece of Georgia's history as well. I have worked tirelessly these many days and have been given several pledges from dozens of organizations to put toward the reward." She stopped and looked at both of them expectantly. "Well, what do you think?"

"I think it's wonderful," Meredith said. She wondered how Beatrice could possibly raise enough to entice the thief to give it up. "Thank you, Beatrice. It's very thoughtful of you."

"I wish I could say it's a selfless act on my part, but I must have that diary for the historical society gala at the end of this month. The whole theme of the event hinges on the diary."

"Whatever the reason, I'm thankful for your offer." Meredith smiled and then proceeded. "Now, about the night the diary was stolen. I know we asked you before, but—"

"That's all I came to say." Beatrice rose and put her clutch purse under her arm. "I'll alert all the media outlets about the reward. Hopefully we'll have the diary back soon."

"Beatrice." Julia also rose. "We'd like to know where you were the night the diary was stolen. It's a very simple question and shouldn't be that hard to answer."

"Hmm." Beatrice scrunched up her face and lifted her hand in a dismissive motion. "I can't recall. Silly me." She waved and walked to the door. "Ta-ta, ladies. I'll be in touch."

Without a backward glance, she left, calling goodbye to Carmen on her way out.

"She's definitely hiding something," Julia said. "And I'm getting more and more curious about what it is."

"You don't think it has to do with the diary, do you?" Meredith asked.

"I have no idea, but it's juicy, I do know that."

Julia went to the window to watch Beatrice walk down the street.

Carmen entered Meredith's office with her cell phone in hand. "Here's something you'll both want to hear."

Julia and Meredith turned to face Carmen.

Carmen looked up at them, her eyes round and large. Then she looked back at her phone and read, "'A man named Troy LeBlanc has claimed he found an eighteenth-century musket, similar to those used by the pirates in this area. He found it in a cave on Blackbeard's Island over the weekend. He left it where he found it and took a team of archaeologists from the Georgia Historical Society to the site yesterday morning.'"

Meredith rose from her spot on the couch and looked at the article on Carmen's phone, her pulse ticking higher. "Are you serious?"

"Here's a picture of him holding the gun." Carmen clicked on the picture.

It was Troy LeBlanc standing near a cave, a musket in hand, grinning as if he'd just won the lottery.

"The archaeology team plans to start excavating the area as soon as next week," Carmen said.

"Does it say exactly where he found the musket?" Julia approached and studied the picture as well.

Carmen scrolled through the article and stopped when she came to the spot she was looking for. "It says he found it on the south side of the island."

Meredith frowned. "I wonder why he looked there. When we were at the library, Rebecca found a map that indicated the treasure might be on the north side."

Carmen shrugged. "Who knows? But isn't it exciting?"

Julia looked at Meredith. "I think we should pay a visit to Mr. Troy LeBlanc. Didn't Nicole say he was staying at the Olde Harbour Inn?"

"I believe she did."

"Shall we go?"

"I believe we should."

Meredith had a few more questions for LeBlanc, especially now that he'd found something that could have belonged to Blackbeard.

***

It wasn't hard to locate Troy LeBlanc when Meredith and Julia arrived at the Olde Harbour Inn on the Savannah riverfront thirty minutes later. The lobby was small and intimate, and LeBlanc was there, near the fireplace, speaking to reporters. His face was shining, and his eyes were aglow as he animatedly told the five people around him how he'd located the musket.

Meredith and Julia stood on the outskirts of the room listening, but LeBlanc was so wrapped up in his story, he didn't seem to notice their arrival.

"I ascertained the location of the treasure by studying several books about Edward Teach over the years. One book was a well-researched work chronicling his life from 1716 to 1718. Using that information, I narrowed my search to Savannah and visited the Carnegie Library on East Henry Street. There, the librarian shared with me several newspaper articles and a map made in 1886 with directions to the treasure. I spent several days on the island looking for the treasure, and on Saturday evening I stumbled across a cave that was almost covered by fallen rocks. After I pulled the rocks away from the opening, I found the musket."

"And did you find anything else, Mr. LeBlanc? Any other treasure?" one of the reporters asked.

"I was so amazed at this discovery, I didn't look any further." LeBlanc shook his head in awe. "I immediately called the Georgia Historical Society, knowing they'd want to do the official archeological dig."

"And what will you do now?" another reporter asked.

"I've been invited by the archeological team to visit the site whenever I'm in Savannah. I won't be any help, but I wouldn't mind checking back from time to time to see what they find."

"This is a big discovery for Georgia," said the third reporter. "What does this mean for you, personally?"

"For me?" LeBlanc grew serious. "I'm a lifelong fan of pirate history. Finding this is a dream come true."

"Are you disappointed you won't have a stake in any of the treasure they uncover?" asked the first reporter.

"No." LeBlanc smiled, his white teeth flashing. "Knowing I had a hand in finding the treasure for the rest of the world is enough reward for me."

The reporters quickly jotted down the sound bite and stood to leave. "Thank you for your time, Mr. LeBlanc," one said after the other. "It was a pleasure to meet you."

"Thank you all for coming," LeBlanc said. "Have a good day."

As the reporters started to file out of the lobby, LeBlanc finally noticed Meredith and Julia standing off to the side.

He smiled and motioned them to join him. "Have you come to hear all about the musket?"

Meredith and Julia took seats in the plush chairs near him. A low, round coffee table sat in the middle of the seating area.

"We're interested in how you found the treasure," Julia said. "But we also have a few more questions for you, if you don't mind."

"Of course not." He put his arms on the armrests and looked contentedly at them. "What would you like to know?"

"I'm surprised you found the musket on the south side of the island," Meredith began. "I thought the map said the treasure might be on the north side."

"It did." LeBlanc leaned forward and clasped his hands eagerly. "But then I noticed a small note on the map that looked like it had been added later. It mentioned a location of interest on the south side of the island, about where I found the musket. I decided to start my search there, since others had looked on the north side already. I traversed the spot all day Friday and Saturday, and I was about to give up when I noticed the pile of rocks. When I started to move them aside, I realized it was the entrance to a cave, and that's when I found the gun."

"That's amazing," Meredith said. "And someone authenticated the musket?"

"Yes, one of the archaeologists." LeBlanc shook his head. "Isn't it wonderful?"

"Very," Julia agreed.

"So, what do you plan to do now?" Meredith asked. "Weren't you due back to work today?"

"Yes, but as you can imagine, I'm not quite ready to head back yet. I'll leave this afternoon and plan to return to work in the morning." He yawned. "Pardon me. I haven't slept much these past couple of days."

"We won't keep you much longer," Meredith said. "We just wanted to congratulate you and hear a little more about the discovery."

"Thank you. I appreciate that."

The three of them rose from their chairs, and LeBlanc followed them to the door.

"Any more leads on the diary?" he asked them.

Julia glanced at Meredith, questions in her eyes. Did they want to share information with him?

"It's still an active investigation," Meredith said. "We'd rather not share any details."

"I understand." He smiled at them. "Thanks again for stopping by to see me."

Meredith and Julia left the hotel and crossed over the bridge that led to the parking lot just off East Bay Street.

"It's almost hard to believe," Julia said, "that after all these years, someone has finally found an eighteenth-century artifact on Blackbeard's Island."

"I suppose if someone was bound to find it, it would be a treasure hunter like Troy LeBlanc who is skilled at locating them." Meredith thought back to the map and the man who had written it. "I wonder if Markus Wheaton planned to look on the south side of the island but died before he had a chance."

"I suppose it's possible."

"And because the family thought the diary was cursed after his death, they hid it away and never looked for the treasure again."

"Seems strange that they were so close to the truth," Julia mused. "But then they let fear stop them right before they found the treasure."

Meredith couldn't imagine how different the Bellefontaine fortune would have looked had they found Blackbeard's treasure. "I wonder if they'll unearth the whole thing over the next few weeks."

"It'll be amazing to see how much it's worth, if they do."

"I suppose we're getting ahead of ourselves," Meredith conceded. "We don't know if this musket was a single object or if it will point to other things."

"That's right. Only time will tell."

"Did you notice something?" Meredith asked.

"What's that?"

"Mr. 'Nelson' used his real name."

Julia laughed. "So he did. I guess he knew the news and his picture would be in the papers."

They stepped into Julia's car, and Meredith looked out the window as they pulled onto East Bay Street and then turned left onto Whitaker Street.

"Doesn't it seem interesting to you," Meredith mused, "that the very first artifact found on Blackbeard's Island came after Anna's diary fell into the hands of someone outside her family?"

Julia glanced at Meredith. "You think LeBlanc has the diary, and he used it to find the musket?"

"I don't know." Meredith nibbled her bottom lip. "He claims he found it using the map from the library, and that might be true, but I suppose he could have used Anna's diary as well."

"You think he's still a suspect?"

"I can't rule him out."

"He seems pretty content with what he found. Do you think he'll return the diary?"

"If he does, he'll have to do it anonymously."

"I don't know," Julia said cautiously. "He doesn't come across to me as a thief."

"In all your years as a criminal court judge, I'd think you, of all people, would realize that not everyone is as they appear," Meredith said. "You have to remember, we already know he's a liar."

"That's true," Julia answered.

"Either way," Meredith said, "if he did take the diary and use it to find the musket, I hope he gives it back. If he didn't take it, and now the real thief realizes they're too late, I hope they decide to give it back."

"Ever the optimist, Mere."

"There's always hope." At least, that's what she liked to believe. With Beatrice's reward money now out there, maybe the thief would have the incentive to give the diary back.

Chapter Fourteen

As Meredith and Julia drove down Whitaker Street toward Magnolia Investigations, a woman caught Meredith's eye. She wore a multicolored jumper exactly like the one Beatrice had worn earlier, but this woman had a scarf wrapped around her head, with dark glasses hiding her eyes. She stepped out of a dermatology clinic, cautiously looking in all directions before she moved toward a parked car.

"Julia, slow down a minute."

Julia let off the accelerator, and the car slowed.

The woman looked left and right and then left again as she walked toward the car.

Frowning, Meredith tried to get a better look. *Was* it Beatrice? But if it was, why was she trying not to be seen?

"What's happening?" Julia asked.

"I think that's Beatrice over there." Meredith pointed to where the woman was walking down the street.

"Should I pull over so we can see if it's her?"

"Sure."

Julia found a spot to park the car not too far away from the woman, and they watched as she took off the scarf and glasses and shoved them into her bag. She ran her hand over her hair several times and then took out a handheld mirror and looked at her appearance.

"It *is* Beatrice. But why the funny getup?" Julia asked.

"Let's go find out." Meredith didn't wait for Julia but opened the door and approached Beatrice.

Julia wasn't far behind.

"Hello, Beatrice," Meredith said.

Beatrice jumped and dropped the mirror with a screech. "Meredith!" she said. "What are you doing here?"

"Heading back to work." Meredith stood with a smile on her face as Julia came up beside her.

"What are *you* doing here?" Julia asked Beatrice.

Beatrice slowly picked up the mirror and then smoothed her jumper. "I—I was just, ah…" She stopped talking and lifted her chin. "It's really none of your business."

"I suppose you're right," Julia said. "When we saw you coming out of the dermatology clinic, we were just curious."

Looking over her shoulder at the clinic, Beatrice swallowed hard. "You saw me leave the clinic?"

Meredith nodded, though she couldn't imagine why Beatrice was being so strange about the situation.

"Promise me you won't tell anyone," she said, her face filling with color. "I'd die of embarrassment if anyone found out the truth."

"The truth about what?" Meredith frowned. "What's going on, Beatrice?"

Beatrice took each of them by an elbow and led them over to the side of a building. "If I tell you the truth," she whispered, "are you required to keep the information a secret—client confidentiality and all of that?"

"Um..." Julia blinked several times. "Have you broken the law? Because if you have, then we can't keep that to ourselves—and you're not our client."

"Oh goodness. It's nothing like that." Beatrice sighed. "I might as well tell you, since you won't stop bothering me about it until I do." She looked at them, her eyes serious. "Promise me this stays between us."

"Of course," Meredith said.

"A week ago Thursday, when the diary was stolen, I was in Atlanta. I wasn't even in Savannah. I left almost immediately after I was at your house, Meredith."

"Why were you in Atlanta?" Meredith asked.

"Seeing a specialist."

"What kind of specialist?"

Beatrice mumbled something under her breath.

Meredith and Julia leaned forward.

"What was that?" Julia asked.

"A hair loss specialist," she said just barely above a whisper.

"A hair loss specialist?" Meredith asked.

"Shh." Beatrice looked around them. "Not so loud."

"You were in Atlanta the Thursday before last?"

"Yes." She sighed again. "I had a treatment done there on Thursday afternoon and remained there until Friday morning. My husband was with me, and I have receipts to prove where I was." She stared at both of them, her eyebrows raised. "Well?" she asked.

"Well, what?" Julia frowned.

"Can you tell the difference?"

Beatrice's hair looked exactly like it always looked.

"They did an amazing job," Meredith said. "I can't even tell you've had anything done to your hair."

"Not on my head," Beatrice said with an exasperated breath. She pointed at her eyebrows. "I had an eyebrow transplant."

Meredith and Julia stared at Beatrice.

"Your eyebrows?" Julia asked.

"Yes." She motioned to the clinic. "I was just here for a checkup, since it's such a long drive to Atlanta. They said the transplant went well, and I should expect a full recovery."

"A full eyebrow transplant recovery?" Meredith pressed her lips together, forcing herself not to smile. If she did, she might burst out laughing.

She didn't dare look at Julia.

"It was more painful than you can imagine," Beatrice said, suddenly looking defensive. "I'm happy the follicles took, since I wouldn't want to endure the procedure again any time soon."

"We saw you just two days after your, um, procedure," Julia said. "You weren't even swollen."

"I was fortunate." Beatrice ran her hand over her hair again. "There was a small chance for swelling and bruising, but I didn't have either."

"That is fortunate," Meredith said.

"So." Beatrice crossed her arms. "You know my dirty little secret. I didn't take the diary, and I'm actually quite offended that I was even a suspect. I thought we were friends."

Friends? Meredith wasn't sure she would classify their relationship as "friends," but she could understand why Beatrice was unhappy about being a suspect.

"It wasn't personal," Julia said, with more patience than she usually exhibited with Beatrice. "We were just doing our job. We didn't mean to offend you."

"Bless your heart." Beatrice smiled, her Southern charm starting to drip all over again. "I can't stay mad at y'all for long." She wrapped her arms through theirs and walked them back to Julia's car. "I fully expect my reward to bring the thief running back with the diary. I'm so convinced, I've gone forward with all my plans for the historical society gala as if the diary is in our possession again."

"If you hear anything," Meredith said, disentangling her arm from Beatrice's, "please let us know immediately."

"I sure will, honey." She waved. "Bye, now."

Julia got into the driver's side and Meredith into the passenger side, and they pulled away from the curb.

Neither one spoke for several minutes, and then Julia said, very slowly, concealed laughter in her voice, "That was interesting."

"Never a dull day on the job," Meredith conceded, trying not to laugh herself.

"You would think that Beatrice Enterline would cease to amaze me." Julia shook her head. "But I'm pretty much shocked every time I encounter her."

Meredith finally laughed. "I don't think I've ever met any two women who were more dissimilar than you and Beatrice."

"She's a good woman," Julia said. "And I know she means well, I just—"

"Don't understand her."

"Exactly."

"That's okay, Julia. You don't have to understand everyone and everything."

"It would be nice though, wouldn't it?"

It would be nice, and it would make Meredith and Julia's job a lot easier.

"I hope Beatrice's reward will help," Meredith said. "I'm starting to run out of ideas as to how we're going to recover the diary."

"Maybe it's time we chatted with Maggie Lu again. See if she remembers anything else about the diary."

"She said she read it and doesn't recall anything that would be of interest to us or anyone else." Meredith let out a frustrated sigh. "She doesn't remember any mention of pirate treasure. Just personal information about Anna and her family."

"Maybe there's something else," Julia said. "Why did Temperance decide to put the diary back into hiding? Was it because she believed it was cursed—or was there another reason?"

"That's a good question." Meredith tapped her finger on her chin. "I'll call her and see if she's available to talk."

If Maggie Lu couldn't remember anything else about the diary, Meredith would have to think of another angle they hadn't considered to recover it.

***

Julia and Meredith pulled into the parking spot in the back of Magnolia Investigations and entered through the rear door. The building was blessedly cool and smelled of fresh coffee.

"I have a few emails to answer," Julia said as she left Meredith in the hall and went toward her office. "Let me know if you need me."

Meredith went to the coffee stand, where she poured a cup for herself.

"Meredith?" Carmen called from the front room, the tone of her voice different than usual. "You have a visitor."

Holding the hot cup of coffee, Meredith entered the front parlor, but Carmen was alone.

"Who's here?" Meredith asked.

Carmen nodded toward the front door. A man stood on the porch. "James Bellefontaine is back. He's been waiting for you for almost an hour."

James was back?

Meredith stood for a moment, contemplating what she should do. Part of her wanted to know why he'd returned, but the other part thought about Chase's warning not to trust the wayward cousin. Was he here for more information? Would he try to get money out of her?

"I'll get Julia," Meredith said. "And we'll talk to him together." She wasn't afraid to be alone with him on the front porch—but she appreciated Julia's experience with criminals and was always thankful for a second set of eyes and ears when she talked to a suspect.

After telling Julia who was back, Meredith opened the front door, and they walked onto the porch.

James turned and quickly looked from Julia to Meredith.

"Hello, Mr. Bellefontaine," Julia said. "What brings you back?"

"I didn't think I'd be speaking to both of you," James said. "I thought it would just be Meredith."

"If you have something to say to me," Meredith said, "then you can say it in front of Julia."

He shuffled from one foot to the other. "Could we sit down?"

A porch swing hung from four chains bolted into the ceiling, while a single rocking chair sat beside it. In between was a small table with potted wax begonias that Carmen cared for religiously.

"Have a seat," Meredith said as she indicated the rocking chair. She and Julia shared the swing.

James sat on the rocker and leaned forward, putting his elbows on his knees. He didn't say anything for several moments.

"What can we do for you?" Meredith asked. Was he here to return the diary and collect the reward? Was he going to try to manipulate her into giving him money to return to California?

"After I left here the other day," he began, "I couldn't shake the feeling that you didn't trust me, Meredith." He met her gaze. "I came home to Savannah to set things right with my family, and I can't leave until I do."

"What do you need to set right with us?" Meredith asked.

"I'm not proud of who I was," he said, letting out a long, low breath. "I didn't get a chance to ask my father or Aunt Temperance for forgiveness before they died, and I didn't want to let that happen with Ron too." He swallowed and looked down at his hands. "Turns out, I lost that opportunity as well."

Despite her misgivings, Meredith said, "I don't think Ron held anything against you, James. He never even mentioned your name."

James shook his head. "That seems worse than if he'd held a grudge against me all these years."

"I appreciate your desire to set things right." Meredith leaned back in the swing. "But you don't need to ask my forgiveness—unless, you broke into my house and took my diary."

"You mean, the family diary." He looked up at Meredith. "I didn't take the diary, but I can't lie. I was upset to hear it had passed to someone who wasn't a Bellefontaine by birth."

Meredith stiffened at his words.

"At the very least, it should have gone to Gwyn or Barb—or even me. Maybe it wouldn't be gone now."

"Do you feel the diary should be yours?" Julia asked cautiously.

"I understand why Aunt Temperance would choose not to leave it to me—but that doesn't mean I'm not a Bellefontaine. I should have something from my family—shouldn't I?"

"Mr. Bellefontaine," Julia said slowly, "I'm going to ask you once again. Did you take the diary from Meredith's home?"

"No." He stood.

Meredith's muscles tensed at his sudden movement.

"I didn't come here to get into a fight about what should and shouldn't be mine." He walked toward the opposite end of the porch. "Like I said, I wanted to make things right with my family." He returned to the rocker and put his hand on the back. "A week after my last arrest, I checked myself into a rehabilitation center in Santa Ana. It was a twelve-month program, and I just graduated in May." He took a moment to gather his thoughts and continued. "Part of the program requires me to face my past and try to make amends, where I can."

Was this another attempt to manipulate Meredith into caring for him and his plight? Would he try to convince her he was a reformed man—even if he wasn't?

"I don't know you," he said to Meredith, "but you're the closest person I have to Ron, and so I'm asking you for your forgiveness. If I ever hurt Ron, I'd like to know you forgive me for that."

Ron had never once mentioned this cousin, so she couldn't imagine that James had ever done something to really hurt him. But who was she to withhold forgiveness when it was in her power to give it freely? Hadn't Jesus said that a man should forgive his brother seventy times seven? "Of course I forgive you," Meredith said.

James lowered his head. "Thank you."

"Have you talked to any other family members?" Meredith asked, wondering if he planned to talk to Gwyn or Barb.

"Not yet, but I don't know if I'll have time before I have to head back to California." He lifted his chin. "I have a job interview on Thursday. I don't want to miss that."

"I wish you well." Meredith rose, and Julia followed.

"Do you?" he asked.

"Of course."

James put his hands in his pockets. "I was wondering." He paused and looked away, squinting one eye. "If it wouldn't be too much trouble, I have a job interview, but I used everything I had to buy a ticket to get here, and it's been expensive to stay in Savannah. Would you, or, that is, could you, spare a little money?"

Julia glanced at Meredith, and Meredith knew what she'd say, even without saying it. Julia had probably seen situations like this a thousand times in her days as a criminal court judge. Once a family member started to enable another one, the cycle was hard to break.

"I'll send you to my church," Meredith said. "There's a benevolent fund available for temporary support. I know they'll be happy to help this one time." Meredith gave faithfully to Wesley Chapel. It had been her home church since she was a child and was within walking distance of her house. Their mission work within the community was one of the reasons Meredith loved being a member. Surely they'd help James.

Julia smiled, letting Meredith know she'd given the correct response.

"Thank you," James said.

Meredith gave him directions to the church and watched him walk away.

"I hope he's sincere," Meredith said. "I pray he's finally gotten his life together."

"I do too." Julia opened the door. "It's a long and painful road for some people."

They entered the office and found Carmen standing in the entry, her arms crossed.

"Were you watching out for us?" Julia asked with a smile in her voice.

"Sí. If he tried something funny, I was ready to defend you." Carmen lifted a fist in mock defense.

Meredith laughed and put her arm around the young lady in a side hug. "A secretary, chef, friend, *and* bodyguard. What did we do before we met you, Carmen Lopez?"

Carmen smiled and returned Meredith's hug. "You didn't know what you were missing, boss."

Each of the ladies went back to her respective office space, but the encounter with James left Meredith a little shaken. She still wasn't convinced they'd seen the last of him.

Chapter Fifteen

January 18, 1734
Colony of Georgia

I do not know how to begin this diary entry or how to get up the courage to write these words. Even now I sit here, with a single candle to guide my hand across this page, and I am uncertain what, if anything, I should share. Every noise I hear outside makes my heart leap within my chest, making me fear for my life. I wonder how to describe the sad and horrific events that have unfolded. I cannot reveal everything, for fear that someone will find this diary and know the full truth—yet I cannot keep it inside any longer. Perhaps I am more like my father than I first thought. He used his words to communicate with the world, and I am doing the same. The only difference is that his words have been read by thousands, and mine will probably never be read by anyone but me. If that be so, then it will be enough.

I have spent days crying, fearing for the future and mourning the past. My life has changed so suddenly that I am now in a state of complete uncertainty. What are my options? Do I have any? My mind and heart are so numb, I am afraid I will never feel again, and that is my greatest worry. Mayhap now is the time to write. To share the events without my own pain clouding the account.

I will attempt to tell the story exactly as it occurred, praying God will direct my words.

It began one week last, when I could no longer deny what my heart had feared. Joseph left the night of our fight and did not return. At first, I was thankful he was gone. His words had been so harsh and filled with hatred that I was afraid that when he returned we would argue again, and he would hurt me even more. To be honest, I did not want him to return. In the deepest, darkest part of my heart, I hoped he would stay away forever and leave me to my own devices. But now I fear that it was my own hatred that brought about his demise.

The longest he had been away was a week, but this time, a week turned to two, and then three, and finally four. My fear that he would return suddenly became my fear that he would not. I had already finished licking my wounds and had resolved to be the best wife I could be when he returned. I would continue to love him, no matter how much he despised me, and I would make the most of our marriage. When I became concerned that he had not come home, I went to Anna's husband and told him I was afraid that Joseph had died. He put together a search party and asked if I knew where Joseph might have gone. I always saw him leave the colony and head south, and I remembered that Joseph said he was searching for the treasure on an island, so that's where I told John to start looking. Within two days, they found Joseph's body on a barrier island, some forty miles to our south. From what the search party could ascertain, he had been crushed under the weight of a tunnel he was digging. It had collapsed on him, and that's where they found him.

I cannot begin to convey the guilt that weighs my heart like a millstone, tethered to the bottom of the sea. I feel as if I will be drowned in my own sorrow and shame. I wished ill upon my husband. Did God hear my hatred and chose to punish me because of it? I confessed my thoughts to the chaplain who resides in the fort, and he told me that God is not a vengeful God, and that I am not responsible for Joseph's death. I have begged God to forgive me, but I know it will be a long time before I will believe He has.

John tells me Joseph was living in a small shelter he had built, and that there were dozens of holes all over the north end of the island, dug over these many months by my husband. Along with his body, they returned to me almost all of his personal effects, though there were a few things missing, and I wonder if they were buried with him, or if the men have kept them for themselves. They did bring back my father's book, for which I am grateful.

The rumors surrounding Joseph's time on the island began swirling even before he was buried. It was obvious what he was doing there. Everyone assumes I knew Joseph's business, so they have tried, relentlessly, to get me to confess what I know. But I refuse to engage in these conversations, because I have no wish to perpetuate the lust for treasure in anyone else. They also suspect that Joseph was using the book to look for the treasure, though out of respect for me, no one read it before it was returned, or so they claim.

After the burial, I was approached by several men who asked me to hand over the book. They said if they found the treasure, they would share the spoils with me. But I have no wish for treasure and would rather see the end of all this. The quest for this treasure is the very thing that created pain and grief in my life. It is the reason Joseph married me, the reason he brought me here, and the reason he lost his life. No treasure on earth could make up for the great loss I have endured.

After I refused to hand over the book, they tried to take it by force, breaking into my house, harassing me on the street, and threatening to harm me if I do not acquiesce. But I have hidden it from prying eyes and put it somewhere no one will ever find it. General Oglethorpe has tried to put an end to the matter, demanding that everyone stop this nonsense, but they refuse to listen to him. He told them to put their energies into their homes and crops, but they would rather spend their days pestering a widow to give up the one thing that connects her to her family and the old world.

I have begun to fear for my life, so Ann and John have taken me into their home. I have come to respect and admire Anna's husband. He is a God-fearing man who has no wish to look for the treasure either. He is a good, honorable man, and I am so very grateful he came into Ann's life. He has promised to shelter and protect me as long as I need his assistance. I do not want to always depend on him, but I am thankful I have family to lean on in this difficult time.

The colonists have begun to call the barrier island where Joseph died Blackbeard's Island. It is all anyone wants to speak about. Colonizing Georgia has taken a desperate toll on their hearts and minds, and this sudden fever for treasure has gripped their weary souls with hope. Several men have already gone to Blackbeard's Island to continue the search, but no one has returned, as yet. I wonder if they will find anything, though it matters little to me. General Oglethorpe is angry that they have gone, neglecting their work here, but there is nothing he can do to stop them.

As for the book they seek from me, the book my father called The Devil, *I should have tossed it into the sea, or buried it with Joseph, or burned it in the fire, where it belongs, but I could not part from the one thing that I now own that belonged to my father. The information it contains is of no concern to me, but to know my father held it in his hands and crafted each letter on every page, that is the real treasure. For those reasons, it is priceless and irreplaceable. I wish Joseph would have realized the same.*

I long to close this chapter in my life, but I fear it will not be that easy. There will be many days and nights ahead of uncertainty and mourning, because though Joseph did not love me, I cared for him and spent fifteen years of my life as his wife. I do not know what the future holds for me, but I do know that I will be far wiser as I go forward.

And the book they seek? It will forever stay hidden, traveling from one generation to the next, tucked away, out of plain sight.

It didn't take long for word to spread of Troy LeBlanc's success on Blackbeard's Island. The very next day, Meredith received half a dozen phone calls and emails from reporters asking for a comment on the discovery. Several people cast doubt on his methods, suggesting that he had taken the diary, since his discovery had come on the heels of it being stolen. Meredith had chosen to refrain from commenting and didn't return their messages. She wasn't quite certain herself.

"There's another reporter on the phone," Carmen said to Meredith over the intercom system the next morning. "This one is from Charleston. Would you like me to patch him through?"

Meredith pressed the intercom button on her phone. "No, thank you."

"You got it, boss."

The sky was a bit overcast, but inside Magnolia Investigations, Meredith didn't have time to think about the weather. She'd spent her morning doing as much online research as she could about James Bellefontaine, Troy LeBlanc, and Anna Coles. There had to be something she was missing, somewhere.

In the front hall, the bell over the door jingled, indicating a new arrival.

Meredith hoped it wasn't a reporter.

"Hello, Miss Maggie Lu." Carmen's voice was faint. "What brings you into the agency today?"

"I'd like to speak to Meredith and Julia, if I may."

Carmen buzzed Meredith's phone, though it wasn't necessary. "Maggie Lu is here to see you. Should I send her in?"

"Of course," Meredith said into her intercom. "Please ask Julia to come to my office."

"Sí, señora."

Meredith rose and ran her hand over her slacks to press out the wrinkles. She stretched her neck to loosen a kink and then went to the door to greet her friend.

Maggie Lu stood in the foyer in a pretty floral dress and a blue hat. She looked like she was dressed for church, and Meredith wondered if she had been to a meeting or social function before coming to see her.

"Hello, Maggie Lu," Meredith said. "It's good to see you again."

"Same to you, honey." Maggie Lu walked into Meredith's office with a big smile on her face. "I'm glad you're here. I've got something important to tell you, and it can't wait."

Julia entered the room a moment later, a smile on her face even before she saw Maggie Lu.

"Hello, Julia," Maggie Lu said as she took a seat on the sofa.

"Hello. Can we get you something to drink? Some of Carmen's fresh coffee?"

"No, thank you. I've just had breakfast with the ladies' aid, and I'm filled to the top."

"Maggie Lu has something she'd like to tell us," Meredith said to Julia.

"I do, indeed." Maggie Lu's face became serious as Meredith and Julia took the seats across from her. "I would have come sooner, if I didn't have other plans this morning."

"Did you remember something else about Anna's diary?" Julia asked.

"I sure did." Maggie Lu nodded. "I don't know how I forgot, but I'm glad it came back to me now. I was puttering around my house yesterday, putting some things away, thinking back to my days with Miss Temperance. As I said before, I pushed all those memories away for many years, but now that I've brought them back, lots of things have returned to me."

"I hope there have been some good memories with the harder ones," Meredith said.

"Some." Maggie Lu crossed her arms. "But there's a reason I pushed the memories away and put them into hiding, just like that diary."

Meredith loved listening to Maggie Lu share stories from the past, and she was especially excited to hear what had brought her in today.

Chapter Sixteen

An eerie quiet seeped through *Miss Temperance's large home as Louvenia ran the duster over the mantel in the front parlor. The steady* ticktock *of the grandfather clock in the foyer gave her a painful awareness of the passage of time, though in some ways, it felt as if time had stopped here at the Bellefontaine plantation. When Louvenia was away from the house, her life went on as usual. She saw her friends, helped Granny Luv, and did her homework. But on the days she worked for Miss Temperance, it felt like there was no one else in the whole, wide world but her, Betty, Franklin, Robbie, and Miss Temperance.*

The fire that had torn them out of the house just a week ago had damaged the back of the house but wasn't as bad as they'd first thought. Robbie and Franklin had already repaired the siding and cleaned up the mess. The smell of smoke still permeated the home, and Louvenia wondered if it would ever leave.

"Louvenia?" Miss Temperance called from the top of the stairs. "Are you about done?"

"Yes, ma'am." Louvenia had been done twenty minutes ago, but couldn't bring herself to find Miss Temperance and tell her. Instead, she had started to dust all over again, returning to surfaces she'd

cleaned earlier that day. "I'll just put this duster away and join you shortly."

"Be quick about it," Miss Temperance said, appearing at the entrance to the parlor, Anna Coles's diary in her hand. "We're getting close to the end." She took a seat near one of the shaded windows.

Louvenia went into the kitchen and put away the duster. Betty sat at the kitchen table with a bowl of peapods from the garden. Louvenia would rather join the old cook and mindlessly shell the peas than return to the parlor.

"Planning to read to Miss Temperance?" Betty asked with a smile.

Louvenia nodded. She hadn't told any of the other help what she read to Miss Temperance. They thought she was reading a work of fiction to their employer. Louvenia had kept her promise and not told anyone. Not even Granny Luv.

"Did she ever tell you why she can't read herself?" Betty asked in a quiet voice.

Louvenia stopped on her way out of the kitchen. "She said her eyes were weak."

"She's got perfect eyesight," Betty said as she picked up another shell. "She can see a speck of dust on the top of a shelf, twenty feet away."

Louvenia frowned and walked over to Betty. "Didn't she get her schooling?"

It seemed preposterous to think a woman as wealthy and smart as Miss Temperance was unschooled.

"She got her schooling." Betty met Louvenia's glance. "I worked for Miss Temperance's mama and daddy and watched her grow up. I remember the hours of tutoring she had." She shook her head. "But

she could never learn to read. They brought in half a dozen teachers, but when she looks at the words, they get all messed up on the page. Her daddy used to tell her she was lazy and stupid, and no man would ever want to marry her, but no matter how hard she tried, she couldn't do it."

Compassion squeezed Louvenia's heart for Miss Temperance.

"It's a good thing you're doing," Betty said to Louvenia. "I know Miss Temperance appreciates having you read to her, especially now that she's not leaving the house."

Guilt plagued Louvenia as she walked back to the front parlor. Instead of grumbling about reading the diary to Miss Temperance, she should be thanking God she could read. Books were Louvenia's favorite things on earth. She couldn't imagine not being able to read and get lost in a good story.

From now on, no matter how much she disliked reading to Miss Temperance, she'd be patient and understanding.

"We don't have much time left," Miss Temperance said as she sat in her chair and watched Louvenia approach.

"Time?" Louvenia frowned.

"If we don't find the treasure soon, someone else will."

The diary hadn't mentioned treasure even once. Why did Miss Temperance still hold out hope? Besides, if there was treasure on Blackbeard's Island, it had been there for centuries. What was the hurry?

"The last entry we read the other day," Miss Temperance said, "they were about to celebrate Ann's fourteenth birthday."

Louvenia approached Miss Temperance and held out her hand for the diary. As always, Miss Temperance paused for a heartbeat before letting it go. Louvenia smiled at Miss Temperance and then took her seat.

As Louvenia began to read, she found Mrs. Coles sharing her hopes and dreams for her daughter on the eve of her birthday. She ended the entry with a short prayer for Ann. The next entry, on December 15, 1733, revealed a new development. Ann had been married to John Gready. As Louvenia read the entry, her heart started to pound, and out of the corner of her eye, she noticed Miss Temperance sit up straighter.

Anna detailed the fight she and Mr. Coles had and the revelation that Mr. Coles was using her father's diary to look for Blackbeard's treasure.

"Ah!" Miss Temperance said, coming out of her chair. "I knew it! Keep reading, Louvenia." She moved to the spot next to Louvenia on the sofa, as if to read the words for herself, though Louvenia knew she could not.

Louvenia continued to read, passing through page after page of Anna's pain. Her heart broke for Anna, knowing she was not loved by the man who had married her. But then, she shared that he died, and Louvenia held her breath. "'Within two days, they found Joseph's body on a barrier island, some forty miles to our south,'" she read. "'The rumors surrounding Joseph's time on the island began swirling even before he was buried. It was obvious what he was doing there. Everyone assumes I knew Joseph's business, so they have tried, relentlessly, to get me to confess what I know. But I refuse to engage in these conversations, because I have no wish to perpetuate the lust for treasure in anyone else. They also suspect that Joseph was using the book to look for the treasure, though out of respect for me, no one read it before it was returned, or so they claim.'"

"There's another book," Miss Temperance breathed. "Anna's diary doesn't point to the treasure, it's her father's book. The one Joseph had."

Louvenia paused, unsure what to say.

"Keep reading," Miss Temperance demanded. "Perhaps she'll tell us where the other diary is located."

Louvenia continued to read. "'And the book they seek? It will forever stay hidden, traveling from one generation to the next, tucked away, out of plain sight.'"

"Tucked away, out of plain sight?" Miss Temperance frowned. "What does that mean?"

Louvenia didn't answer. Not only because she didn't know, but because she didn't think Miss Temperance really wanted her to answer.

"It's a riddle," Miss Temperance said, nibbling on her bottom lip as she frowned. "It's hidden, but it's traveling from one generation to the next." She shook her head. "If she buried it, it couldn't travel." Suddenly her head shot up, and her eyes grew wide. She rose on shaking legs and held her hand out to Louvenia.

Louvenia jumped off the couch and took Miss Temperance's trembling hand.

"The traveling desk," she whispered. "It's in the desk."

Miss Temperance started toward the study, holding tight to Louvenia's hand for support. The woman was so thin and so exhausted from sleepless nights, she had very little strength left in her.

Louvenia flipped on the lights in the study. The writing desk sat exactly where they had left it, unnoticed these many weeks as they'd poured over the diary.

"Tucked away, out of plain sight," Miss Temperance said again as she went to the desk.

Standing back, Louvenia watched as Miss Temperance opened the writing surface and looked inside.

"It's empty," Miss Temperance said. "Just as I thought."

"What about the other side?" Louvenia asked. "Where you can keep pens and pencils."

Miss Temperance began to jiggle the pencil holder—and it suddenly gave way, coming out of the desk with a little tug.

Without a word, Miss Temperance pulled at the other pieces of wood. They came out, one by one, like a jigsaw puzzle, each piece fitting together in a specific way.

Miss Temperance paused as she stared at the desk.

Louvenia couldn't stop herself. She walked over to the desk and looked inside. A small notch was carved into the bottom piece of wood.

"Do you think it's a secret compartment?" Miss Temperance asked quietly.

"There's only one way to know," Louvenia replied on a shaky breath.

Miss Temperance placed her finger in the small notch and pulled. The piece of wood moved, but stuck with age. It took some prying, but she was finally able to pull the wood away, revealing a small book which fit perfectly inside the little compartment.

"It's her father's diary." Miss Temperance's voice was filled with awe.

Louvenia's heart pounded hard at the sight of the book that had caused Anna Coles and her husband so much pain and heartache. Did it really contain the information Joseph Coles had sought? If it did, why hadn't he found the treasure?

Miss Temperance stood perfectly still, staring at the book.

For several minutes, neither one moved or spoke. Louvenia was almost afraid to ask Miss Temperance why she didn't take it out.

"Do you know what that is?" Miss Temperance asked Louvenia.

"Yes, ma'am." She couldn't wait another moment. "Would you like me to read it to you?"

Miss Temperance still held the piece of wood that had hidden the book from their sight. It trembled in her hand. After another moment, she slowly lowered the wood back into the box and pushed it into place.

She didn't speak as she replaced the other pieces, one at a time, until they were all in place again.

Louvenia held Anna's diary in her hands, and Miss Temperance took that as well. She placed it into the writing desk and secured the writing surface over it, then she closed the desk, bringing both halves together.

When she finally looked at Louvenia, there was clarity in her eyes for the first time in weeks. "Please ask Franklin to pull the Buick out of the garage."

"Yes, ma'am." Louvenia wanted badly to ask her employer what she planned to do, but it wasn't her place. Why didn't she take the other book out and see what it had to say?

"Tell him I'd like to go to the bank and return the desk to the safe."

"Ma'am?" Louvenia frowned. After all this time, she was going to put it back where she'd found it? But why? Didn't she want to find the treasure?

"There's a reason this book has been kept hidden all these years," Miss Temperance said. "I almost fell prey to its lure, just as Joseph Coles did, but I have no wish to succumb to the same fate he did. I

believe Anna was right to hide it away and never speak of it again. And I believe my aunt was right when she said it only brought trouble to those who own it."

Louvenia's desires warred deep within her chest. If she were Miss Temperance, what would she do? Would she be strong like Anna, and put the diary away, never knowing where the treasure was? Or would she be weak like Joseph, allowing the temptation of wealth to consume her better judgment?

Louvenia didn't say another word as she walked to the study door, but her stooped shoulders must have spoken volumes to her employer.

"Remember what I told you, Louvenia." Miss Temperance's voice was low and serious. "Never speak of this again, for as long as you live. It will only bring death and destruction to those who fall under its curse."

The ominous words wrapped around Louvenia's heart as she left the study in search of Franklin.

How had a diary that had held no interest for her suddenly become something she couldn't stop thinking about? But, more importantly, how would she return to her normal life, never knowing what the second book said?

As Louvenia went to find Franklin, she had to force herself to bury her disappointment along with the book.

***

Meredith sat across from Maggie Lu, her eyes wide as the older woman finished her story.

"There's another diary?" Julia asked. "Hidden in the writing desk?"

"Yes, ma'am. At least there was last time I saw the desk." Maggie Lu watched Meredith closely. "I don't know how it will help you, but I thought I should tell you, in case the thief figures out the riddle and comes looking for the second book."

The writing desk hadn't been moved since Meredith had brought it home to her study. It was still sitting on her oak desk, inconspicuously hiding a second diary—one even more dangerous than the first. She'd already checked the other compartment and found it empty. Had she missed something? She scooted to the edge of her seat.

"So Blackbeard's Island got its name because of Joseph Coles," Julia said, almost to herself. "Obviously, other searches on the island proved fruitless."

"Until Troy LeBlanc's discovery," Meredith said.

"And that's how the rumors started about Anna's diary," Julia added. "It was actually her father's diary that people were trying to get at, but over the years, people probably forgot about the second diary and just assumed the one with the information was Anna's."

"That would definitely explain a lot," Meredith agreed.

Julia's phone sounded, and she pulled it out of her pocket. She frowned. "It's Beau," she said to Maggie Lu. "Will you excuse me?"

"Sure, honey. You go ahead."

As Julia left the room, talking low and quietly to Beau, Maggie Lu moved to the edge of the couch and pushed herself to her feet. She sighed and shook her head. "This business of getting old is for the birds." She laughed. "I need to go, Meredith. I hope I've been helpful. I wish I'd remembered that second diary before, but some things take time to rattle out of this old brain of mine."

"Thank you for your help, Maggie Lu. I appreciate all the information you've given us."

"I wish I could be more helpful. If I think of anything else, I'll be sure to call."

Meredith walked Maggie Lu to the front door, anxious to go home and see if the second diary was still tucked away inside the old desk. If it was, the possibilities were endless. Not only would the Daniel Defoe Library be thrilled, but it could shed light on so many other things, the greatest of which was Blackbeard's treasure. Were there other treasures written about in the book? What about other pirate secrets, long since considered lost?

Her heart beat quickly as she said goodbye to Maggie Lu and watched her walk down the steps and out of sight.

As Meredith closed the door, Julia left her office, lines around her mouth. "Beau asked if I could meet him at home. He said he has something to tell me that he didn't want to say on the phone." Julia's face was pale, and she looked like she was about to be sick. "What could he possibly have to tell me?"

Meredith shook her head, unsure what to say.

"I'm heading home," Julia said. "I-I'll call you later."

She didn't wait for Meredith to say goodbye and left through the back door.

Carmen came into the hall, a frown on her face. "Is Julia going to be okay?"

"I don't know." Meredith hoped Beau wasn't going to tell Julia something horrible. "I hope so." She said a quiet prayer for her friend and then turned to Carmen. "I'm going to run home. I have something I'd like to check."

She was tempted to tell Carmen about the second diary, but the fewer people who knew about Daniel Defoe's book, the better. She could trust Carmen, but it didn't pay to get her hopes up unless the book was still there. Any number of things could have happened to it. "I might need to run a few errands, so I don't know if I'll be back to the office today."

"Got it, boss."

Meredith went into her office and grabbed her purse and cell phone, and then she went out to her car. Nerves tingled up her spine as she pulled out of Magnolia Investigations to head home.

If the diary was still in the desk, she wouldn't make the same mistake twice. She'd immediately take it to the historical society where they could guard it far better than she ever could.

Chapter Seventeen

THE CLOUDS MOVED ON, MAKING the day warmer and more humid as Meredith pulled into the parking spot behind her house. Sweat dripped from her brow as she pushed open the door into her back entry, making the wonderful air-conditioning inside a sweet relief.

GK sat at the top of the stairs and greeted her with a *mrow* as she closed the door behind her. He swung his tail back and forth but didn't bother to get up at her arrival.

Meredith set her purse on a hook and went down the stairs into the study. Anna's writing desk was exactly where she'd left it, just waiting for another discovery. Meredith hoped and prayed the second diary was in the false bottom. It could shed light on so many things, both past and present.

Maggie Lu had said the false bottom was under the pencil holders, so Meredith started by tugging on the small pieces of wood that crisscrossed to form boxes. No wonder she hadn't considered dismantling this side of the writing desk before. It took a little work, but she was able to remove each piece. They came out in a specific pattern, each one fitting inside the other just so. They'd have to be put back the same way, or they wouldn't fit properly.

When she finally had all the pieces out, she looked down at the bottom and found the small notch in the wood. It was just big enough for her to put her index finger in. As she did, she couldn't help but think about Anna Coles doing the very same thing, almost three hundred years ago. Hopefully, if Maggie Lu's story was accurate, the book would still be where Aunt Temperance had left it in 1959.

With a gentle tug, Meredith dislodged the false bottom and held her breath.

There, sitting exactly where it was left, was the book.

The mantel clock ticked, and the cars on East Charlton Street drove by, but everything else felt as if it stood still, waiting.

Her heart pumped hard as she set the false bottom aside and then gently removed the book. It was old and fragile but in surprisingly good shape. The blue fabric cover was worn at the corners, and the edges of the paper were yellowed. But from a quick inspection, nothing was torn or damaged.

"Incredible," Meredith breathed as she held the book in her hand and lifted the cover to look inside.

"My sentiments exactly," a man said from the doorway of the study.

Meredith spun on her heels, the cover of the book slamming shut in her hands, and faced Troy LeBlanc.

He stood in an outfit similar to the ones she'd seen him in before. Khaki pants, a purple polo shirt, and casual brown shoes. He had on a light jacket, which was odd for this humid weather. There was nothing menacing or threatening about his stance—but the sheer fact that he was in her home without her permission made her heart pound harder than before.

"Wh-what are you doing here?" she asked.

"It took me a while, but I finally figured out Anna Coles's riddle." He started toward Meredith, and she backed up, her thighs pressing into the desk. "I read her diary three times through before it dawned on me."

"It was you?" Meredith asked. "You broke in and stole Anna's diary?"

"'Borrow' is the term I'd prefer. I fully intend to give it back, after I find the treasure."

"Where is it now?"

He smiled, as if this were all a game. "Don't worry about that right now."

Meredith's cell phone was in her purse, on the hook in her entry. The landline was on the desk and she eyed it, wondering if she'd have time to grab it and dial 911 before he stopped her.

"I'm not going to hurt you, Mrs. Bellefontaine," LeBlanc said, holding up his hands. "There's no need to do anything drastic."

"You've broken into my house—twice." She tried to control her breathing, to steady her beating heart. "I don't know what you plan to do."

"I didn't break in this time. You left the back door unlocked. I only came to borrow the second book. I was hoping you wouldn't be home, and I could take it without you even noticing."

Meredith clutched the second diary.

"I'll return it once I'm finished with it," he said. "No harm done."

"I thought you already found the treasure." Wasn't that what he'd said? He'd found the musket and was convinced the rest of the treasure was close at hand.

"A simple distraction. I used one of the muskets from my personal collection and planted it in the cave. Everyone will be so busy excavating the south end of the island, they won't pay any attention to what I'm doing on the north end, where I believe the real treasure is buried."

"You won't get away with it. Don't you think Anna's husband would have found it, if the book held the clues?"

"Modern technology will make it so much easier to find. Anna's diary said he'd been digging holes all over the north end of the island. I have high-tech infrared equipment to help me, and if I can pinpoint its approximate location. I'll only have to dig one hole."

Meredith wasn't about to give up the diary—but how far would LeBlanc go to get it?

"Hand it over nicely, if you please," LeBlanc said, taking another step toward Meredith. "I don't want to use force, but I will, if I must."

Meredith's throat went dry at the threat.

"We don't want anyone or anything to get hurt, now do we?" he asked.

Her hands trembled as she clutched the book, and her heart rate sped up even more when he pulled a small gun from his jacket pocket.

She immediately extended her hand, and he took the book, a gleam of excitement in his eyes.

"Go," she said. "But you won't get far."

"Unfortunately, you're right." He sighed and lowered the book as he studied her. "I can't leave you here alone to call the police. They'd find me within an hour—which isn't nearly enough time to locate the treasure."

Meredith stared at him. What did he plan to do with her?

"I really wouldn't want to tie you up and leave you here either," he said as he wrinkled his nose and shook his head. "That seems so uncomfortable and unnecessary. I could use your help, so if you'd like, you could come with me of your own free will."

She had no wish to go anywhere with LeBlanc. He wasn't stable, she could see that. What would he do with her, alone, on a secluded island? With little thought, Meredith made a mad dash for the door—but he was younger and stronger than she was, and he had her in his rough grasp before she even left the study.

"Don't do that," he said with a sigh. "I don't want to hurt you. If you'd just cooperate, you could make this so much easier for both of us." He leaned close, as if telling her a secret. "I'd even consider sharing the fame with you."

"I have no wish for fame," she said, her voice shaking.

He started pushing her toward the stairway to the back entry, nudging her in the back with his gun as they walked. "Then there's only one thing to do with you. I'll have to take you with me to the island."

Desperation clawed at Meredith's heart. She had to think of some way to reason with him. "Kidnapping is a crime."

"Only if I get caught. Once I have the treasure, and you see how valuable it is, you'll thank me." He stopped pushing her and produced a pair of handcuffs from his pocket. He told her to put her hands behind her back, and then he snapped the handcuffs on her wrists. "Just think what a contribution Blackbeard's treasure will make to history. Can you even imagine? You of all people should appreciate that."

Tears stung the back of her eyes. Would he hurt her?

"Don't fret, Mrs. Bellefontaine. Once I have the treasure, I'll let you go, and we'll become friends, just wait and see."

The man was delusional.

"Don't try to scream as we walk to the car." His voice grew dark and dangerous for the first time since he'd arrived. "Don't make me do something I'll regret."

Panic welled up in her chest as he prodded her up the stairs toward the back entry. Her purse hung on the hook, so close, yet impossible for her to reach with her hands behind her back.

GK sat on the top step, watching as LeBlanc opened the back door.

"Remember what I said," he told her. "Don't make a scene, and I won't hurt you. I'll let you go as soon as I have the treasure."

Uncertainty warred within Meredith's heart as she walked outside and entered the courtyard. If she called out for help, would anyone even hear her? Was it worth the risk?

"My car is parked near yours," he said to her. "The doors are unlocked. I'm going to help you into the passenger side, and you'll sit nice and quiet for me, do you understand?"

"You don't need to do this," she said. "I won't tell anyone you have the diary. If you leave me here, I won't say a thing, and you can take all the time in the world to look for the treasure. If you take me, and someone realizes I'm missing, they'll come looking for us."

He paused, as if considering her offer.

Meredith's heart soared with hope—but then he pushed her to the courtyard door. "I can't take the risk. I don't know if I can trust you to stay quiet."

"They'll come looking for me."

"If I'm lucky, I'll find the treasure before they get there. I've narrowed it down to a couple of possible locations, and this new diary should solidify my suspicions."

"That won't stop you from being arrested."

"Not if I've found the treasure." He grinned, as if he truly believed the treasure would make his crimes null and void. "Keep quiet." He opened the courtyard door and looked left and right, then he pushed her through and walked close behind her to the passenger door of his black Cadillac.

Meredith looked desperately around for someone who might see her, but there wasn't anyone within sight. The square was empty, the sidewalk was empty, and no one was walking down the street behind her house. Where was everyone? Hopefully someone was watching from a window, but the chances of that were also slim. So many people were at work in the middle of the day.

"In you go, Mrs. Bellefontaine," LeBlanc said. "No more stalling."

Meredith got into the car, though it wasn't easy to sit with her hands behind her back. LeBlanc reached over her and secured the seat belt, which stunned Meredith.

"Safety first," he commented, almost to himself.

If he was worried about her safety, surely he wouldn't hurt her. At least, that's what she hoped.

He walked around the front of his car, the second diary in hand, and tapped the hood of the car as if buoyed by excitement before getting into the driver's side to take her to Blackbeard's Island.

***

Blackbeard's Island was only forty miles south of Savannah by coast, but by car, it took them over an hour to reach Harris Neck Wildlife Refuge, where LeBlanc parked his car in an empty lot.

"I've been going out to the island every day," he said to Meredith. "So I rented a slip and a boat for the week and kept it here."

Meredith had never been to this wildlife preserve or Blackbeard's Island preserve, though she was familiar with the Savannah Coastal Refuges Complex, which maintained the seven wildlife preserves that stretched over the course of a hundred miles of coastal lands, including over fifty-six thousand acres.

LeBlanc left the car and came around to help Meredith out of the passenger side. Her hands had long since fallen asleep, and she was sore from sitting in such an awkward position for over an hour. She tried not to grimace as she swung her legs out of the car and stood.

"If you had just agreed to come with me, I wouldn't have handcuffed you." His voice was accusing, as if it were her fault. "If you promise not to try to run now, I'll take them off."

She was very aware of how alone they were in the nature preserve. There wasn't a house or business for miles. There was no ranger station close by either. Where would she go? Whether she liked it or not, she was at LeBlanc's mercy. The most she could hope for was a bystander to come by, using the boat landing. "I won't run."

"Good." He unlocked the handcuffs and threw them into the car.

Meredith rubbed her wrists and rolled her shoulders to remove the ache.

Sunshine beat down on them, the heat almost unbearable. The slacks and blouse that she had chosen to wear that day weren't conducive to outdoor activities, nor were her low-heeled pumps.

The ride from Savannah to the preserve had been filled with LeBlanc's constant babbling about Anna Coles and Edward Teach. If

Meredith hadn't been bound and kidnapped, the conversation would have been interesting. As it was, she hadn't contributed to the conversation once, but it didn't seem to hinder his enthusiasm.

As Meredith watched, LeBlanc opened the trunk and pulled out a large duffel bag and several bottles of water. "It's hot today," he said as he threw the bottles into his bag. "We'll need to stay hydrated."

He didn't put down Daniel Defoe's diary, but held it like it was a small child.

She followed him to the boat, and he set his duffel bag inside, then he offered her his hand to help her in. She didn't want to take his help, wanted to run in the opposite direction, but she had little choice—and she didn't want to end up in the Barbour Island River.

Meredith sat in the bow of the boat while LeBlanc stepped into the back and took a seat on the long bench. The boat tilted and swayed as he worked on getting the motor started, but after he'd pulled the starter cord half a dozen times, the motor sputtered and turned over.

Did anyone back in Savannah know she was missing yet? Julia had gone home to talk to Beau, and Carmen wouldn't know she wasn't home until she got to Meredith's after work, which was still several hours away. When would someone come looking for her? Would LeBlanc let her go if he didn't find the treasure today?

How long was she at his mercy?

He maneuvered the boat through the river, east toward the coast. The preserve was made up of several barrier islands, crisscrossed with dozens of rivers and streams.

"The only way to access Blackbeard's Island is by boat," LeBlanc said, speaking loudly over the sound of the motor and the wind.

"You can unload people at Blackbeard's Creek, but there isn't a place to dock the boat. We'll have to lay anchor on the beach, instead."

"What about high tide?"

"Not until this evening. We have hours."

What if they didn't get out of there before the tide came in? Would they be stuck on the island for the night?

It took about thirty minutes for them to navigate the river before coming into Sapelo Sound.

"There's Blackbeard's Island," LeBlanc said, pointing to the land ahead. "We'll go around the island to the coastal side."

Meredith loved the ocean, but there was nothing enjoyable about the boat ride. Uncertainty and fear wrapped around her heart as she clutched the edges of the boat. She hoped and prayed they'd come across someone who might help, but there was no one to be seen.

"Anyone who planned to come to the island today is probably on the south end," LeBlanc said with a satisfied smile. "The lure of treasure is too irresistible to ignore. That leaves this side of the island all to us."

Waves pushed against the boat, and the sun reflected off the water, blinding Meredith and giving her a headache. Her skin would start to burn if she didn't take shelter or put on sunscreen. And she hadn't eaten since breakfast—though she didn't know if she could eat, given the chance.

Twenty minutes later, they approached the ocean side of the island. Hundreds of dead trees lined the sandy beach, their gray, gnarly branches reaching toward the sky and sea, as if asking for help. The sight was spectacular, if not eerie.

"It's one of the most remarkable boneyard beaches on the East Coast," LeBlanc said to Meredith as he pointed the boat toward the beach. "Some people think Blackbeard still haunts the island, roaming in and out of the boneyard, protecting his treasure."

Despite the heat, a chill ran up Meredith's spine. She didn't believe in such things, but she couldn't deny that the beach looked like the perfect place for such stories to develop.

LeBlanc ran the boat aground and cut the engine.

"You'll have to take off your shoes," he said, "or you'll get them wet."

Meredith did as he said and took off her heels. She rolled up her pant legs and climbed into the ocean water. The waves lapped against her legs, pushing the boat closer and closer to shore. The water was cool and refreshing. Meredith lifted several handfuls to wet her cheeks and neck as she walked onto the beach, thankful for this one bit of respite.

LeBlanc also exited the boat, the diary in his right hand, and used his left hand to pull the boat all the way on shore. He tied it to a dead tree and took out his duffel bag.

Dozens of seagulls soared and dipped overhead and dotted the beach, but there were no people anywhere here either. After three hundred years, the island was just as remote as it had been when Blackbeard visited. The dozens of creeks and inlets would be a perfect place for a pirate crew to hide.

But had they hidden a treasure there as well?

"This book was referred to as *The Devil*," LeBlanc said as he looked down at it in awe. "Blackbeard once said that only he and the—"

"Yes, I know." Meredith didn't wish to hear it again. "Did it occur to you that he might not have been talking about the book?"

"There's too much evidence to support the claim." LeBlanc started walking across the beach, toward the jungle-like woods beyond. He turned and frowned at Meredith. "Don't make me drag you with me." He patted his jacket pocket and raised his eyebrows at her. "I'll use this if I have to."

Unfortunately, she believed him. "I need to put my shoes back on."

He frowned as he seemed to notice her heels for the first time. "Be quick about it."

Meredith sat on the trunk of a downed tree and wiped the sand off the bottom of her feet. It stuck in every little crease and crevice. She put on her shoes, taking as much time as possible, hoping and praying someone would come upon them. But there was no one.

"Hurry up," he said, his voice short and irritated. "We have a lot to do."

She finished and stood to join him.

He pushed through the vines and underbrush, going deeper and deeper into the trees.

With one final look back at the beach, Meredith followed.

Chapter Eighteen

HOURS PASSED AS THE SUN made its slow descent toward the horizon. Meredith sat on a rotting tree trunk as she watched LeBlanc traverse a fifty-foot square with a handheld infrared gun. He'd spent some time skimming Daniel Defoe's book before he'd narrowed his search to the area where he'd spent the past three hours hunting. Several times, he'd stopped and started to dig, but had come up with nothing but rocks. The ground was wet and sloppy, filling her nostrils with the stench of mildew.

From time to time, Meredith rose to stretch her legs and back, but she didn't join LeBlanc's search. He'd tried to get her input, but she evaded his questions.

She wasn't sure what time it was, or if anyone had become aware of her disappearance. She hoped and prayed Carmen or Julia had started looking for her, but there was no way of knowing. If they started looking, would they know to come to the island? Even then, with over five thousand acres to search, how long would it take them to find her?

With dusk came the mosquitos. They bit Meredith's burnt skin and buzzed around her head. She swatted them away, irritated, frustrated, and scared to think about being on the island overnight. Alligators frequented the barrier islands, and with a marsh only thirty yards away, she was certain they were nearby.

"I don't understand," LeBlanc said as he kicked at a soggy clump of dirt. "The treasure should be right here."

Meredith didn't respond as he set the infrared gun down and picked up the shovel once again. Sweat stains marred his shirt, and mud stuck to his wet skin. He growled as he struck the earth with the shovel. The wet earth must be extremely heavy. "Defoe's book points right to this area."

The island had several hiking and biking trails, but there were many places marked as off-limits to help protect wildlife and flora and fauna and for the safety of visitors. LeBlanc and Meredith were in one of the off-limits zones, and she could only guess why. The chances of someone stumbling across them were scarce.

"The tide will start to rise soon," Meredith said to LeBlanc, wanting desperately to be home. "Shouldn't we head back?"

"I'm not leaving this island until I find the treasure." He grunted as he dug, tossing sloppy mud to the side.

Dozens of subtle indentations surrounded them, and Meredith wondered if they were the places others had dug for the treasure before. Had Joseph Coles died in this very spot?

LeBlanc wiped his brow and glanced at the ever-darkening sky.

Meredith held her breath, waiting to see if he'd realize the folly of his actions and take her home. Instead, he turned back to the hole and continued to dig.

Several times that afternoon, she'd thought of running off while his back was to her, but she'd never been on the island before and didn't know where to go. If she returned to the boat, she doubted she'd be able to get it started before he caught up to her. If she tried to find one of the trails and head south, hoping someone was on the other end of the island, she'd have to either run in her heels or her bare feet, and she suspected LeBlanc was faster than she. No doubt he'd overtake her. If he did, there was no telling what he might do.

"Why don't we head home and try again tomorrow?" Meredith asked. "I'm starving and have no wish to remain on the island over—"

"No!" LeBlanc jammed the shovel back into the ground. "We're not going anywhere until I have the treasure." He looked at her, distrust in his eyes. "You'd go to the authorities and tell them I kidnapped you, and then I'd have to deal with that mess when I have better things to do."

"If someone comes looking for me and finds me, you'll be charged with kidnapping and won't have a choice."

"They'll be too overcome with the treasure to care." He leaned on the handle of the shovel. "Most people believe Blackbeard's treasure is worth ten to fifteen million dollars, but the historical value of it would be worth far more. I'll become a hero."

"What if you don't find the treasure?"

He clenched his jaw as he stared at her. "That's not an option."

"What makes you think you can find it when everyone else has failed?"

"Because I have the book. They didn't." He started to dig again. "Make yourself comfortable. We're here until I find it." His shovel hit something solid, and he stopped. "It feels like wood." He hit it again. "Hollow wood."

Meredith's heart started to pound harder, and she stood to get a closer look.

LeBlanc dug furiously around the object, sweating profusely and breathing heavily as he worked.

"It's a box," he said, excitement in his voice. "And it's in really good shape."

He dug for a few more minutes and then threw the shovel out of the hole and reached down to remove the box.

It was about one foot by two feet, with a latch on one side and hinges on the other.

"That looks exactly like Anna Coles's writing desk," Meredith said with a curious frown.

LeBlanc stared at her, disappointment and disbelief in his gaze. "You think it's just a writing desk?"

"It doesn't look like a treasure chest to me."

He set the box on the ground and grabbed a rag from his duffel bag. He used it to wipe the mud off, and then he inspected the box for a moment. The clasp and hinges were rusted with age and moisture, but the wood was in remarkably good shape—especially if it was as old as Anna's desk.

LeBlanc unlatched the clasp and tried to open the box. The hinges didn't work properly, and he was forced to pry it open.

Meredith cringed when one of the hinges snapped.

The inside of the box was identical to Anna's writing desk, and on the top right-hand side were carved the letters *JWC*. Were those Joseph's initials? Had Mr. Defoe given a desk to Joseph upon his wedding to Anna as well?

"This must be Joseph's writing desk," Meredith said. "Perhaps it was buried when the earth caved in on him and killed him."

"It's not the treasure." Troy sat back on his haunches, shaking his head. "I can't believe I haven't found it yet." He lifted the writing surface, but all that remained inside was the remnants of rotten paper. He pulled the small pieces of wood out of the pencil holders, just as Meredith had done with Anna's desk. "Maybe something's hidden in the compartment underneath."

Meredith doubted it was the treasure he was seeking, but she recognized desperation in his voice and didn't want to make him more upset.

"Nothing." LeBlanc pushed the desk aside. "Nothing, nothing, nothing."

The desk wasn't "nothing" to Meredith. It showed her that LeBlanc had identified the same location as Joseph, and that if the treasure was going to be anywhere on the island, there was a good chance it would be here.

But it wasn't.

LeBlanc straightened and went back for his infrared gun.

"What are you doing?" Meredith asked.

"I'm going to keep looking."

The last of the sunlight rimmed the edges of the sky. They didn't have time for LeBlanc to keep looking.

"How do you expect to work through the night?" she asked. "It'll be impossible."

"I brought flares."

Desperation started to rush through Meredith's limbs as panic set in. "Then I'll return to the boat and—"

"No." He stopped fiddling with his infrared gun and frowned. "You can't go anywhere."

Meredith was tired of playing his game. Would he really hurt her if she tried to leave?

"I'm leaving now, before the tide rises," Meredith said as she started to walk back the way they'd come. "I'll return for you tomorr—"

LeBlanc rushed toward her, and she started to run, a scream escaping her throat of its own free will.

But he was too quick, and he grabbed her around the waist. She kicked and screamed, trying to break free, but he put his muddy hand over her mouth.

"I don't have time for this," he said against her ear, his voice tight. "I'll have to tie you up."

She shook her head, clawing at his hands. If she was tied up, and an animal came upon her, how would she escape?

He hauled her to his duffel bag and grabbed a rope. She tried to fight him, but she was no match for him, and she was growing wearier with the effort. She was tired, hungry, and sunburned. Her joints aches, and her head pounded.

"Please." She tried to plead now that his hand was occupied with tying her wrists together and no longer over her mouth. "I won't try to run away again."

"I can't trust you."

"I haven't tried to run all day."

"You just did."

"I won't do it again." Tears stung the backs of her eyes, but she wouldn't cry. "I promise."

He hauled her to a large cypress tree, bent with age and wind, and tied her to the trunk. The rope bit into her wrists, and she was forced to stand with her back to the tree as he wrapped the long rope around her waist.

"This isn't necessary," she said.

"Keep quiet." He finished tying the rope and then went back to his infrared gun, which he picked up and turned on.

Meredith had been praying all day, but her prayers increased now. The last of the daylight disappeared, and the woods around them were now cast in shadows. What had been familiar all day took on a new, menacing form. A bird cried out and the wind picked up, but LeBlanc didn't seem to care.

As Meredith stood and prayed, she became aware of noises to her left, from where she and LeBlanc had come earlier. At first she thought she heard voices, and then the rustling of undergrowth.

LeBlanc worked on another hole, the shovel slopping into the mud, his back to her, and he didn't appear to notice the sounds.

Then a flash of light in the woods. It was there one second and then gone the next.

Meredith held her breath. She didn't dare cry out—not yet—and alert LeBlanc that someone was in the woods with them.

She just hoped whoever it was would continue coming toward them.

Another flash of light, and this time, Meredith realized it was a flashlight.

Her heart pounded, and she swallowed the rush of relief, hoping and praying it was a search party.

More voices, more rustling, and then there were three flashlights—and then four.

LeBlanc finally glanced up, his attention no longer on the hole he dug, but on the new arrivals.

An officer in a US Coast Guard uniform emerged from the woods into the small clearing, followed by another. Just behind them, Chase and Carter rushed onto the scene.

"Mom!" Chase and Carter both yelled.

Julia was just behind them, her face pale and her eyes wide.

Soon, there were other officers on the scene.

LeBlanc stood motionless as the officers descended on him. He didn't try to run or hide, but he did shake his head. "I'm only looking for the treasure," he said. "I know it's around here somewhere."

"Troy LeBlanc," one of the officers said, "you're under arrest for the kidnapping of Mrs. Meredith Bellefontaine." He began to read LeBlanc his rights as another officer put him in handcuffs.

"You don't understand." LeBlanc ignored the officer speaking to him. "I didn't kidnap her. She came with me to help find the treasure." He looked at her, his eyes wide. "Tell them, Mrs. Bellefontaine."

Chase worked to untie Meredith's hands as Carter removed the rope from around her waist. It was clear to everyone that Meredith was not there of her own free will, and she had no wish to even speak to her kidnapper.

"Are you okay?" Julia asked Meredith. "Did he hurt you?"

Meredith rubbed her raw wrists and shook her head. "I'll be fine."

Carter pulled Meredith into a tight hug. "I'm so happy you're okay. When Julia called me and said they were setting out to search for you, I didn't even stop to tell anyone I was leaving. I'm surprised I didn't get into an accident—I hardly remember driving here."

"I'm glad you came." The tears Meredith had been fighting finally came now.

Chase was the next to hug Meredith, and then Julia.

"When did you realize I was missing?" Meredith asked them as she wiped away her tears. She must have looked a mess, but she didn't care. She was so relieved to have them with her.

"A few hours after you left the office," Julia said. "Carmen tried calling you to see what you'd like for supper, and you didn't answer. After trying for an hour, she went to your house. Your car was there, the back door was unlocked, and your purse was hanging on the hook, but you weren't there. She called me, and I told her why you went home. She checked the study and saw the open writing desk with the contents pulled out—but you weren't there. That's when we knew something wasn't right.

"So, I called the police and Chase and Carter," Julia continued. "When the police arrived at your house, Harlowe came over and asked what had happened. He said he was walking a block away and saw you get into the car with a man, but didn't get a good look at him with his poor eyesight. He said it didn't look like you were struggling, but again, his eyesight isn't what it once was."

"We guessed that whoever took you probably brought you to the island," Carter said. "And when we got to the boat landing and saw the black Cadillac, the Coast Guard ran the license plates and learned that the car was registered to Troy LeBlanc."

"Then we knew for sure," Chase said to Meredith.

"Why didn't you go to the south side of the island to look?" Meredith asked. "Since that's where he said he found the musket."

"I remembered what you told me about the north side of the island," Julia told her. "So that's why we started here—though, there are other law enforcement looking there as well."

"I'm so happy you found me." Meredith hugged each one again.

"Ma'am." One of the officers approached. "We need to head back. The tide is rising, and we don't want to get stuck here."

Meredith nodded and then remembered Daniel Defoe's diary and the second desk. "There's an old writing desk over there," she said to the officer, pointing at the small box. "It's been waterlogged and preserved all these years and must be properly handled, or it will start to break down quickly. Could we take it to the historical society for proper preservation?"

"Yes, ma'am."

"Thank you. And there's a book in Mr. LeBlanc's possession that belongs to me. It's three hundred years old, and I'd like to make sure it's properly handled."

One of the officers went to LeBlanc's duffel bag and opened it. "There are two books in here."

Was Anna's diary in the bag as well?

The officer brought both books to Meredith, and more tears threatened to fall. "It's the other diary," she said. "The one LeBlanc stole from my house a couple of weeks ago. It's almost as old as the other one."

"I didn't steal it," LeBlanc said. "I was borrowing it until I found the treasure."

"Unfortunately," the officer said, "I'll need to keep these items as evidence until the case is closed."

"I understand." Meredith nodded. She would speak to her attorney and see if she could get them returned to her as soon as possible.

Given their age and condition, they could petition the judge to release them into her care for preservation's sake.

Several officers stayed at the site to document and gather evidence, while the others escorted LeBlanc, Meredith, her relieved sons, and Julia back to the beach where a Coast Guard boat was waiting for them. The tide had already started to rise, but the large boat could handle the fluctuating water levels.

LeBlanc was taken to a holding room in the hull while Meredith and the others were given a place to sit on the deck to be questioned by an officer.

There would be several rounds of questioning, complaints to file, and a trial to endure, but Meredith was thankful she was safe, and she finally had the diaries back in her possession.

As soon as she was able, she'd put them on permanent loan at the historical society, where they'd be safe and secure. Though they were invaluable, and she was so thankful to have them again, they were nothing but trouble for anyone who owned them.

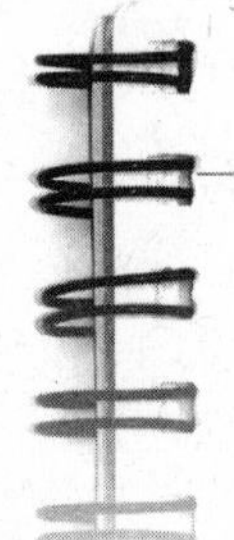

January 31, 1788
Savannah, Georgia

It has been many years since I have last written in this diary—over fifty, if I am not mistaken. I had thought to never lay eyes on it again, but my darling daughter, who is herself a great-grandmother many times over, found the old writing desk tucked away in my attic this very day. She brought it to me and asked if I would like to keep it by my chair, since I do not stray far from it often, and I so love to write. I pulled this book out and relived the early years, marveling at how much has changed—at how much I have changed.

The two-story clapboard house I sit in now is not far from the one Joseph Coles built for me all those years ago on Johnson Square, when I was young and so lonesome for England. It seems like a dream now, and all the people I had longed to return to are dead and gone. I am the oldest of the original colonists to Savannah. Whenever there is a parade or celebration, they make a big fuss over me, though I try not to encourage them. If I had known when I arrived what I know now, I wonder if I would have been so eager to return to my homeland. If I had, I would have missed some of the greatest blessings in my life. How many years were wasted on unhappiness and regret? I am too old to worry about such things now. Instead, I take comfort in the blessings God has bestowed upon me and thank Him for the dawning of each new day.

Less than a year after Joseph died, my Ann gave birth to the first of her eight children. She and John invited me to live with them to help care for the children, which I did joyfully for fifteen years until Joseph's cousin, Mr. Robert Coles, arrived in Savannah from England in the year 1750.

He was a printer and had been eager to come to the new land to start his own printing and book shop, which he did, quite successfully. He also printed the first newspaper in Savannah, gathering news from the bustling ports nearby. Though we had never met before his arrival, we were his only family. He had been widowed several years before he came, and we had much in common, with our affinity for books and writing. Though I was a widow and over fifty years old, Robert made me feel like a young woman again. We discussed books, news, and history, and I found in him a kindred spirit. He asked me to write articles for his paper, and I did so with an eagerness driven by a sense of purpose. I quickly came to know and love him with all my heart, and he returned my love, lavishing it upon me in ways I had never known.

He built the beautiful home I am sitting in now, and then he asked me to marry him. Ann's oldest children were almost grown by then, and I was ready for my own home once again. Robert and I were married in a small ceremony, and then Ann and John gave a wedding luncheon in our honor. After that, Mr. Coles and I retired to our home on Johnson Square, and here we have been living very happily ever since. It has been thirty-eight years since I married Robert, and there has not been one day of regret for either of us.

With Robert by my side, we have celebrated and mourned over four generations of our family. Six of Ann's children lived to adulthood, and they all have children and grandchildren of their own. They have thrived here in Georgia, building businesses, homes, and families. We have also watched this city grow and multiply, until I can hardly recognize it anymore. We watched a nation be born and witnessed the horrors of war. I lost five grandsons to the fight for independence, and not a day goes by that I do not think of them and all they gave for our freedom from England's rule. They would be honored to know that just this very month, Georgia became the fourth state of the United States of America. Though they did not live to see that day come, those of us who have know we owe everything to them and their sacrifice.

Robert calls to me now from the front parlor, where he is writing a letter to the editor of the Savannah Gazette, *and has asked me to come and read it to see if it is ready to submit. He has long since sold the newspaper and printing shop, but they indulge my dear husband with an occasional commentary on the affairs of the day.*

But I do not want to leave this diary without sharing one last thing. I have lived long enough to know that change is inevitable, that very little stays as it is, and that progress is a double-edged sword. But I also know that the things that really matter never change, like love, faithfulness, and courage. I do not know who will read this diary one day or how long these frail pages will last, but I do know that the legacy of family and faith will continue for eternity.

This book is full of the troubles of a young woman who lost a husband because of greed and who suffered for years because she was not loved. The story could have been so much different if the lure of treasure had not captured Joseph's heart. But I am thankful that God, in His infinite and mighty power, knew the end from the beginning and saw me through each difficult hour. What the enemy intended for evil, God has used for good.

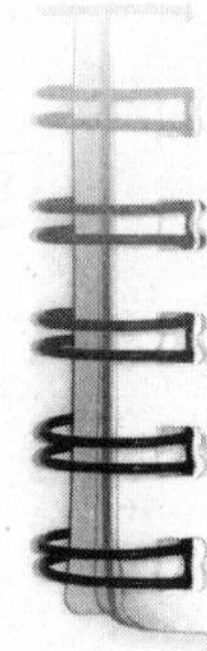

I want to caution whoever reads this diary to remember that our earthly treasures are fleeting, but our heavenly treasure exists where moth and rust do not destroy. As I draw closer and closer to my eternal home, knowing all that is in store for me there, I have no doubt that the real treasure is yet to be found.

Chapter Nineteen

SUNSHINE WARMED MEREDITH'S CAR THE next day as Chase drove them west on East Charlton Street and took a left onto Whitaker. Anna's writing desk was safely secured in the back seat, and both diaries, which Meredith had retrieved from the police station that very morning, were in acid-free envelopes on her lap. Though the case was not yet closed, everyone had agreed that the diaries should be properly stored and handled, and that would not happen at the station.

Meredith had not had time to read the books thoroughly, but she had read the end of Anna's diary and was pleased to know that Ron's ancestor had lived a long and happy life on Bull Street, near Johnson Square.

"Is the historical society expecting us?" Chase asked as he stopped for a red light.

"Yes, Beatrice will be there with the Director of Acquisitions and Preservation to accept the donations on permanent loan. They're eager to finally have them in their hands."

"It's amazing that after all these years in hiding, the diaries will finally be on public display." Chase shook his head. "I wonder what Anna Coles would think of that."

Meredith had wondered the same. Though Anna had written in great detail about her personal life, there were hints that she was a private person at heart. Would she want to know that strangers were combing through her heartache to find clues from the past? Or would she be proud to know that her writing would be read by thousands, just as her father's had been?

Chase found a place to park not too far from the historical society on the corner of Whitaker and West Gaston Streets. And while he removed the desk from the back, Meredith held the diaries like newborn babies in her arms. They'd been through a great deal the past couple of weeks, and Anna's diary had suffered some damage.

"I talked to Carter this morning right before he left to go back home," Chase said as they walked down the street toward the historical society. "I reassured him, again, that your home security system is being installed soon and that I won't leave again until it's fully operational."

"Thank you, Chase. I appreciate you and Carter more than you'll ever know."

"I do have to warn you that he's going to try to convince you to give up your investigations agency once and for all."

Meredith sighed. "I know."

"But I'll defend your decision one hundred percent."

She smiled at him, thankful that at least one of her sons was on her side.

"Have you heard from any reporters?" he asked.

"Several, though I've refrained from commenting until after the trial is over." Meredith had been the center of attention far too much since she'd inherited the diary—and now even more so once word had spread that she'd been kidnapped by the thief. "Of course, they're now aware that LeBlanc's first discovery was a hoax, and they're itching to find out what, if anything, was found on the north side of the island."

Beatrice stood at the side entrance to the building and opened the door the moment she saw Meredith and Chase approach. She wore a bright blue sundress with matching blue heels, and she grinned when she met Meredith's eye.

"Hello, darling! Come in, come in." Beatrice held the door open for them, her eyes aglow. "I can hardly wait to see those diaries."

Sean O'Neil, the director of preservation, was also there to greet them, though his dark suit and sour disposition were a stark contrast to Beatrice.

It took a few minutes while Meredith filled out some paperwork, but then Sean took the items and brought them to his workstation in a back room. With white gloves and extreme patience, he examined the items, asking several questions and writing notes.

"Have you heard?" Beatrice asked Meredith. "There's talk of sending a team of archaeologists to the north side of the island where LeBlanc was digging. Since the second desk was found there, some think there might be other artifacts of interest—or even the treasure itself."

Would the rumor of treasure never cease?

"I hadn't heard," Meredith said.

"Perhaps you can consult on the matter," Beatrice offered. "Wouldn't that be exciting to go back to the scene of the crime?"

Meredith shook her head. She had no wish to ever return to Blackbeard's Island.

"We will transcribe the diaries as we conserve them," Sean said to Meredith. "I will personally send you copies of the manuscripts when they are finished, and you're more than welcome to come and see the artifacts at any time."

"Thank you." Meredith was glad there would be an easy-to-read transcript available.

"And we've been in contact with the Daniel Defoe Library in England," Sean continued. "They will be sending the president of the library to Savannah later this year to look over the diaries."

"Thank you, again." One of the stipulations Meredith had given the historical society when she agreed to place the items on permanent loan was that they give the Daniel Defoe Library complete access to the books. "I know Mr. Foxgrove will be delighted to work with you."

"We're hoping to have most of Anna's diary transcribed by next week," Beatrice said with giddy excitement. "And highlight some of the information we gather at the midsummer gala."

"Will the diary be at the gala?" Chase asked.

Sean shook his head, and Beatrice pouted her bottom lip.

"Unfortunately, it's too great a risk," Sean said. "We wouldn't want anything to happen to it, now that we have it in our collection. I'll be sure to take several pictures, which Beatrice will exhibit at the event, but I cannot approve of putting it on display."

Beatrice continued to pout, but she didn't try to debate with the serious Sean O'Neil.

"It will be wonderful, regardless," Meredith tried to reassure her. "I'm just happy we finally have it back in our possession."

It was time to leave, though Meredith hated to part with the diaries again so soon after finding them.

"We need to go," Chase said. "Carmen and Julia are waiting for us at the diner."

"Lunch?" Beatrice asked. "I'm starving. Do you mind if I join y'all?"

Meredith shook her head. "Not at all."

They left the historical society, and Beatrice followed them to the diner. It didn't take long to arrive and find Julia and Carmen at one of the tables near the back.

"We have a surprise for you," Julia said when they entered and gave Meredith a quick hug. "Maggie Lu will be joining us shortly. She heard what happened yesterday and wanted to come and hear all about it."

"I have a surprise guest too," Meredith said.

"Hello, Julia, darling," Beatrice said as she breezed through the doorway a second later. "Thank you for inviting me to lunch."

Julia met Meredith's gaze and shook her head, though a smile hovered over her lips. "Just for today, because I'm so happy you're safe, I will put up with just about anything," she whispered for Meredith's ears only.

Carmen greeted Chase and patted the seat next to her for him to sit down, while Beatrice sat across from them and started to chatter on about the diary and the kidnapping and the gala. Charlene walked up to the table with some cups and fresh coffee, and Maggie Lu appeared at the door with a big smile on her face. They all fussed about Meredith and her ordeal, and she told them everything she remembered, but it was Julia who Meredith was most concerned with at the moment. It wasn't the time or the place, but with everything that had happened the day before, Meredith hadn't had a chance to find out why Beau had wanted Julia to come home in the middle of the day.

After Meredith finished her tale and Charlene had served them their lunch, Carmen and Chase started a side conversation, and Beatrice chatted incessantly with Maggie Lu, leaving Meredith to take a little breath and enjoy the moment.

Julia took a sip of coffee and then turned just enough to look at Meredith. "I know you're dying to find out what happened with Beau and me yesterday."

"I didn't want to ask," Meredith said quietly. "Here, with everyone else listening."

Julia set her cup down and smiled, a happy, dreamy kind of smile. "I was completely wrong about my Beauregard."

Relief seeped through Meredith, and she sighed. "I'm happy to hear it."

"Do you know what he's been up to?" Julia asked.

Meredith shook her head.

"He's been secretly taking ballroom dancing lessons for me."

"Beau?" Meredith laughed. "I thought he had two left feet."

"He did!" Julia also laughed, joy radiating from her face. "That's why he decided to take the lessons. He wanted to surprise me at the gala, but he knew I was getting upset and suspicious, so he called me home yesterday to tell me what he'd been doing."

"Why didn't he just tell you over the phone?"

Color tinted Julia's cheek. "Because he made me a special lunch to make up for the anniversary meal he missed, and instead of telling me he was taking lessons—he showed me. We danced in the living room. I've wanted him to learn since we were married."

"And the woman at Leopold's?"

"His dance instructor." She laughed again. "He's not very good at keeping a secret."

"That's a good thing." Meredith smiled. "I'm happy for you, Julia. And I can't wait to see you and Beau dance together at the gala."

"Neither can I."

They enjoyed their lunch, laughing and visiting with their friends, and when Meredith's phone buzzed a few minutes later, she half expected it to be another reporter—but it was Quin calling.

"I'm going to take this call," she said to the others. "I'll be right back."

She stepped outside the diner into the heat of the July afternoon and answered the call. "Hello?"

"Hi, Meredith. It's Quin."

She smiled. "Hi, Quin."

"I just heard the shocking news about yesterday." His voice was tight with concern. "Is it true Troy LeBlanc kidnapped you?"

"Yes, but I'm fine. Nothing to worry about."

"I'm so relieved to hear that." He paused for a heartbeat. "I had thought to stop by and check on you but didn't know if you'd be up for company."

"I'm always up for company." She smiled. "I heard a rumor that Chase and Carmen are pairing up this evening to make an Italian meal."

Quin laughed.

"Would you like to join us?" she asked.

"I'd love to." He paused again. "I should wait until this evening to ask this, but I can't wait."

Meredith held her breath, wondering what he'd say.

"Do you have an escort to the historical society gala next week?"

A rush of nerves filled her stomach, and she shook her head, suddenly feeling like an inexperienced teenager again. "No."

"Would you like one?"

She bit her bottom lip to stop from grinning foolishly. "It depends on who the escort might be."

"How about me?" he asked.

She couldn't deny the rush of happiness she felt at the invitation. "I would enjoy that, Quin."

"Good." He seemed relieved. "So would I."

They spoke for a few more minutes and then said goodbye.

Meredith took a deep breath and smiled at the world around her. It was a good day.

***

A beautiful, starry evening greeted Meredith as Quin opened the passenger door and extended his hand to her. She took it and stepped out of his Land Rover, readjusting her long gown.

"Have I told you how beautiful you look tonight?" Quin asked her.

She smiled, her cheeks growing warm under his praise. "Twice now."

Appreciation glowed in his eyes. "I'll probably say it several more times before the night is over."

"Thank you, Quin." It had been a while since someone had complimented her, and she realized she would never grow too old for a little praise.

Quin handed his keys to a valet and extended his elbow to her. "Shall we?"

She took his offered assistance with one hand and lifted the hem of her gown with the other. She'd chosen to wear a sleek red gown with a long silk scarf flowing to the hem of the dress. Her matching red heels clicked on the concrete as they walked up the steps to the Jepson Center where the gala would be held. The large glass windows and doors revealed the beautifully decorated tables, sparkling lights, and bright white walls within the art center.

Already, dozens of people had started to gather, some dressed in gowns inspired by the colonial era. Even a few of the men were wearing colonial-inspired suits, complete with black buckled shoes and curled wigs.

Beside Meredith, Quin wore a simple black tuxedo. He looked amazing, and when he caught Meredith admiring him, he smiled.

"Meredith!" Beatrice noticed her the moment they entered the museum.

Meredith led Quin to Beatrice's side. Beatrice wore an elaborate colonial gown with a tall, white wig with ringlets falling over her shoulders and a painted mole on her left cheek.

"You look lovely, darling," Beatrice said as she kissed Meredith's cheeks. "I'm so eager for you to see the exhibit we created with the pictures from the diaries."

"Beatrice Enterline," Meredith said, "I'd like you to meet my friend Quin Crowley, who is a lawyer here in Savannah."

"Yes, of course," Beatrice said, shaking Quin's hand. "It's so nice to meet you, Mr. Crowley."

"The center looks amazing," Quin said to Beatrice. "Well done, Mrs. Enterline."

Beatrice beamed under his approval as her eyes scanned the room. Tall, fresh-cut flower arrangements adorned the white linen tabletops, gold chairs with white seat cushions were placed around each table, and along the walls were oversized pictures of the diaries.

"Take your time and enjoy the evening," Beatrice said. "There are refreshments circling."

Meredith smiled at their hostess and then took Quin's arm again. He led her to the pictures, where several others were gathered. A professional photographer must have been hired to photograph the diaries, because the pictures were very artistic, showing the details of the binding, the cover, the handwriting, and even the damage to the books. Beside each picture was a transcription of a different page of the books, telling only a brief part of the story. The exhibit was very well done and gave Meredith such pride, knowing Anna was Ron's ancestor.

"I have to admit," Julia said as she came up beside Meredith, wearing a beautiful navy blue ball gown, "Beatrice outdid herself."

"You're impressed?" Meredith raised her eyebrows. "With Beatrice?"

"She tries so hard," Julia said. "It was bound to happen eventually."

Meredith smiled and shook her head. "You're impossible, Julia Foley."

"Don't encourage her," Beau said as he came up behind his wife. "She's taken great pride in being impossible her whole life."

Julia smiled at her husband and took his hand in hers. "I like to keep people on their toes."

"Hello, Beau," Meredith said.

"Hello, Meredith. You look well."

"Thank you." She indicated Quin. "Have you met Quin Crowley?"

"I don't believe I have." Beau extended his hand to Quin. "It's nice to meet you."

"You too," Quin said.

"Do you golf, Mr. Crowley?" Beau asked.

"Quin," Quin said to him. "And yes, I do."

"Wonderful!" Beau grinned. "I'm always looking for a new golfing partner."

Julia rolled her eyes and shook her head. "You've done it now, Quin. He won't let it rest until he has you out on the course."

Quin smiled. "I'm looking forward to it." He looked at Meredith. "Do you golf? Could we make it a foursome?"

It had been years since Meredith had golfed, but she liked the idea of spending an afternoon with Julia, Beau, and Quin. "I have a set of clubs. I wouldn't mind dusting them off."

"Then it's set," Beau said. "I'll make a tee time for Saturday afternoon."

"Hold on," Julia said, putting her hand on Beau's shoulder. "Let everyone catch their breath."

They laughed as they walked down the row of pictures together and took their time reading each of the transcribed pages.

"Excuse me." Beatrice spoke into the microphone set up at the front of the room, a big smile on her face. "Will everyone please take their seats?"

It took a few moments, but everyone found a place to sit. Meredith and Julia sat side by side with Quin and Beau to their right and left. Anthony and Nicole Stone were at a table nearby, and when Meredith caught Mr. Stone's gaze, he gave her a simple nod.

"Before the meal begins," Beatrice said, clasping her hands together, "I'd like to make a presentation."

The room finally quieted, and Beatrice took a beautiful bouquet of flowers off a side table. She returned to the microphone, her white wig slightly tilted to the side.

"Recently, three very important items were put on permanent loan with the Savannah Historical Society. The board and I would like to publicly thank Mrs. Meredith Bellefontaine and her family for the generous donations."

The room erupted in applause. Meredith's cheeks warmed as everyone turned to look at her.

"Meredith, darling, please come up to the microphone," Beatrice said.

Meredith had not prepared a speech, so she hoped Beatrice didn't expect one.

Everyone continued clapping as Meredith stood.

Julia smiled, and Quin winked at her as she left their table and made her way to the front of the room.

"As everyone has probably heard," Beatrice said when the room quieted again, "Anna Coles's diary was stolen from Meredith's home shortly after she inherited it, and both she and Judge Julia Foley worked tirelessly to retrieve it. In the process, they were able to locate a second diary, one that is believed to be written by Daniel Defoe, and is full of information pertaining to the history of pirate activity in colonial America."

Again, the crowd applauded.

"So," Beatrice said as she handed the flowers to Meredith, "please accept this simple gift as a thank-you for the donation and the work you have done for the City of Savannah. You've made us all very proud."

Embarrassment at the public praise warmed Meredith from head to toe, but she graciously accepted it and then went back to her table, where Julia clapped the loudest.

"You should have been up there with me," Meredith said to her.

"No, thank you," Julia said with a big smile.

The evening progressed with a lovely meal and a very brief annual meeting, which was more of a formality than anything else, and then the orchestra set up and the dancing began.

"It's the moment you've been waiting for," Julia said to Beau.

Beau took a deep breath, and then he stood and offered his hand to Julia. "May I have this dance, my dear?"

"I thought you'd never ask." Julia rose and took Beau's hand.

"Have fun," Meredith said.

They walked onto the dance floor, and Beau took Julia into his arms. They began to dance, and Julia glowed.

"Would you like to dance?" Quin asked Meredith.

"You dance too?"

"My mother made me take lessons when I was a child." He stood and extended his hand to her. "I used to hate going—but on evenings like tonight, when there's a lovely woman in a beautiful red dress, I'm so thankful she insisted."

He led her onto the dance floor and twirled her around to the sound of the orchestra. Meredith laughed as she allowed herself to get lost in the moment. It felt good to be in Quin Crowley's arms and to let all her troubles fade away for the evening.

"I'm happy she insisted too," Meredith said a bit breathlessly. "You're a good dancer."

"I'm only as good as my partner."

Meredith smiled and met Julia's gaze from across the dance floor. It was much like a business partnership. She was so thankful Julia had agreed to partner with her to start Magnolia Investigations. So far, it had been a wild ride. She couldn't wait to see what happened next.

Dear Reader,

In March of 2019, my husband and I had the opportunity to travel to Savannah for the first time. One of the things that most intrigued me about the city was the pirate lore. Savannah abounds with amazing legends, and it's hard to separate fact from fiction as you listen to the tales. We enjoyed a delicious lunch at the Pirates' House restaurant, which is housed in one of the oldest buildings in Savannah and was, at one point, an inn for seafaring sailors and pirates. It was there that I first imagined my own pirate tale, complete with diaries, lost treasures, and rumors!

Much of the history I've shared in this book is true; however, the real colonist, Anna Coles, had no connection to Daniel Defoe, as far as I can tell, and did not leave behind a diary for us to discover. Daniel Defoe is rumored to have written *A General History of the Pyrates*, and there is a real Blackbeard's Island south of Savannah, but I do not know if Daniel had any knowledge of the treasure. As far as Savannah is concerned, I tried to depict the early days of colonization as accurately as I could, given the limited information available. What I do know is that General James Oglethorpe did outlaw alcohol, slavery, lawyers, and Catholics—but all four were eventually allowed to enter. It is but one of the many interesting facts you'll learn from any tour guide you meet.

Pirate history is only one aspect of Savannah's amazing past. The citizens call the city My Savannah, and it's not hard to start feeling like you belong as soon as you walk through the beautiful squares, taste the delicious southern food, and bask in the lavish hospitality. It has been my great pleasure to share this story, and this city, with you.

Sincerely,
Gabrielle Meyer

About the Author

GABRIELLE MEYER LIVES ON THE banks of the upper Mississippi River in central Minnesota with her husband and four children. By day, she's a homeschooling mama, but at night, she escapes to imaginary worlds to pen tales of hope and inspiration. As an employee of the Minnesota Historical Society, Gabrielle fell in love with the rich history of her state and enjoys writing fictional stories inspired by real people, places, and events. You can learn more about her and her books by visiting gabriellemeyer.com, or connect with her on Facebook at facebook.com/AuthorGabrielleMeyer.

The Truth Behind the Fiction

EDWARD TEACH, BETTER KNOWN AS Blackbeard, was a fascinating pirate who was only active for two brief years (1716 to 1718), but left a lasting impression on American history. To this day, the vast fortune he collected has yet to be found, and is rumored to be worth at least ten million dollars. I chose to use Blackbeard in this story because of the island named after him just outside of Savannah (where some believe his treasure is still hidden), and because I have a personal family connection to this infamous pirate.

My maternal grandmother's ancestors began to arrive in America during the Great Puritan Migration between 1620 and 1640, and among those ancestors, I have three colonial governors in my family tree. One of those men was Charles Eden, the governor of South Carolina between 1713 and 1722. He was most well known for trying to rid South Carolina of pirates and for offering the King's Pardons to both Blackbeard and gentleman pirate Stede Bonnet, when they promised to turn from their evil ways. Both pirates, however, fell back into pirating, and died soon after.

Some people believe that Governor Eden and Blackbeard were friends, perhaps because the governor performed a wedding ceremony for Blackbeard and his wife, Mary Ormond, and they had homes near each other. Whatever the case may be, in 1719, after Blackbeard's death, Eden was accused of colluding with Blackbeard because of a letter found on Blackbeard's body that was written by Governor Eden's secretary of the council, mentioning the governor's name. Eden was able to prove his innocence to the provincial council, but the rumors still persist, three hundred years later.

Southern Fried Chicken

Ingredients:

3 eggs

⅓ cup water

About 1 cup hot red pepper sauce

2 cups self-rising flour

1 teaspoon pepper

House seasoning (recipe follows)

1 (1 to 2½-pound) chicken, cut into pieces

Oil, for frying, preferably peanut oil

House Seasoning Ingredients:

1 cup salt

¼ cup black pepper

¼ cup garlic powder

Directions:

In a medium-sized bowl, beat the eggs with the water. Add enough hot sauce so the egg mixture is bright orange. In another bowl, combine the flour and pepper. Season the chicken with the house seasoning. Dip the seasoned chicken in the egg, and then coat well in the flour mixture.

Heat the oil to 350 degrees Fahrenheit in a deep pot. Do not fill the pot more than half full with oil.

Fry the chicken in the oil until brown and crisp. Dark meat takes longer than white meat. It should take dark meat about 13 to 14 minutes, white meat around 8 to 10 minutes.

House Seasoning:

Mix ingredients together and store in an airtight container for up to 6 months.

Read on for a sneak peek of another exciting book in the Savannah Secrets series!

Whispering Bells

BY SHIRLEY RAYE REDMOND

"ANOTHER CREEPY OLD HOUSE." JULIA Foley shuddered.

Meredith Bellefontaine ignored the comment as she parked her SUV behind Pastor Ed Markham's minivan. Stepping out of the vehicle, she paused on the gravel of the circular driveway in front of the rambling, three-story historic mansion. Faded green shutters framed the tall, yawning windows. One of the five chimneys jutting from the roof appeared to have crumbled to nothing but rubble.

"Creepy," Julia insisted as she emerged from the passenger side of the vehicle. She glanced at the flat roof, the white fluted columns, and sprawling veranda. Spanish moss, hanging from a large oak tree, draped itself across one edge of the roof like a veil. "But certainly not as decrepit as the old Besset plantation house the historical society is renovating. I don't think it's as old as the Besset place either," she added, referring to the historic home at the center of the first case she and Meredith had solved together.

Meredith nodded. "River View was constructed at the beginning of the Civil War."

Julia guessed that her business partner knew exactly how old this mansion was. As the former president of the local historical society, Meredith knew pretty much everything there was to know about Savannah and the city's historic homes. This grand old house, with its elegant proportions, must have been a sight to behold in its heyday. Now, neglected and rather forlorn, it appeared to droop in the heat of the August morning.

"I wonder why your pastor wanted us to meet him out here," Meredith said.

"I can't even begin to guess." Julia slung the strap of her chestnut-brown Jenny N. tote bag over her shoulder. "According to Carmen, he called asking that we join him here as soon as possible. It's fortunate that we were both free. Ed said it was important."

Actually, what their wisecracking receptionist had said was that Pastor Markham needed to chill out and they'd better get out to the old River View place *muy rapido*—very quickly.

"It looks haunted, but I'm willing to take on any ghosts we encounter to get a clipping from that." Julia pointed to a late-blooming purple clematis vine clinging to a tall ornate trellis on the side of the house. "Miss Dicey used to tell me stories about her house, but I've never actually been here before. Have you?"

Meredith chuckled as she crunched over the path of ground shells toward the mansion. "Of course. Miss Laodicea Oglethorpe used to entertain in grand style many years ago. When I was just a girl, Mama always held up Miss Dicey, with her air of daintiness and refinement, as a model for all the young ladies to aspire to. She's always ready to tell anyone who'll listen that she's a direct descendent of General James Oglethorpe, who brought the first settlers here in 1733. Her favorite line is, 'He established three rules for the new settlement of Savannah: no slavery, no liquor, and no lawyers.'"

Julia came to a halt on the path. Grinning, she said, "I never heard her say that. Is it true?"

"Yes indeed." Meredith grinned back as she pushed against the old gate. It yielded with a reluctant groan. "General Oglethorpe considered lawyers to be 'the scourge of mankind.' And that's a direct quote in writing by the general's own hand."

Shaking her head admiringly, Julia said, "Of course, you would know." She followed Meredith through the gate and up the long path to the veranda.

"I once asked Daddy why Miss Dicey never married," Meredith said. "He said it was because she was too proud of the Oglethorpe name to give it up."

"Do you think she's at home?" Julia asked. "Perhaps Ed has come to visit her?"

"Miss Dicey is definitely not here," Meredith replied. Julia's shoulders slumped with disappointment. "The old dear is a hundred years old, if she's a day, and now lives in a nursing home."

Julia cast a sidelong glance in the direction of the lush vine with its deep purple blooms.

"Do you think Miss Dicey would mind very much if I took just a snip or two of her clematis? I'd like to transplant a sprig on the side of our house." She loved her rambling home with its spacious green lawn. When her hubby, Beau, wasn't cutting the grass on his riding mower, he spent his retirement years fishing and golfing. She had taken up gardening—when she wasn't assisting Meredith with Magnolia Investigations, of course.

She and Meredith had been college roommates once upon a time at Georgia Southern University. They'd kept in touch with Christmas cards and the occasional birthday phone call. When Julia moved back to Savannah fifteen years ago, the two friends had met by accident at the Sentient Bean. Julia had been thrilled. She and Beau enjoyed Ron and Meredith's company, and the couples had become close friends. After Ron's death, when Meredith considered reopening his detective agency, it seemed only natural that Julia, with her background in criminal law and her experience as a judge, should join her. So far, the Lord had blessed their endeavors.

"Miss Dicey wouldn't mind if you took a snip or two, I'm sure," Meredith told her as they mounted the front steps. "She loved her garden and was always happy to share iris bulbs or cuttings from a particularly lovely rose or flowering vine."

The front door swung open then. Ed Markham stood on the threshold to greet them. The pastor's face glistened with perspiration, and his blue broadcloth shirt was damp with sweat. There were sweat patches under his arms too. "I've been keeping my eyes peeled, looking out for y'all. Thank you for coming on such short notice." He grinned. "I've got a bit of a conundrum, ladies, and I need your expert advice. C'mon in. We're going to the music room." His brown eyes sparkled with good humor. He didn't appear worried or troubled.

Julia felt puzzled. She'd known Ed for years. She and Beau worshiped regularly at the New Beginnings Church. They had quickly come to respect Ed's sound theological sermons and lively preaching style. His wife, Naomi, was a sweetheart who did everything from leading the choir to teaching Sunday school with grace and good humor.

"So, what's up, Ed? Our receptionist said it was urgent." Julia wiped the perspiration from her upper lip. It was hot enough to melt butter in here. She guessed the place was overly warm and stuffy from being closed up for so long. "Has there been a break-in?"

She glanced around as they passed from one spacious room to the next. She took in the cobwebs in the corners near the ceiling and the furniture protected by cotton dust covers. Meredith was right—Miss Dicey hadn't lived here in years. Was it possible that trespassers had been tempted to steal some of the valuable antiques? She paused to admire an elegant staircase and portraits of long-dead Oglethorpes mounted in gilded frames upon the walls. "Oh my," she muttered with awe. "Miss Dicey certainly lived high."

"I've always loved this old historic home," Meredith said with a sigh. "It was one of the finest in its day."

Glancing down at the faded rug and the specks of chipped paint along the baseboards, Julia felt a twinge of sadness. It seemed a shame that a place so beautiful should become the victim of time and neglect. River View was an architectural gem filled with treasures—even if it did look spooky from the outside. One of Ed's recent sermon passages came to mind then—one from Matthew. "For where your treasure is, there will your heart be also." She hoped the Oglethorpes had been storing their real treasures in heaven. River View was just a house after all. Still, it was quite a house. "If only the walls could talk," she mused aloud.

"If only," Meredith agreed.

Together they followed Ed into the large music room. The baby grand piano in the center of the room was coated with dust. Julia noted stacks of sheet music piled high on the window seat, the end tables, the bookshelves, and every other available surface.

"This is why I'm here." Ed made a sweeping gesture with his arm. "I was visiting Miss Dicey at the nursing home, and she asked me to come by to pick up some of her sheet music. Thankfully, she didn't specify any one piece of music in particular." He smiled. "She's been feeling puny-like, so she said, and wanted something to ease her days."

"This is a fine collection," Julia observed. "I knew Miss Dicey loved music, but I didn't know she played the piano." She pointed to the baby grand. "That piano is a Bösendorfer."

Meredith nodded. "She could have been a lauded concert pianist, but most women didn't pursue careers back in the day."

Julia picked up a sheet yellowed with age. "'Chickery Chick,'" she read. "The copyright date is 1945."

"Here's one with a picture of Bing Crosby on the front." Ed held up another piece of faded sheet music. "'Zing a Little Zong,'" he read. "I'm not familiar with that one. Doesn't sound much like classical music, now does it?"

Picking up another sheet with ragged edges, Julia read the title, "'The Band Played On.'" She opened the page and read the copyright date: 1936. It was hard to imagine proper, straitlaced Laodicea Oglethorpe playing such lively popular tunes of the day rather than Mozart and Chopin. But it made sense that she would want her music with her at the nursing home. No doubt each tune brought back fond memories.

"I don't know much about music, except for hymns and country gospel," Ed volunteered. "And the occasional lively ragtime piece.

Perhaps I should have y'all go through the stacks and pick out some of the classical music."

"No, she'll want these, I bet," Meredith guessed. "Just grab a handful from several different stacks and take them to her. You can tell just by looking at these sheets that the songs were played often. I'm sure they'll bring back happy memories for Miss Dicey, bless her heart. As she said, it will help to ease her days."

Heaving a sigh, Julia fanned her face with a piece of vintage music. "But surely you didn't ask us to come help you rummage through Miss Dicey's sheet music?"

Ed fished a snow-white handkerchief from his back pocket and wiped the perspiration dotting his face. Regarding them with an expression both sheepish and mildly eager, he said, "I want to show y'all something. It's a secret I need to share—just in case something…er…should happen."

Julia cast Meredith a sidelong glance. Her friend widened her blue eyes meaningfully.

"What might happen?" Julia wanted to know. "You're being mighty mysterious, Ed."

"And the suspense is killing me," Meredith piped up. "If the temperature in this room doesn't do me in first." She too had claimed a piece of music to use as a makeshift fan.

Ed cleared his throat. "All right then. Julia, would you come over here?" He stepped toward the fireplace with its handsome mantel made of green marble. A series of footed vases in various shades of blue and green made an eye-catching display across the top. Wedgwood jasperware, if Julia had to guess. Antiques, and quite valuable.

As she stepped toward the fireplace, Ed said, "Y'all watch closely now." He told Julia to place her hand on one of the carved rosettes on the side of the mantel. "Now push and turn it to the right at the same time."

Julia pushed and twisted. As she did so, she cast Meredith a questioning glance. There was a slow swishing sound, and suddenly, a dark gap appeared between two dusty bookshelves. Julia's pulse raced. "Stars and garters!" she exclaimed with bated breath.

"A secret panel!" Meredith declared.

Smiling, Ed shook his head. "Dear ladies, it's not the secret panel that's so amazing." His tone was now tinged with undisguised excitement. "Wait until y'all see what's inside."